CW01455168

SHADOWS OF BETRAYAL

THE SHADOW REALMS
BOOK 3

BRENDA K DAVIES

BRENDA K. DAVIES

Copyright © 2021 Brenda K. Davies
All rights reserved.

Warning: All rights reserved. The unauthorized reproduction or distribution of this copyrighted work, in whole or part, in any form by any electronic, mechanical, or other means, is illegal and forbidden, without the written permission of the author.

This is a work of fiction. Characters, settings, names, and occurrences are a product of the author's imagination and bear no resemblance to any actual person, living or dead, places or settings, and/or occurrences. Any incidences of resemblance are purely coincidental.

CHAPTER ONE

COLE RELEASED Lexi as soon as he stepped out of the portal. He stalked over to one of the window openings overlooking the Gloaming. The glow of the approaching flames cast shadows across the land and lit the night as the opposing fae army came over the top of a hill.

There were hundreds of them marching on *his* home. His hands fisted as he glared at the traitors. When he found out who was behind this, he would make them pay.

"Stay here," he said as he turned away from the window.

"I'm staying with you until you leave this palace," Lexi said.

Cole didn't have the time to argue with her. "Stay close to me."

He strode toward the door to his room, flung it open, and swiftly descended the stairs. Her soft footsteps followed him down. Once they reached the first floor, she ran beside him as he raced for the weapons room.

He grasped the handle and pushed open one of the doors to the cavernous space. He waved Lexi inside and pressed his hand to the wall before closing the door behind him.

He wasn't sure the palace was going to welcome her into this room. It had allowed her into one of the other weapons rooms, but this was the King's room, and few were allowed here. It had accepted her far more than most others, but the palace was an endless mystery He would know soon if it allowed her to stay or if he'd have to ask her to leave.

The second the door closed, the wall beneath his hand heated. Lexi would be allowed to stay. The weapons room was a separate building adjoined to the palace. Its pointed ceiling was fifty feet off the ground.

As the wall warmed, the ceiling lit with the dim glow of moonlight. It spilled around the room to illuminate the hundreds of weapons lining the walls. More weapons were stashed inside the trunks around the room and hidden in containers set into the walls and floor. Few knew how to access those containers, but he was one of them.

"What? How?" Lexi breathed as the room grew brighter.

"Few are allowed in here, so there is no one to keep the torches lit. Instead, the ceiling draws energy from the rays of the moons, stores it, and uses it to light the room when those who are allowed into it enter. It recognizes our touch on the wall."

"Amazing," she whispered.

Over his many years and countless hours of training in this room with his father and brothers, he'd forgotten how amazing it was. But then, the whole palace had a life of its own.

He didn't make a sound as he strode out to the middle of the white marble floor before stopping to kneel. After his father told him how to access the weapons in this hidden spot, it had taken many tries for him to locate them without fail.

When he was younger, he had to count the steps from the door to this secret cache. All the while, he worried he'd stepped too far to one side or the other. Many times, he did, and his father would have him start all over again.

One tiring day, he'd attempted to find the spot nearly two dozen times. Under his father's watchful eye and endless patience,

Cole tried and tried again until he finally located it. He never missed again after that.

When he placed his palm on the floor, it warmed against his skin until a golden glow shone around the edges of his hand. The familiar sensation wasn't unpleasant as the palace recognized his touch and gave up one of its secrets.

Lexi gasped when the ground slid back to reveal the thick steel case beneath. Once the floor was completely out of the way, he pulled open the case to expose the weapons inside.

Numerous lethal weapons lay within, but he sought the sword in the center. The black, oplyx stone in the middle of the exquisitely crafted hilt shone as he twisted the long sword in his hands. He pulled the weapon halfway from its sheath to examine the honed blade.

It was as lethal as he remembered.

"Is that yours?" Lexi asked.

"It was my father's."

His father had spent countless hours sharpening and polishing this blade. And now that it was his, Cole would do the same. Numerous kings had held this sword in their hands, countless enemies had lost their lives to this sword, and Cole would take more of those lives tonight.

"Is it fae metal?" Lexi asked.

"No, but whoever started this rebellion will not survive this blade."

Not even during a rebellion would he use fae metal against his kind. Those rebelling against him would not survive, but he refused to break one of the most sacred rules amongst the fae.

These assholes might deserve it, but the dark fae did not wield fae metal against their own.

Of course, some didn't always respect the boundary. He was sure some of them were on that field now.

Cole dropped the sword on his back to the ground and slung his

4 BRENDA K DAVIES

father's sword over his shoulder. He would go into battle wielding his father's weapon.

When he lifted his head, he discovered Lexi watching him with dread. Her sun-kissed skin was much paler than normal, and her full lower lip quivered before she stiffened it.

Bending, he clasped her cheeks in his palms. "I must go. Don't leave this palace."

"Go? What about battle armor?"

"I don't wear any."

"You *can't* go out there without armor."

"I never wear armor into a battle. It's too constraining, and I can't move as fast in it."

"Cole—"

"I've never worn it before, Lexi. I'm not about to start now. I have to go."

She looked about to argue more but closed her eyes and nodded. "Please, be careful."

"Always."

He kissed her forehead, her nose, and finally her lips before releasing her and walking away. As he crossed the room, the floor over the hidden cache slid back into place with a familiar click.

He didn't look back as he opened the door and left the room.

CHAPTER TWO

LEXI STARED after Cole as he left the room. She didn't move until she heard the front door open and close. She was afraid if she moved before then, she would sprint after him and beg him not to go.

He's not wearing battle armor.

It didn't matter if he never wore it or not and had survived the war. He was going out there more exposed than most of the others on that field. *All* of him would be open and susceptible to an attack.

How could he not wear battle armor?

Lexi tried to rein in her terror before it got out of control. It was too late to stop him. He was already going out there, already charging out there to fight an enemy that should *never* have been an enemy.

What were these dark fae thinking to rise against him? Didn't they have enough troubles with the Lord and the war that just ended without having to create *more*? She would never understand some immortals or mortals.

Once the front door closed, she sprinted across the room. She stopped in front of the weapons that first caught her attention when the lights came on. Lexi examined them before removing a small sword and the leather belt hanging with it.

The sword was small enough she'd be able to wield it without tiring for a little while. It wasn't too heavy and would do some serious damage to anyone who tried to harm her.

Ignoring the sting of the healing burn on her palm from Orin, she slid the belt around her waist and buckled it before sheathing the sword. Lexi had no intention of leaving this palace. She wouldn't become a distraction to Cole, and despite all the training Brokk had been putting her through, she wouldn't last on that battlefield, but she wouldn't remain weaponless either.

Searching the walls, she discovered throwing stars hanging fifteen feet away. She smiled as her fingers itched for them. Unlike the sword that she had little practice with, she was good with throwing stars, and they wouldn't tire her out as fast as using a blade she'd never wielded before.

She ran over to the stars and started to reach for them. She froze when she saw the intricate designs marking the thick metal. The sword she'd selected was not welded from fae metal, but the stars were.

However, she wasn't fae. It wasn't against the rules for *her* to use fae metal against them. Of course, it probably wasn't the best idea for her to use fae metal against the fae she might one day rule over, but it had been a worse idea for them to rise against Cole.

And she would make them pay for that if it became necessary.

She removed a brown satchel from a hook next to the stars and tied it to the other side of her waist. When she was sure it was secure and wouldn't interfere with the sword, she shoved the stars inside.

～

GATHERED BY THE GATES, the hundred or so soldiers of the king's army stood as they waited for Cole to arrive. Their horses pranced as the torches drew nearer and the noise of the approaching army, and those fleeing it, increased.

Shouts from the fae folk living in the homes on the hills resonated through the night as they fled toward the palace. Refugees from the town were already pouring through the side door next to the gates.

Sobs and screams filled the air. Women hugged their children as their husbands ushered them forward. Some of the single men, and a few of the husbands, asked for weapons to join against the rebellion.

Normally, Cole would not welcome untrained farmers, merchants, smiths, and artisans on the battlefield, but at one time, the king's army numbered much higher. That was before the Lord's war decimated their numbers. And now, he couldn't turn a willing fighter down.

The army marching against him would be filled with many of the same as what was gathering near his gates. There would also be skilled fighters amid the group, but not as many as before the war.

Cole fought with many of the king's men during the Lord's war, but his father was king. Their loyalty was with his father, and he had no idea how many now considered themselves loyal to *him*.

During the war, he'd saved many of these men's lives, but that didn't mean he could count on them not to stab him in the back. He had no way of knowing how long this rebellion had been in the works, who organized it, or whose loyalty might have been bought by the traitor. Any number of these men could also be a relative of the organizer or *organizers*.

He was about to ride into battle with his enemies ahead of him and countless more at his back. His skin prickled as he studied the men. Their faces all blended as their horses twisted and turned.

He was about to leave Lexi behind as he rode into battle. Though he hadn't said anything in front of her and Orin, he did find her silver markings odd. He recalled the silver mark he saw on her forehead after he'd nearly killed her while in the grip of a nightmare.

He'd blown it off then as having come from the bed when she fell out of it. But could he blow off another silver mark on her?

And how could she possibly be anything more than what she believed herself to be? She didn't have any powers.

Unfortunately, right now, he couldn't stop to figure out what was going on. He despised the idea of leaving her here alone, especially with all the questions churning in his mind, but the palace would keep her safe, and he had to stop this rebellion.

"Bring me a horse!" Cole shouted to the stable boy running between horses.

He'd much prefer to ride Torigon into this battle, but he left his steadfast mount at Lexi's manor. It was one more thing working against him at the moment.

More screams and shouts rolled down the hills as the fae fled their homes for the safety of the palace. Those cries echoed throughout the courtyard and rebounded off the palace walls, the houses in the bailey, and stables.

"Milord," Niall greeted as he rode up and stopped his mount in front of Cole.

Out of everyone here, he trusted Niall the most. They were the same age, and his father was once a general in Cole's father's army. When they were children, they played on top of hay bales together, ran through the fields, skipped rocks, shared dreams of being mighty warriors, and later trained in the art of war.

They spent countless nights together carousing with women, drinking, and fighting. Niall had saved his life nearly as many times as Cole saved him during the war. He was one of Cole's most trusted friends.

The stable boy ran up to him. He was holding the reins of a bay stallion who stood calmly by, as confusion ruled in the courtyard. The animal wasn't as large as Torigon, but his legs were in good shape, and he wouldn't shy away during the fight.

All the horses in the stables were battle tried and trained to withstand the noise and chaos sure to follow. That was what mattered most.

Grabbing the pommel, Cole swung himself onto the brown leather saddle and settled himself onto the horse's back. He seized the reins as he surveyed the men surrounding him.

He was about to find out who was loyal to him and who planned to stab him in the back. He nudged his horse and raised his voice to be heard over the cries of the innocent while he rode before his men.

"Destroy all those who rise against me but, if possible, leave the leaders of this rebellion to me. I will see to their deaths!"

A cheer went through the soldiers, and the horses stomped their feet in anticipation of the battle to come. Turning his horse's head, he rode up to the palace gates. When he gripped one of the bars, the gates sprang open.

CHAPTER THREE

As HE RODE through the gates, he pushed them further open so the rest of them could follow. He didn't bother to close them; they would do so on their own once all the men were through.

His horse's hooves thundered across the earth, eating up the ground as they galloped up the hills toward the approaching enemy. When he leaned over his horse's neck and urged the animal faster, the wind blew his hair back and plastered his clothes to him.

Unlike him, many of his men wore armor to keep them protected; the silver mesh and chains making up their armor rattled in the wind. The glow of the four moons illuminated the land and bathed it in a beautiful, silvery light.

When shadows jumped and swayed all around, the ones within him responded to their movements, swelling within him. He sensed the strength in the shadows surrounding him, but he didn't draw on them or release the shadows inside him. That was still his secret to keep and spring on the Lord when the time was right.

He kept waiting for an arrow or sword to pierce through his back, but so far, he wasn't feeling the sharp pain of betrayal. The fae still trying to flee the approaching traitors raced past him and toward the palace as the rebel army topped the crest of the next hill.

Cole was closing in on the fighters when the first arrow flew at him. But it did not come from the approaching army. No, as he'd suspected, there were traitors amongst his men too, and they wanted him dead.

The bolt whistled past his ear and struck the ground twenty feet in front of him. It quivered as it stood straight up from the earth. Shouts sounded from behind him, and when he glanced back, some of his men were closing in on one of their own.

A blow from one of his guards knocked the traitorous fae from his saddle. He disappeared beneath the pounding hooves of the horses surrounding him, but Cole knew he would not be the last enemy to come from behind.

Since he didn't have eyes in the back of his head, he would have to rely on those who were loyal to keep him safe. He turned back in the saddle and focused on the enemy galloping down the hill toward him.

Cole swung out with his sword and sliced the head from the first fae to reach him. Another arrow came from behind him. The whistling sound of it alerted his lycan senses that it was coming.

He turned in the saddle in time to avoid taking the bolt to his shoulder. Since none of the rebels had gotten past him yet, he knew it had come from another one of his men.

Then, he was surrounded by the enemy as they collided in the middle of a hill that became their battlefield. The clash of steel against steel resonated across the land; the shouts of men fighting and the screams of the injured and dying filled the night.

The scent of blood and horse sweat filled his nostrils, as did the rich aroma of the earth churning up beneath the horse's hooves. Warm blood splattered his face and clothes as he cut down one dark fae after another.

The sights and sounds of this battle would haunt his nightmares, but for now, he remained focused on one thing… surviving.

He did not allow fear or pity to take him over, and he didn't hesitate as he delivered blow after blow to his enemy. He didn't know how many he killed outright and how many he maimed, but when this was over, none of the rebels would be left alive.

His horse's hooves pounded over bodies as they stomped them into the ground. Despite the noise, the blood, and the death, the animal never shied away or attempted to bolt.

Cole deflected the blade of one fae but missed the sword of another one. It split open his flesh as it sliced across his bicep, and blood spilled down his arm.

Spinning in his saddle, he was about to destroy his attacker when Niall's blade swung out and severed the man's head from his shoulders. Niall's black eyes shone with fury when they met Cole's, and blood dripped from his black hair.

Though he was pure dark fae, Niall was a little broader and heavier than most others. That came from years of honing his fighting skills.

Cole nodded his thanks to him, and Niall's grin revealed all his white teeth. And then, he was pushed back and swallowed by the sea of enemy racing between them.

Despite the sheer number of them, Cole didn't tire as he used his sword to cut them down. When a ball of fire shot at his head, he ducked and threw up a hand to catch the flame in his palm. He had no idea where it had come from, but it was now his to wield.

Flipping his hand over, he flicked his wrist and flung the ball into the face of a dark fae charging at him. The man screamed, and his hands flew to his face. As they did so, Cole drove his sword into the man's heart.

With a savage shout, he sliced upward, cleaving the man in half from his chest through his head. Once his sword was free, he chopped off the fae's head to ensure his death, before twisting in the saddle to face the pounding hooves coming at him from behind.

He jerked his horse's reins to the side, and the horse instantly obeyed his command to twist away. The animal was fast and sure and managed to avoid being plowed into by the horse charging them. Cole recognized the attacker as one of his men.

The betrayal burned like acid in his throat, and as the horse raced toward him, Cole shifted his hold on his sword. This bastard would never expect what was coming at him.

When the man was close enough, Cole swung out with his free hand, and extending his claws, he embedded them under the fae's chin. He ripped the man from his horse.

The man kicked and made gurgling noises as his fingers tore into Cole's hand. With his sword still in hand, Cole gripped the man's shoulder and tore his head off. Retracting his claws, he palmed the head and threw it at the next fae coming at him.

It bounced off the man's forehead and sent him tumbling from the saddle. The horse continued toward them but veered away before it ran into Cole's horse. He aimed his horse at the fallen rider; the animal didn't hesitate before trampling him.

From somewhere further up the hill, a fire blazed to life. It whipped across the lush grass and down the hill toward him and a dozen other riders.

Cole almost laughed out loud as the fire encircled them. He was sure that whoever controlled the flames probably thought they'd intimidate him, but after what he endured during the trials, this fire was pathetic.

Kicking his feet free of the stirrups, Cole jumped from his horse's back and strode toward the flames. On the other side of the fire, he spotted Durin standing with Nissa and Fiadh, Aelfdane's brother and sister.

A smile curved his lips as he realized who had organized and was leading this rebellion. He would make them pay for their treachery.

As he stalked toward them, the three dark fae lifted their arms, and the flames leapt higher. The dark fae could control the elements, and they were using the air to whip the fire into an inferno, one that still did nothing to intimidate him.

If he stopped and took the time, he could take control of the fire. It would be tiring since there were three of them and they were powerful fae, but he could do it. He wouldn't waste the time or energy it would take.

Besides, he thought with a grim smile, *these assholes think they have me cornered, and they're in for a big surprise.*

Cole bellowed as he raced toward the three of them.

CHAPTER FOUR

LEXI HELD her breath as Cole charged toward the flames. Blood splattered him, and his torn clothes were little more than rags as their remnants clung to his broad frame. The growing fire pushed the men trapped with him closer together.

The dark fae could control the elements, but someone else already controlled this fire. *Three* someone else's... or so that's what it looked like from her viewpoint.

She didn't know if Cole could wrest control away from them. She suspected he could, but it would take too much time or energy for him to do so.

As she watched him battle the enemy with unwavering strength and determination, she'd understood why the troubadours sang about his feats during the war. Why others whispered about his fighting skills and the legends of him were larger than life.

And he didn't fear the flames; every part of her froze as he ran toward them. He was so incredibly powerful but still killable.

He was almost to the fire when he sheathed his sword. She couldn't move; her hands ached from clutching them, and a scream lodged in her throat as, with his next steps, Cole transformed into a wolf. His powerful haunches bunched as he leapt into the air.

As the wolf flew above the conflagration, it twisted to avoid the inferno surging higher into the air. Soaring above the flames, fire licked at its fur but didn't catch as the wolf spun in midair.

The beautiful creature was so powerful and mesmerizing that Lexi forgot to breathe as the sword slid from his back and toppled to the ground on the other side of the fire. While the wolf was falling on the other side of the flames, his massive jaws snapped down on a fae man. Cole twisted and, landing on four feet, smashed the fae into the ground.

The man didn't move again.

"Miss?"

Lexi jumped when someone spoke from behind her. She spun away from the window to discover Amaris standing in the doorway of the empty room Lexi occupied. She'd searched the palace until she found a room she could enter that would give her a good view of the battle.

"Ye-yes?" Lexi whispered tremulously.

"Miss, why don't you come away from the window?"

"Call me Lexi."

"Lexi then, please come away from the window. You shouldn't watch this."

"No, I shouldn't, but I'm going to."

Lexi turned back to the window and rested her hands on the stone sill as she leaned out to watch. The growing flames and moonlight illuminated the bodies littering the field. Horses ran through and over those bodies while the injured tried to crawl away.

The blood soaking the ground had turned it from a vibrant green to a gruesome maroon. Horses were down amongst the fallen fae; their screams mingled with the cries of the wounded and dying.

She'd never heard such sounds before and hoped never to hear them again.

Her nails dug into the stone as one of the fae nearest Cole

unleashed a dagger. It spun through the air before embedding in the wolf's shoulder. It had to hurt, but it didn't stop him from tearing the head off the fae he'd smashed into the ground.

COLE SPIT out Fiadh's head and spun on Durin and Nissa. *One down. Two more to go.*

"No!" Nissa screamed.

She lunged forward, but her fighters fell between them to keep her separated from Cole. He'd lost his clothes when he transformed, but he didn't care. All he cared about was destroying these fuckers.

"I'll kill you!" she shrieked.

Cole transformed, and as he rose, he ripped the dagger from his shoulder. A hot rush of blood poured down his back, soaking his flesh. As he turned the blade before him, he wasn't surprised to discover it was fae metal.

Hefting the weapon in his hand, he lifted his head and smiled at Nissa as the rebels charged at him. He didn't throw the blade at them; it would find its home in Nissa. He'd entered this battle without fae metal, but if one of his enemies were stupid enough to use a fae metal weapon against him and lose it to him, then it was only fair they got it back through their heart.

The charging rebels were almost to him when he sank Nissa's blade into the ground and knelt to rest his fingers on the earth. He drew forth the shadows surrounding him and smiled when they slid over his flesh; his attackers were nearly to him when he vanished, reclaimed the blade, cloaked it, and danced away before they arrived at where he'd been.

They gazed around in confusion as they skidded to a halt in the spot where he once stood. He didn't set the shadows within himself free; there were too many here who would report what they saw to the Lord if he did.

He'd done what any other dark fae could, but he'd cloaked himself in shadows far faster and more thoroughly than any of them. Not only that, with the amount of power he possessed, none of these assholes could see him. A dark fae stronger than another could see through their cloaking, but he was more powerful than anyone else in this realm.

Moving faster than a shadow fleeing the light, he reclaimed his father's sword and its sheath. Their eyes swung toward him as he lifted the sword, but it was only a couple of inches off the ground before it vanished too. He slid the sword into the sheath and swung it onto his back.

With the stealth of a spirit slipping through the night, he came up behind one of the rebels and plunged the blade straight through his heart. As the man went down, Cole caught the sword he'd been holding and turned it over.

The flames caught and reflected off the pristine metal forged by the hands of a dark fae. And the dark fae were the best weapons makers in all the realms. They were also the only ones who melded dark fae metal, which was exactly what this man held.

All of the rebels were wielding fae metal.

The betrayal of that was a worse sting than the rebellion. Even if it infuriated him, he could understand this uprising. Powerful men and women, who sought revenge for the death of their brother and who believed they should be the ones to lead, engineered it.

But using the only weapon that could kill a dark fae against their kind—this breaking of the unwritten rule—was something far worse.

And he would make them pay for it.

They couldn't see him, but the rebels saw the fae going down as blood spread across his chest. They spun and started coming toward him, but he darted to the side and away from them before they could arrive.

The rebels stopped moving and exchanged uneasy looks. Even if he weren't completely silent in his movements, the screams of the dying and the crackle of the flames would hide them. He sliced the head from one of the fae before driving the dagger through the heart of another.

"Unleash the arrows!" Durin commanded and pointed at the fae he'd just slain.

He didn't have enough time to get out of the way of a volley of arrows as many of the rebels pulled crossbows free from their sides and lifted them. Wrapping his arm around the throat of a rebel, Cole jerked his body around to use as a shield.

The twang of the arrows releasing was barely audible over the sounds of the battle, but they rang in Cole's ears. The fae struggled in his hold, but as the arrows pummeled his body, his resistance faded until he went limp in Cole's arms.

Continuing to hold the limp body, Cole ran at the men with the crossbows. From behind them, Niall and a group of the king's army came into view. Bloody and battered, they still released a bellow as they charged toward the rebels, Durin, and Nissa.

"The arrows are fae metal!" Cole shouted.

He threw down the dead dark fae and spun to wave his hand at the circle of fire that originally imprisoned him. Now that his enemies had become distracted and given up their control of the fire, he could seize it.

When the flames jumped out of the way, they created an opening that allowed more of his men to spill free. As soon as they emerged, Cole released the shadows to reveal himself.

It was *him* these traitorous bastards wanted most, and he would not let his men suffer and die while he remained hidden.

CHAPTER FIVE

"No," Lexi whispered when the shadows peeled away to reveal Cole.

She couldn't take much more of this uncertainty. She couldn't stand to see him out there, surrounded by so many enemies and exposed to them again. Her fingers dug into the stone of the windowsill as she chewed on her bottom lip.

She'd hated not being able to see Cole, but she hated seeing him more.

"Miss," Amaris said. "I mean, Lexi. Please, come away from the window. It will be better for you."

When Amaris grasped her arm, Lexi pulled it away. "I have to go down there."

Lexi spun away from the window and ran from the room. Her booted feet barely hit the floor as she raced down the hallway. She had no idea what to do; she couldn't go onto the battlefield. She'd never survive and would probably get Cole killed if she did something foolish, but she couldn't stand there and watch anymore either.

Once on the stairs, she moved so fast she tripped over her feet and only managed to keep herself from plummeting to the bottom by throwing herself against the wall. Catching her balance, she paused for only a second before continuing down the stairs.

When she made it to the hall, she ran for the door as something outside released one of the most awful shrieks she'd ever heard. Lexi's head shot up as the sound came from all around them, but of course, she couldn't see through the ceiling to whatever lay beyond these walls.

A dragon hadn't made that noise; she'd become accustomed to their roars. This was something she'd never heard before; it was high-pitched, angry, and *hungry.*

The noise slowed her enough that Amaris caught up to her. The fae woman held her side as she panted for air.

"What was that?" Lexi breathed.

"There are many ravenous things in this land," Amaris said.

In her head, Lexi heard the echo of Cole's words from the first night they met… *"There are all kinds of creatures in this land. Some are like the human realm, and others… well, others would give you nightmares for a week."*

"The fight has probably awakened their hunger," Amaris said.

"What…?" Her question trailed off as another echoing screech reverberated over the land. It echoed off the walls until it came from all around them. "Cole."

She ran for the front door again.

"Wait!" Amaris shouted after her.

Lexi didn't hesitate before she threw open the door. She skidded to a halt when she saw she wasn't looking at the courtyard but thick woods. Despite the light of the moons, an impenetrable blackness obscured anything beyond the first row of tree trunks.

The chirrup of what sounded like crickets on steroids came from the trees. From behind one of the tree trunks, eyes the color of a rotten peach blinked at her.

Before she could decide what to do, the door ripped away from her hand and slammed shut. Lexi stepped away from it as it vibrated in its frame.

"That's not the way out," Amaris said as she skidded to a halt beside her. "You do *not* want to go out there."

"It looks the same as the main door, and I swear those stairs...."

She glanced back at the stairs that were duplicates of the ones she'd climbed after leaving the main hall behind. The ones she'd climbed with Cole before.

"It's easy to get turned around in here. Sometimes, I think the palace does it on purpose," Amaris said.

Lexi didn't doubt it, but she didn't think that's what happened now. She didn't understand why, but the palace protected her before, and it did pull the door from her.

It wanted her to see what was out there, or maybe it was hoping she would still think this was the main entrance and wouldn't go out there. She had no idea how the palace worked, but it had a mind of its own.

"This way," Amaris said and clasped her elbow.

She led the way around the stairs and down another hall before they turned a corner, and another double set of doors came into view. When she glanced at Amaris, the helot nodded, and Lexi sprinted for the exit.

Flinging the doors open, she nearly recoiled when the stench in the air hit her. It must not have drifted up to the room she was in before, but down here, it reeked of blood and death as well as the rich aroma of churned-up earth.

Normally, that last part wasn't an unpleasant scent, but it made her stomach turn when mingled with the other aromas. The air also held the odor of something else, something feral and rotten. Something she'd never encountered before.

Another screech drew her attention to the sky as a massive bird-like thing swept into view. Its enormous, bat-like wings briefly obscured one of the moons. Designed to tear the flesh from its victims, it had a long, pointed nose.

Is that a pterodactyl?

No, it can't be.

But it looked so much like one that, for a second, she wondered if she'd stepped back in time. However, there were some differences between this thing and the long-dead dinosaur. Like this thing was a vivid red, but then perhaps the dinosaur was red too.

Bones didn't exactly reveal the color of things, or maybe they did. She wasn't an archeologist, but she was looking at something ancient. Something that had never walked or flown in the human realm.

This was something straight out of the Shadow Realms as it opened its mouth to reveal hundreds of razor-sharp teeth the size of her hand.

"It's a craz," Amaris whispered. "They usually stay in the caves of Wright Mountain, where they feast on the wild goats. The battle must have drawn them out."

As she spoke, two more vicious-looking things flew into view and dove toward the field. The fae below scattered to get out of the way, but one of them wasn't fast enough.

The craz's powerful beak clamped down on his upper body, and the man's legs kicked in the air as the craz soared upward. Its throat worked like a pelican consuming a fish as it gulped the fae down.

The dark fae, who'd fled into the courtyard for protection, screamed as they threw up their hands and ran for shelter. Many of them ran for the stables while others fled into the homes of the king's soldiers.

She almost shouted at them to come to the palace but bit the words back. She had no idea who any of these immortals were or if she could trust them. Inviting them into Cole's home was probably a horrible idea and one that Cole, and probably the palace, would not take kindly to.

"Shit," Lexi whispered as more of them flew into view.

Her gaze found Cole on the field as he battled through the men trying to destroy him. He had to know these monsters were here, but he didn't look up as another rocketed down to claim another victim.

Another round of arrows launched at him. Cole spun in time to deflect many of them with his father's sword while dodging the others with a fluid grace none of the others possessed. Though none of the arrows hit him, she saw what they'd truly intended to do with those bolts... distract him.

"No!" she screamed as half a dozen dark fae charged at him from behind.

Cole spun and took down three of them. He ducked back from a fourth who lunged at him, but the fifth had come up behind him. The steel of the fae's sword glinted in the firelight as Cole spun toward him, but he wasn't in time to stop the fae's blade from plunging into him.

CHAPTER SIX

THE BLADE PIERCED through Cole's shoulder and burst out the other side. Whatever it hit in there caused his nerve endings to send a command he did not issue as his hand went lax, and he released his sword. It hit the ground as the fae twisted the blade within him.

Cole gritted his teeth as, instead of trying to tear himself free of the sword as the fae expected, he pushed his way forward and toward the fae. As he moved, the blade cut through sinew and muscle while plunging deeper into his body.

The man was so shocked that Cole was impaling himself, he stood and gawked at him. When he looked away, Cole knew he was contemplating releasing the sword and running, but it was already too late.

His claws extended, and with one swipe, he cut the fae's head from his shoulders. Others ran toward him as he gripped the sword handle and tore it free.

It was made of fae metal, but he didn't hesitate before turning it on his attackers. With one hand, he swung the sword at the fae charging toward him, disemboweling one and cutting the hand from another before the others jumped back.

His dominant hand remained unmoving at his side, but he'd spent years training with both hands and was as good with his left hand as he was with his right. Another screech from above drew the fae's attention to the skies as the craz soared into view.

Cole didn't look up. The creatures were hunting, and they had plenty to feast on down here. Instead, he used his enemy's distraction to throw the sword that had impaled him into the fire and retrieve his father's sword. He'd secured Nissa's dagger in the sheath for his sword by plunging it into the side to keep it in place.

When one of the craz plummeted from the sky and streaked toward them, the fae closest to him turned and ran. Behind them, Durin mounted his horse as more fae turned and started to flee from the malicious birds.

With his weapons secured, Cole finally looked up to discover nearly a hundred craz crowding the sky and choking out the moonlight. Nissa turned and started to run too.

Cole shifted his hold on his sword and pulled the dagger from his sheath. Once it was free, he sheathed his sword.

He could not let her and Durin escape. They would only try to regroup and continue the rebellion if they did. Without them as leaders, this uprising would come to a fast and bloody end. If one of them survived to lead, it could continue for weeks or months.

There was no way he would allow the loss of life that would result.

A craz dove at him as he sprinted after his enemies. When it landed before him and opened its mouth, he shifted the dagger into his other hand. The feeling was starting to return, and his fingers closed around the dagger's hilt.

Without missing a step, Cole lifted a lost sword from the ground and plunged it straight down the craz's gullet. The animal choked, but he didn't see what it did next as he sprinted past it.

Nissa climbed onto her horse and gathered her reins. Most of her guards had fled from the craz, but some remained. A few turned toward him as he approached.

Cole ducked beneath the first sword arcing toward him and swung up with the dagger. It plunged into the man's solar plexus before Cole ripped it free. The fae grasped at the wound as he staggered back, but more fell in to take his place. And they all wielded weapons made of fae metal.

When another swung a sword at him, Cole blocked the arc with the forearm of his still-healing arm. The metal sliced through his flesh and embedded in muscle. He bit back a shout as he used his arm to keep the fae from tearing his sword free.

Cole stuck the dagger into the fae's belly, grasped the sword's handle, and jerked it free. He swung the blade out in time to clash with the swords of more rebels. Over their shoulders, he saw Niall thundering across the ground with his sword raised high.

Behind him, more of the king's army closed in on the others, but as they encircled the leaders, the craz descended. Some of the king's men were plucked straight from their horse's backs; others managed to avoid the creatures as they clashed with the rebels.

Cole yanked the dagger free of the fae's gut and, lowering his shoulder, attempted to charge through the ten fae who remained. He used the sword to block their lethal blows, elbowed them out of the way, pushed them aside, and punched to the best of his ability.

They swarmed over him like locusts, kicking and stabbing as he deflected one sword after another. He was determined to make it through this even if he couldn't see beyond their barricade.

And as he was about to break free, fiery pain lanced across his nerve endings.

One blade had gotten through to find its mark.

Throughout all his battles, he'd endured countless blows, cuts, gashes, and slices to his body. He'd been stabbed, burned, and buried alive beneath the sand of the trials.

But he'd never felt pain like that of fae metal piercing through his muscle and bone to embed deep in his heart. The organ lumbered to beat around the intrusive blade as the fae who stabbed him bared his teeth in a twisted smile.

"That was a short reign, *milord*," he spit the word "milord" as if it were a foul taste on his tongue.

Cole grinned back at him as he leaned forward and plunged the dagger into the fae's heart. The man's eyes widened; a gurgled sound issued from him as blood bubbled out of his mouth.

Cole punched the man in the face, knocking him away from the sword. He didn't grasp the handle to rip the blade out as he staggered forward and went down.

CHAPTER SEVEN

"Oh no," Amaris whispered before gripping Lexi's arm. "Come, we must get you out of here."

Lexi pulled her arm free of Amaris's hold. "No."

"Miss... Lexi. You shouldn't be here when the council arrives to claim the palace. They won't... they won't appreciate your presence here."

Becca really wouldn't appreciate it, but Lexi didn't care what they wanted as she watched Cole go down. She'd never experienced such terror and sorrow as a steel vice gripped her heart and squeezed until she was sure she'd go to her knees as Cole had.

But she couldn't do that. He needed her to remain strong, and she would.

"The council is not coming in here," Lexi stated.

"With the king dead, the council has a right to the palace."

"He's not dead!" Lexi retorted.

When Amaris recoiled, Lexi regretted the harshness of her words. But he *wasn't* dead. He would *not* die.

"Lexi," Amaris said tenderly. "I know you aren't of our world, but a dark fae cannot survive fae metal through the heart. And that sword was fae metal."

But a lycan can. Or at least she hoped they could. Brokk was half vampire, and he'd survived when he took a fae sword through the heart; Cole would too.

If she could get him off the battlefield. The others would all think him as good as dead. Some might try to retrieve his body, but with everything going on out there, not many of them would risk their lives for what they believed was a dead man.

Amaris rested her hand on Lexi's arm again. "Lexi—"

"I have to go."

Except she didn't turn and flee into the palace like Amaris wanted. Instead, she ran out the door and into the courtyard. If she somehow survived this, Cole would kill her, but she couldn't leave him out there.

The others would all count him out, but not her.

Sprinting across the open courtyard, Lexi grasped the reins of a large, gray horse that had trotted back in with some of the other riderless animals. She'd homed in on the one least covered with blood, grasped its reins, and vaulted onto its back as her mind raced and her heart hammered.

Cole has a blade through his heart!

And so did Brokk.

She kept reminding herself of this as time crawled by. If Cole survived the blade through his heart, the longer he was out there, the more vulnerable he was and the more likely he was to die.

Seconds became hours as all the minute details around her stood starkly out. The earth and blood scent of the battle became so acute, she could taste them both. The screams of the dying faded as the rapid beat of her pulse drowned them out.

She turned the horse toward the open side door that the horses, and some of the injured had returned through. The main gates remained locked, and she suspected the palace wouldn't open them for her or the council.

She didn't want them to open anyway. She would get to Cole,

but she couldn't leave those inside the palace vulnerable to an attack. That side door was her only way out.

"Lexi, no!" Amaris shouted after her as she dug her heels into the horse's side.

The small sword and throwing stars bounced against her sides as she nudged the horse into a gallop. Its hooves thundered across the earth as she neared the small side door. When she was still twenty feet away, it started to close.

It didn't surprise her. The palace had protected her against Becca and whatever lay in those woods. It was seeking to protect her now, but she would not have it.

"NO!" she shouted, and for a second, the door hesitated, but then it continued to close.

Lexi leaned over the horse's neck as it galloped faster. She would crash into that door before she stopped, something the palace seemed to realize as the closing door slowed before swinging open again.

Then she was going through it. The door brushed her side but didn't knock her from the horse as she raced onto the battlefield. Most of the fleeing civilian fae had already arrived at the safety of the palace; the ones still fleeing now were fighters.

The wind tore at her hair and plastered her clothes against her as the horse flew across the ground. A craz landed in front of them and released a hideous shriek. The horse leapt to the side as it twisted away from the monster.

The sudden motion nearly unseated her, but years of riding had made her capable of handling most anything when it came to horses. She righted herself and regained control of the horse as it danced away from the craz.

The glow of the fires played over the monstrous beast, illuminating its leathery flesh and yellow eyes. It was revolting and determined to eat them.

When the craz lunged for them, Lexi slid her hand into her pocket and removed one of the skin-melting potions she'd taken from Sahira's stash. She ignored the twinge of discomfort that came when she shifted the reins into her burned hand.

She steadied the horse and threw the vial as the craz came at them with its jaws hanging open. The vial burst in its mouth before its jaws clamped around it.

The creature screeched hideously, but she didn't look back as she steered the horse toward where she last saw Cole. And then, she topped a rise in the earth and spotted him on the battlefield.

~

COLE SHOVED ASIDE another dark fae as he strained to get at Durin and Nissa. He clenched his teeth against the agony of the blade in his heart as every movement caused it to shift and cut deeper.

Fuck! He inwardly snarled and nearly went to his knees when someone stumbled back and hit the hilt of the sword.

Durin and his men were trying to fight their way through Niall and some craz. Nissa's men were struggling to get her free of the king's men and the craz. He used his claws to decapitate a dark fae who ran at him before plunging the dagger into the heart of another.

He nearly went down again but managed to catch himself by grabbing the arm of Nissa's man. The blade of a sword whistled through the air, and though he couldn't see it, a breeze cooled his cheek as it arced toward him.

He swung his head to the side in time to avoid losing an eye. The blade slicing across his temple spilled more of his blood. He didn't think he had much left in him to lose.

The craz above screeched excitedly as they dove out of the sky. With their talons fully extended, they impaled their victims into the ground and picked their skin away like crows on carrion.

He was about to hammer his fist into another fae's chest when a craz crashed into the man's side and tore him away to expose *Nissa*.

CHAPTER EIGHT

Cole sneered as he lunged forward. His claws extended, and fangs filled his mouth as the lycan sought to break free. Unsure of how much more damage it would cause him if he transformed, he suppressed the impulse.

Nissa scrambled to get on her horse, but she wasn't fast enough. Grasping her shoulder, Cole yanked her back as one of her men sank a sword into his ribs.

He grunted as it pierced through bone and embedded in his lungs. He tried to draw in air, but the sharp pang the motion caused made it impossible.

Releasing Nissa, he twisted as much as he could with the fae still holding the sword, seized the man's throat, dug his claws into it, and tore it out. When the man staggered away, he pulled the sword with him.

Cole winced as the sword scraped across his ribs before tearing free of his flesh. Blood filled his lungs while he gasped for breath. He didn't know how much longer he could remain standing, but he would take his enemies down before he fell.

He lunged for Nissa. This time, when he got his hands on her, he didn't let go. Pulling his hand back, his fingers clamped around her throat, and he sank the dagger into her heart.

Nissa's mouth parted, and her hands shook as she clawed at Cole's face. Cole smiled as he twisted the blade deeper.

"Fuck you," she spat, and blood sprayed his face. "You're already dead too."

Cole didn't reply as he yanked the dagger free. Blood gushed forth, and Nissa's hands went to her chest as she sank to her knees. Cole turned to fend off the rest of the men protecting her, but they'd already turned to flee when their mistress fell.

More were fleeing the craz and the king's guard as they hacked their way through the rebels. He smiled grimly when Niall cleaved Durin's head from his shoulders. It rolled across the ground before a craz dove down to swallow it.

And just like that, what remained of the rebellion fell apart as its leaders perished. The fighters turned and fled.

The craz killed most of the ones who the king's guard didn't take down, but some fled over the hills. He would have to send men after them, but first, he had to get off this field.

The blade in his heart shifted when he staggered toward Niall, who was carving his way through what remained of the rebellion. He was almost to Cole and extending a hand toward him when a craz crashed onto Niall's back and dragged him from his horse.

Niall and the craz vanished as they rolled across the ground, with Niall battling the craz as they rolled over a hill. Cole released the dagger as he stretched a hand over his back for his sword.

A scream rushed up his throat and clogged there as the movement sent a wave of blackness across his eyes. Straining against passing out, Cole pulled his sword free.`

He panted for air as sweat ran down his forehead and into his eyes. He didn't dare try to wipe it away; he'd probably pass out if he did.

Cole stepped toward where Niall vanished before his legs gave out, and he went to his knees. His sword fell at his side as he remained kneeling with his head bowed as he tried to draw air into his brutalized lungs.

With thick, fumbling fingers, he clawed at the handle of the blade in his chest as the blood seeping around it soaked his chest and dripped onto the ground. He no longer cared if removing it would cause him to bleed more; he couldn't have the thing poking and digging into him every time he moved.

No matter how hard he tried, he couldn't get it out. Giving up on trying to remove it, he lifted his head and gazed at the spreading fire as it leapt higher. Fae and horses fled from the slaughter of the craz as more of the birds dove from the sky.

Lexi. I have to get back to her.

He dug his fingers into the ground as he pushed himself to his feet. He couldn't die out here on this field and leave her behind, not after what happened with the Lord and Malakai.

They would tear her apart.

The possibility of that happening propelled him forward a couple of steps toward the closest horse. Grasping the reins and the pommel, he tried to pull himself onto the saddle, but the blade in his heart made climbing onto the horse difficult.

He released the reins. Teeth clenched, he smashed his fist onto the hilt of the sword again and again.

He grunted, and blood sprayed from his mouth as the blade pierced out his back, and he buried it to the hilt in his chest. Clinging to the saddle, he swayed as he tried not to pass out.

Sweat dripped off his face, his vision blurred, and the horse leaned to the side as he slumped against it. But he didn't pass out, and once he could see clearly again, he could move better now that only the hilt of the sword protruded from him.

Better able to maneuver, he grasped the reins and started to pull himself up when a craz hit the side of the horse. The animal screamed and lurched forward as the craz snapped at it. Rearing, the horse spun and hit Cole.

Flung back by the blow, Cole hit the ground and crashed into a couple of bodies before coming to a halt. The impact knocked the air from him.

He labored to inhale oxygen into his already brutalized lungs as his mind spun and weakness crept through his muscles. His fingers had gone numb, and he couldn't feel his feet, but it wasn't enough to keep him down.

His fingers sank into the blood-drenched earth as he pushed himself to his knees. The thud of something hitting the ground drew his attention as a craz landed three feet away from him.

The creature released a screeching bellow that sounded like a cross between a lion and an irate hawk. As it charged toward him, Cole reached for his sword again. It didn't matter if he could breathe or not; he'd carve this thing to pieces.

It opened its mouth to reveal its flesh-rending teeth as it raced toward him on its two, stork-like legs. He managed to pull the sword free and rise as he braced himself for the impact of the nearly two-hundred-pound creature.

It was nearly to him when it released another screech that could shatter glass. And then, it began to dissolve even as it tried to take flight again.

Its skin sloughed off the side of its face, falling to the ground in a puddle that bubbled as it dissolved. Its wings flapped like a butterfly with broken wings, and it didn't get an inch off the ground before collapsing.

From behind it, a large gray horse came into view as it raced toward him. What remained of his heart lurched when he spotted the red flowing around the horse's neck. He couldn't see her face behind the horse's head, but he'd recognize that shade of red anywhere.

Lexi.

CHAPTER NINE

COLE OPENED his mouth to tell her to leave, but she was already dismounting and running toward him. As she did, another craz landed and ran at her. She spun and threw a vial at it. When the contents exploded over the creature, its skin started to boil before peeling away.

Her long hair, having worked its way free of its braid, whipped around her face as the spreading fire ate the land with deafening intensity. As the dark fae scrambled to escape the battle and the craz, there was no one left to put out the fire. And he certainly wasn't in any condition to do it.

The light of the flames playing over Lexi's face emphasized not only her beauty but also the steely determination etched onto her features.

"Get out of here," he hissed when she arrived at his side. It was difficult to get words out when he could still barely get air into his lungs, and every movement caused the sword to dig deeper into his heart.

"Not without you."

"You shouldn't have left the palace."

"I know."

He hadn't expected the acknowledgment on her part, and for a second, it knocked some of his anger away. He lifted his head to survey the battlefield full of dead men, horses, and craz. Blood, death, and fire consumed the land, and she should *not* be anywhere near any of it.

"We have to go!" she shouted to be heard over the fire.

She clasped his hand and draped his arm around her shoulders. Cole refused to let her see how much agony he was in or the weakness seeping through his body. He steadied his wobbly legs as she led him to the horse.

The animal's head was held high; its ears flicked as it took in the noises around it. It looked ready to bolt from the spreading fire but held its ground.

She leaned him against the saddle as Niall burst through the smoke and raced up to them. Blood streaked his face, and ugly gashes marred his shoulder and left arm. Lexi pulled out another vial and prepared to throw it at him before Cole seized her arm.

"Not Niall," he told her. "You can trust him."

She frowned at him but put the vial away as Niall skidded to a halt beside them. His breath came in rapid pants; he was bloody and bruised but still quick and sure.

His eyes fell on the sword in Cole's chest, and his eyebrows shot up before he met Cole's gaze again. If there was ever a time to try to kill him, it was now when he was weakened and more focused on getting Lexi to safety, but Niall would not try to do it.

"Durin is dead," Niall said.

"So are Nissa and Fiadh," Cole said. "The rebellion's leaders have fallen, and the remaining traitors are running. When we've had time to regroup, send men to hunt down the rebels and destroy them."

He would do it himself, but if they survived this field and made it back to the palace, he wouldn't have much left in him for commands.

"It will be done," Niall vowed before glancing at Lexi.

"Keep her alive," Cole commanded.

"I will."

"Get on the horse," Cole said to Lexi.

"After you," she said.

"Lexi," he growled.

"If you're sitting behind me, you could fall off. I should be behind you. I can avoid the sword."

"And you're going to be strong enough to stop me from falling?"

Lexi lifted her chin as she glared at him. "I made it this far, and I'll do whatever it takes to get you safely back to the palace."

The fire in her eyes eased his dread over having her standing on this field. She *would* do whatever it took to protect him, and she'd made it farther than many others. What amazed him most was she'd done it for *him*.

He knew she loved him, but many immortals and mortals loved another and wouldn't risk their lives for them. Not his Lexi, though; she was brave, selfless, and she loved him as deeply as he loved her.

He clasped her chin and gave it a small squeeze before gathering what little remnants of strength he still had to sheath his sword and grab her waist. With shaking arms, he lifted her off the ground and onto the horse.

She was still sputtering protests when he grasped the reins and pulled himself onto the horse behind her. It was the most awkward and uncomfortable way he'd ever settled onto a horse.

He almost released the lines and fell when he jarred the sword in his chest, but willpower and Niall grasping his foot to push him further up finally got him settled in the saddle. Stars erupted before his eyes as he hissed in a breath.

"Cole?" Lexi asked.

"I'm fine," he grated out.

When he was sure he wouldn't pass out, Cole lifted her a little and settled her on his lap the best he could before grasping the reins.

"I'll lead the way," Niall said.

It was then Cole saw that he'd found another horse and was already sitting on it.

Did I black out for a little bit?

If he had, he couldn't let it happen again. He had to get Lexi safely back to the palace, and if he fell off the horse, she would stop for him. She was not going to leave him out here, and while it only made him love her more, he wouldn't allow her to die because of him.

CHAPTER TEN

IT TOOK everything Cole had to stay on the horse as Niall led the way across the field. The rebels had scattered; all that remained were their bodies and the craz who feasted on them. More of the craz circled overhead, diving toward the remains and the allure of the fleeing fae.

Cole tried not to slump against Lexi, she would only worry if she realized how weak he was, but as the horse galloped across the earth, the sword shifted inside him each time it landed. It was getting more difficult to maintain an appearance of strength while his heart was shredding.

She took the reins from him and, leaning forward in the saddle, guided the horse with the expertise of one born to ride. She steered clear of the obstacles in their way while also managing to throw two more vials of melting potion at the craz.

Niall hacked his way through a few more craz as Lexi removed a throwing star from the pouch at her side. She whipped it side-armed at a craz diving toward them. The weapon shot into the craz's open mouth and knocked the monster on its ass.

He'd known she was training with Brokk, but he hadn't realized how much she learned while he was going through the trials.

He'd fought with men who'd trained for years and weren't as courageous as her on the battlefield.

He slid his arm around her waist and slipped another star from the pouch. He briefly admired the fae metal before flinging it at another craz. The movement pulled at his flesh and spilled more blood, but he reached into the bag and pulled out another one.

∼

THOUGH HE TRIED to hide it, Lexi could tell Cole was growing increasingly weak as he slumped against her more and more. Still, he managed to throw another star that knocked the craz descending toward them off its target.

Blood bloomed across the front of the bird's chest as it spiraled away from them and the closed gates they approached. They had to get through the door and into the bailey; she had to get Cole to safety.

She focused on those gates while Cole and Niall fought off the craz who weren't occupied by eating the dead. As they neared them, the door also came into view, and she breathed a sigh of relief when she saw it remained open.

Digging her heels into the horse's side, she urged it faster as their safety loomed closer and closer. Twenty feet... Fifteen... At ten, she was certain a craz would crash into their back or the door would slam shut.

The palace wouldn't shut them out, but some didn't want Cole to rule. Would the palace open the door for them again if it was closed?

Five feet...

Come on. Come on....

And then they were flying through the open side door and into the courtyard. Many sought shelter when the craz arrived, but it was still crowded with dark fae seeking refuge from the battle and craz.

The injured lay on the ground, and survivors ran around as they tended to them. Her horse's hooves dug up the earth when she pulled up on the reins. The animal skidded to a halt a few feet from the palace stairs.

When Cole shifted behind her, she grasped his forearm as he slid to the side and nearly went down. Kicking her feet free of the stirrups, she leapt off the horse and landed beside him. Cole kept his shoulders back as she wrapped her arm around his waist and led him toward the steps.

"Let me help," Niall offered.

"No!" Lexi snapped. "Stay away."

Her free hand found the last remaining star in her pouch. She didn't care if Cole said she could trust Niall and that he'd helped get them off the battlefield. She didn't trust anyone other than herself around Cole right now. He was far too vulnerable.

"Easy," Cole whispered in her ear. Others might think it was a tender, loving gesture, but she knew it was because he couldn't hold his head up anymore. "I told you, you can trust Niall."

"Can *you*?" she retorted.

His blue eyes swam with pain when he turned his head toward her. Staring into those eyes, etched with lines that weren't there before and surrounded by dark shadows, she was more terrified now than when she was on the field.

"Yes," Cole whispered.

Lexi eased her grip on the star and didn't protest when Niall draped Cole's other arm around his shoulders. The palace doors opened when they arrived at the top of the stairs.

Amaris hovered nervously in the hallway. Her dark eyes were wide as she stared at Cole. He was a bloody, awful mess, pale and barely standing, but any other dark fae would have been dead by now. The fact he was still breathing was mind-blowing; that he was still *walking* was a miracle.

"Can I get you anything?" Amaris asked as she rushed over to Niall's side.

"No," Lexi said.

Cole said she could trust Niall, but she wouldn't trust anyone else with his life. Traitors surrounded them in this realm; she liked Amaris, but she'd be damned if she let anyone else do anything with Cole.

Cole's weight pulled more and more against her shoulders and strained her back as they ascended the stairs. By the time they finally made it to his rooms, his feet dragged across the ground, and when they laid him on the bed, he was unconscious.

Lexi tried not to panic as she stared at his unmoving form. Had it been pure willpower driving him this far?

Is he dead?

CHAPTER ELEVEN

"STAY AWAY FROM HIM!" Lexi commanded in a far too high-pitched voice as Niall leaned over Cole.

She wasn't exactly portraying strength by nearly shrieking at him, but she couldn't control the gallop of her heart or the terror spiking her adrenaline to epic levels. Then Cole inhaled a rattling, wet breath that didn't bode well for his health but told her that he was still alive.

That knowledge didn't ease her stress. He was alive but so vulnerable, and she was the only one she trusted to protect him. She would make sure he stayed alive.

The dark fae rose slightly to study her. He lifted his hands, but she saw the hostility in his black eyes.

"He's my king and my friend," Niall said. "He's safe with me."

He's the love of my life, and I don't care what you say.

But she held the words back. None of the dark fae cared about love or feelings. They respected control and power. To them, love was a weakness.

"I'll take care of him," she said.

"You'll need my help."

"Stand outside the doors and guard them. Do *not* let anyone else in here."

A muscle twitched in his cheek; he didn't like taking orders from her, but when his eyes returned to Cole, his stance relaxed a little.

"He is my king. I cannot leave him with you," Niall said. "How do I know *you* won't kill him."

Lexi was stunned he would consider such a thing. "I am to be your queen. You will do as I say."

His eyes narrowed as Lexi's shoulders went back.

"How do I know you are to be my queen? He has not proposed to you."

She had no power over Niall and certainly wasn't strong enough to force him from the room, but she wouldn't back down either. However, his words reminded her how tenuous her position in this world was.

She was alive and here because Cole had brought her here, and this man respected that; many others wouldn't.

"He brought me here. How many other women has he done that with?" she demanded.

The way his eyes darted away gave her the answer she'd sought.

"I went onto that field to get him. *I* saved him. I would *never* hurt him, and he'd expect you to listen to me," she said.

The irritation on his face made her reconsider her bravado, but when his attention turned back to Cole, his eyes softened. Cole was more than a king to this man; Niall also cared about him.

She still preferred not to have anyone else near him when he was this vulnerable.

"I can help you save him," Niall said.

Lexi wasn't sure anyone could help her save him. At least not without the aid of a witch, and Sahira was hunting for the harrow stone with Brokk. The only other witches she knew were at the new marketplace, and it would take too much time for her to get there.

Sahira had more potions at the manor, some of them must be healing potions, but she couldn't leave Cole alone with another dark fae. No matter how much Cole trusted this man, she couldn't leave them alone while Cole was so weak.

"You can help me by guarding the door," she said. "I'll let you know if I need anything more."

Niall's nostrils flared, and his jaw jutted out, but he stepped away from the bed. Lexi didn't breathe easy until he left the room. She hurried after him and stood in the bedroom doorway as he made his way across the sitting room, opened the door to the hall, and paused there.

He looked over his shoulder at her. "I'm not leaving this hall."

"Good. Don't let anyone in here."

Although, if the palace didn't want anyone in this room, they wouldn't get in unless they battered down the door or set it on fire. But she would take all the extra help she could get to protect Cole, even if it was from the other side of the door.

When he closed the door, Lexi ran across the room and clicked the locks into place. Knowing it wasn't enough, she retrieved a chair from the corner and wedged it under the door handle before rushing back to Cole's room.

He lay on his side with the sword blade still sticking out of his chest. It took everything she had not to rip the weapon out of him, but she couldn't do that without some supplies first.

And then there was the other wound, the one through the side of his chest. She didn't have the time to examine it more closely, but it had to be tended and would require help to heal.

He'd survived when almost all other fae would have already perished, but that injury, on top of his copious blood loss, could still be the end of him. She had to get her hands on some healing potions, but to do so, she would have to leave him here, alone and unprotected.

She stepped back to recheck the chair and door. Neither had moved.

If she went fast enough, she could be back here in mere minutes. But what if she couldn't find anything to help?

That was a chance she had to take. She ran over to the bed, and with tender care, she removed his father's sword from his back. Smoothing his hair from his forehead, she kissed him tenderly.

"I'll be back soon. I love you."

Lexi couldn't look back at him as she ran to the portal he'd left open; if she did, she wouldn't leave. And if she didn't go, he would probably die.

Though her heart screamed at her to turn around and go back, Lexi kept moving. She plunged into the portal that would take her home.

When she burst out the other side, she half expected Orin to be still hanging out, stirring a pot of spaghetti sauce, but the kitchen was empty. She was grateful for that; the last thing she needed was to deal with him right now too.

Lexi flew across the kitchen toward the cabinets where Sahira kept her potions.

CHAPTER TWELVE

"Orin?"

Orin turned away from the closed, metal door when his brother, Varo, spoke. Sometimes, Orin forgot what his brother looked like now, and it would shock him to see Varo again. This was one of those times.

Varo had always been slender, but since the war, he'd lost more weight. His high cheekbones stood out starkly against his pale skin, and the dark circles under his eyes made his white-blue eyes vividly stand out. The war hadn't been kind to his half light fae sibling, and the aftermath was less so.

"Varo," he greeted with a smile.

Varo's eyes shifted to the cell, and a line appeared across his forehead. "What are you doing here?"

Orin jerked his head toward the cell. "I have some questions for our inmate."

"What could you possibly have to ask Del?"

"There are some things I'm interested in learning about his daughter."

"You know his daughter?"

"Yes. She's Cole's mate."

Varo's black eyebrows rose into his hairline. "Cole has a mate?"

At the same time, Del asked from behind him. "What did you say?"

Orin ignored the vampire as Varo glided closer.

"Cole has a mate?" Varo asked again.

"Yes. Apparently, that lycan part of him is stronger than we believed."

"How is he?"

"He's Cole. Stubborn, single-minded, and judgmental. He's also king of the dark fae."

Varo stopped walking. During one of his visits back to this realm, he'd told Varo about their father's death and that Cole would face the trials, but the revelation Cole had survived them was new to Varo.

"He survived," Varo whispered and closed his eyes. "That is good."

"Yes, it's all freaking fantastic, but we've moved on from that. We have more important things to discuss now."

Varo opened his eyes. "What have you done, Orin?"

"Me?" Orin feigned offense as he rested his hand over his heart. "I haven't done anything."

Varo wasn't at all swayed by his protest of innocence. Orin rolled his eyes and turned back to the door. Del's eyes remained a vivid shade of red as he glowered at him.

"It's *his* daughter who's done something." Orin pointed a finger at Del. "So, we're going to have a little discussion, aren't we, Del?"

The vampire's face remained stony. This wasn't going to be easy.

Orin flashed his best smile at the vamp, who didn't react at all, which wasn't surprising as it usually worked best on women.

However, he was a charmer, and he didn't like it when those charms didn't melt others as they should.

Orin continued to smile as he approached the door. "Your daughter is a very interesting young woman, Del. It's been a pleasure getting to know her better."

And pulling on her heart strings to manipulate her into doing what I wanted, but he kept that to himself.

Del didn't reply.

"She has my brother twisted around her lovely, little finger. It's quite an interesting thing to see. I never expected anything like it from Cole. But then, I'm sure you always thought the same about him as you know him well. Did you ever think he'd fall for an immortal who is half human and half vampire or for *any* woman?"

Nothing.

Orin decided to give him a little nudge, even if it was just to piss Del off and more for his amusement. "Did you ever think the man who led you through the war would fuck your daughter?"

The tiniest tic of a muscle in his cheek was the only reaction Del had to those words.

"I mean, you fought with him in the war," Orin continued. "You were one of his most trusted generals. From all accounts, the two of you were close, and he pays you back by crawling into bed with your *daughter*."

"What are you trying to do?" Varo inquired.

"Nothing. I like pushing his buttons."

Del's eyes narrowed. "You're nowhere near the man your brother is."

"Ouch!" Orin cried as he slapped his hands over his heart. "That stings. Oh, wait, no, it doesn't."

He was well aware that when it came to Cole and him, most found him lacking. His older brother was bigger, stronger, more powerful, and far more reliable. He was also *far* more boring, so Orin was happy with being considered "inferior."

Besides, he'd proven most of them wrong during the war. He'd hated standing against his father and brothers, but he made a name for himself on those fields. His side lost, but he'd become such a thorn in the Lord's side that the twisted prick was still trying to hunt him down.

He took great pride in that.

CHAPTER THIRTEEN

"But you sure don't like hearing about your friend, someone you trusted, screwing your daughter or that a dark fae is banging her," Orin continued. "A dark fae with a *lot* of previous sexual partners, as all dark fae have. I bet you saw Cole go through a *vast* number of women during the war. And now our brother is going through your daughter, or should I say"—he made a circle with his left index finger and thumb before shoving his right index finger through it a few times—"*into* her."

"That's enough," Del snarled, and his fangs flashed in the dim light of the nearby torches.

Orin's smile widened. "Does that bother you, vamp?"

"Orin," Varo cautioned.

His little brother never had the stomach for this sort of thing, but mind games were where he excelled.

"He's mated her too," Orin continued. "The lycan part of him has claimed her. I've seen the bite, but then, those lycans always like to mark their territory."

Orin studied the vampire's face for the tiniest reaction.

"The Lord had our father killed because he wanted Cole to assume the throne, and he has," Orin said. "Unfortunately, he had to return to the Gloaming to fight a rebellion there; your daughter went with him."

Nothing.

"But not before the Lord had her brought to Dragonia."

It was like talking to a wall as Del kept his face impassive while he stared at a spot over Orin's shoulder.

"Now that he knows about her, the Lord intends to use her to keep Cole in line. After all, she's his mate, and we all know a lycan will do anything for their mate. The Lord is going to keep a close eye on her. If Cole steps out of line, he's going to let his men rape her."

A small muscle twitched at the corner of Del's eye.

"That's if he doesn't let his dragons eat her like he commanded one to do to our father. Not to mention, I'm sure the Lord will spend some time with her too. She is beautiful, and many men would be happy to take her to bed... willing or not. But, if there was some way to bring the Lord down, some secret only a few knew about, then we could all work together to keep her safe."

Orin paused to let his words sink into the stubborn vamp's head before continuing.

"I saw a silver marking on your daughter's hand, Delano, so I stuck it in some fire."

Del's eyes burned a little hotter.

"Do you know what happened?" Orin inquired.

And *there* it was! The tiniest flicker in his eyes and a small shift in Del's posture was a subtle enough change to let Orin know he held the vamp's full attention. He'd also stopped breathing as he waited to hear Orin's reply.

Del wouldn't have this reaction if there weren't something to react to, no matter how small it was.

"Do you know, Del?" Orin pressed.

Del didn't respond.

"Well, I'll tell you, it burned her," Orin said.

"Of course it did," Varo muttered.

"No, *not* of course," Orin said as he stepped closer to the door. If the metal weren't separating them, he would be standing toe to toe with Del. "Because she's not what she claims, is she, Del?"

Del didn't respond.

"If the Lord has his way, then she's going to be around him and his dragons more often. He's going to rape her eventually; there is no avoiding it, and we all know it, including her. Can you imagine how terrified she must be of that knowledge?"

Del's upper lip curled into a sneer as he finally met Orin's eyes again. Orin suppressed a smile as his needling finally started to chip away at the stubborn vamp's resolve.

"You're a prick," Del spat.

"I'm aware."

They stared at each other for a while before Orin continued.

"Cole can do *everything* that psychopath asks of him and do it all perfectly, but it will *never* be enough, and the Lord will take it out on her. But if she's something else, something we can use—"

"*No* one is using my daughter for anything," Del growled.

Orin didn't agree, but he wasn't going to say so. "Are you ready to talk to me about her?"

"I'm not talking to you."

"To Varo?"

Del didn't speak again.

"Would you trust Cole enough to talk to him?"

The silence stretched on for so long that Orin didn't think Del would respond. And then, he gave a barely perceptible nod.

Orin rocked back on his heels as he contemplated what to do. If Del wasn't hiding anything from them about Lexi, then he was opening himself up to a whole lot of anger from Cole, Lexi, Brokk, and Sahira for nothing.

But if he kept the vamp here, he wouldn't talk. Well... he would *eventually* speak, but it could be a while before his concern for Lexi finally broke him down enough to reveal all to Orin.

And he didn't have that much time; none of them did. They

had to do something about the Lord sooner rather than later. Del and Lexi might be the key to bringing him down.

Or he could be completely wrong, and he was handing one of his prisoners over for no reason. She may be exactly what she claimed, but Orin didn't think so.

And after seeing Del's reaction, he believed he was about to be proven right.

CHAPTER FOURTEEN

BROKK STRUGGLED to hide his shock as he gazed at the young women standing outside their lodges. Best described as tepees, the structures had thick, wood beams sticking out the top of the roomy canvas structures. Different symbols and runes were painted on all of them.

Some of the dwellings had their flaps pulled back to let fresh air into the shadowed interior. He glimpsed bedding stored inside as well as empty and full bottles of potions tucked neatly within.

The assorted ingredients for potions were also stored inside and outside the structure. All of the lodges had fires burning outside their doors. Heavy, black cauldrons hung over the flames.

Many of the lodges were tucked beneath the canopies of beautiful green, red, and orange trees. The sun shining through their leaves cast shadows over the ground and illuminated their dazzling array of colors.

The beautiful, haunting melodies of the pixies floated on the air until the songs intermingled in such a way they all came together as one. The different tunes didn't grate on the nerves but soothed them.

He'd never been to a witch's realm before, but that was

because he was part vampire, and they would probably set his ass on fire if he tried to enter their realm alone. He enjoyed not having toasted buns and liked sitting, but this was different. This was a land for crones and not the witches' kingdom.

He supposed it was still technically a witches' land since the crones resided here, even if he had yet to see one. He kept searching for the old women, but they were all young. Some were beautiful, others weren't so blessed, and others were intriguing or pretty, but none of them were stooped over and old.

Mixed in with the women and the landscape were other immortals. Pixies giggled as they flitted past. Each of them was a different color, and their translucent wings left a trail of multicolored dust in the air. The dust settled across the ground to create a rainbow pathway he and Sahira followed until a small breeze blew it away.

Mermaids basked on the rocks of the lake they passed. On the shore, their tails had taken on the hue of the sun and shone gold beneath its rays.

Once back in the water, those tails would become blue or green as they became the color of the water. Neither the men nor women wore tops.

Unicorns also moved through the lodges. Their hooves were noiseless on the thick, vibrant green grass. Some of them were pure white with gold horns, while others were completely black with gold horns. All of them had eyes the color of sapphires.

Overhead, pegasusses flapped their wings and soared over the land. Like the unicorns, they were either pure black or pure white, but their eyes were the striking color of a violet.

Phoenixes sat on perches outside some of the lodges. Some preened as they cleaned their beautiful feathers and fluttered their wings. Others were missing large clumps of feathers and sat with their heads down like stooped over old men.

Tiny chicks peeped as they accepted food from the older, more vibrant ones. The phoenixes in their prime possessed red bodies with striking red and orange wings and tail feathers. A golden tuft of hair stood on top of their heads.

As they passed, one of the older ones fell off its perch. Before it hit the ground, it erupted into flames.

Brokk stopped as the last ash fell onto the pile that had accumulated on the ground. He smiled when a small peep sounded from the pile's center and a tiny head poked out. At first, the phoenix's eyes were closed; then they opened to reveal its beautiful, amber eyes.

When it released another peep, he almost said *aww* as his heart melted a little. Then he recalled where he was and stifled his amusement. Any sign of weakness in this place might get him killed.

He threw his shoulders back a little and glanced at Sahira, who was staring at him with amusement.

He pretended not to notice as he glanced around. "What kind of an outer realm is this? All the ones I've been to have been barren chunks of rock with little or no life on them."

"This is the land of crones. Witches love to grow things, and the crones have been making this their home for hundreds of years."

"Where are all the crones?"

She frowned at him. "We've passed a bunch of them."

"We have?"

He looked behind him, but he didn't see any crones there. When he turned back to Sahira, she wore that amused expression again. At first, he found it cute; now, it was becoming annoying.

"I know the term crone brings to mind ugly, stooped, old women with warts on their faces, but witches are immortal too. They're not about to cast spells over themselves to make them age, even after they come here to retire," Sahira said.

Brokk chose to ignore her grin as he started walking again. He refused to acknowledge he'd been so focused on his image of a crone that he hadn't stopped to think they were immortal and would therefore look young.

He didn't look at Sahira as he took in more of the realm. On the other side of the lake, a family of sasquatch emerged from the thick foliage of the woods.

The father had to be at least nine feet tall, while the mother was a little smaller. Their two children barely came up to their waists but were probably five feet tall.

The parents sat and drew the kids toward them; they settled their young in their laps before plopping their enormous feet in the water. The children munched on tree branches while their parents worked the mats from their thick, brown fur.

"How did all of these magical creatures end up here?" he asked Sahira.

"Most of them are outcasts from their realms, or they left for some other reason. They all possess things commonly used in witches' spells, so the crones invited them to live here where it is private and safe. It's a win-win for all involved."

"Interesting," Brokk murmured.

They snaked their way through more of the lodges until they came across one at least three times the size of the others. The white canvas stretched taut over the poles sticking out from the top was painted with different sun and moon symbols. Streaks of color, runes, and other witch symbols also marked the canvas.

"Here we are," Sahira murmured.

Five phoenixes sat on a perch outside the open flap. The fire beneath the cauldron had died out, but whatever was inside still bubbled as they passed it. A pixie landed on the planter beside the entrance.

Herbs overflowed the container. The pixie giggled as her wings fluttered, and she smiled coyly at Brokk before settling her wings into place. A trail of orange dust fell at her tiny feet. Most pixies were only three to six inches tall; she was no exception as she stood about four inches tall.

"Hi, cutie," she said in her tiny voice and blew a kiss at him.

Brokk held out his index finger to her, and she clasped it in her minuscule hands. She gave it a small shake.

"Pleasure to meet you," he said.

She giggled again and rested her cheek against her shoulder as she batted her lashes at him. Her orange eyes shone with merriment, and her apricot hair fell to her shoulders in tight ringlets.

"You too," she said in a voice that barely carried to him.

She released his finger and flew away as Sahira ducked to enter the lodge, and Brokk followed. He'd barely taken a step inside when a voice boomed.

"Vampires are *not* welcome here!"

He didn't get the chance to see who the thunderous voice belonged to before a blast of wind hit him. It was so strong and unexpected that it threw him out of the lodge before he could register what was happening.

He flew a good ten feet through the air before hitting the ground. He bounced across the earth on his ass before stopping with his back against a tree. Sahira crashed into his feet as she skidded to a halt in front of him.

CHAPTER FIFTEEN

WHEN LEXI RETURNED to the Gloaming with the healing potions, she rushed back to Cole's side and knelt on the bed beside him. She'd only been gone for a couple of minutes, but he hadn't moved.

That fact—despite knowing a person sleeping normally wouldn't have moved around during that time—only ratcheted up her panic. He barely breathed as she carefully lifted his head and prodded open his mouth.

Pressing the bottle to his lips, she steadied her trembling hands before pouring some of the liquid into his mouth. Her heart pounded as she waited for him to swallow before giving him more.

When the bottle was empty, she stroked his cheek with her thumb as she tried to calm her racing heart. He was too cold to the touch. Far too cold, and his lips had taken on a blue hue.

"Don't you dare die on me," she commanded before kissing him.

Laying him gently back on the pillows, she slid off the bed. She ran into the bathroom, scrubbed her hands, and gathered as many towels as she could before returning to Cole. With tender care, she placed the towels around him to be ready for when she pulled out the sword.

Resting her hands on his back, she carefully shifted him again so she could see the sword embedded in him and the wound in his side. She blinked away the tears blurring her eyes.

He'd been so brutalized and beaten, but he was still alive, which was more than she could say for his enemies. And if the leaders of the rebellion weren't already dead, she'd kill them herself.

But they were dead, and she had to make sure Cole survived. She shifted him again, so the blade rested against the bed but wasn't digging into it. It couldn't get stuck in the mattress.

Taking a deep breath, she wiped her palms on the clean sheets of the bed before gripping the hilt of the sword. She stared at Cole's pale, handsome face as she tried to gather the courage to remove the blade.

No matter what she did, this was going to hurt him, and even though she'd given him the potion, he would not heal while the weapon remained inside him. She braced herself and pulled, but the sword didn't budge.

She couldn't get enough leverage to pull the sword free. After readjusting him a little, she pulled again, but the blade still wouldn't budge. Biting her lip, she shoved aside her frustration as she resisted her impulse to jerk on it; that would only hurt him more.

She studied Cole and the sword. She might be able to get it free if she placed her foot against his chest and pulled on it, but she couldn't do that to him.

Finally, she admitted she would need help to remove it.

Reluctantly, she crawled off the bed, returned to the outer door, moved the chair, and cracked the door open. Niall stood on the other side with his legs braced apart and his arms crossed over his chest.

Beyond him, the hall was empty, but someone could be lurking

there. When Niall glanced at her over his shoulder, the stony coun-
tenance of his face eased a little.

"Is everything okay?" he asked.

"I need your help," she whispered.

"Cole?"

"He's fine, but I can't get the sword out."

She stepped back enough for Niall to enter. She studied the
hall, but if there were a dark fae out there, she wouldn't see them if
they were hiding in the shadows.

She hoped the palace would know and alert them to someone
trying to approach, but she wasn't exactly sure how this place
worked. The magic and mayhem here were all a fantastic mystery,
but one that could backfire on her if she trusted it too much.

Lexi closed the door, locked it, and positioned the chair against
it again. It was then she realized Niall wasn't in the room.

CHAPTER SIXTEEN

LEXI RAN into the bedroom and skidded to a halt when she discovered Niall standing beside the bed. He wasn't doing anything other than standing there, studying Cole, but she stalked over to stand protectively near Cole. She climbed back onto the bed and rested her hand on Cole's shoulder.

"He's going to survive," Niall said. "If he's made it this far, he'll survive. No other dark fae would still be breathing."

She didn't tell him about Brokk having survived a fae sword through the heart, but then Brokk hadn't been this badly injured.

"Yes, he is," she agreed. "I'll hold him while you pull it out."

"He doesn't have much left, but there's going to be a lot of blood."

"I know. I gave him a healing potion and have the towels to help stop the flow."

He didn't ask where she'd gotten the potion from, and for that, she was grateful. *Cole trusts him,* she reminded herself.

She held Cole as Niall gripped the sword's hilt. When he gave her a small nod, her hands tightened on Cole before he pulled the blade free. She tried not to wince as metal scraped bone and Cole grunted.

As soon as the blade was out, blood poured from the wounds. Lexi snatched up the towels and pressed them against his chest and back in an attempt to staunch the flow. Niall set the sword aside and knelt on the bed beside her. When he reached for one of the towels, she almost snatched it away, but the look on his face caused some of her tension to ease.

She let him lift the towel from the bed and reluctantly removed her hand from Cole's chest. Niall held the cloth against Cole's chest while she kept the other against his back. With her free hand, she lifted another towel and pressed it to the hole in his side.

The injuries to his bicep, shoulder, and forearm had already started to heal. Blood seeped from them, but his skin had knitted closed over both.

The wounds he sustained before the fae metal pierced his heart were healing faster than the ones he received during and after the sword went through his heart. The fae metal hadn't killed him, but it was slowing his healing ability.

She released the towel and kept it lying there as she leaned over Cole to lift another potion from the bedside table. To remove the stopper, she had to let the towel go.

When she did, Niall picked it up and held it against the wound. Lexi tipped Cole's head back and poured some more potion into his mouth. When he had no other choice, he swallowed the liquid.

She put the stopper back in the empty bottle and set it on the table before brushing back some of Cole's hair. Some of the color had returned to his face, but he was still far too pale for her liking. Though his lips weren't blue anymore, they were still the bloodless color of a corpse.

His skin was still cool to the touch but warmer than before. As she ran her fingers over his cheeks, she relished the roughness of the stubble lining his cheeks. It felt real and solid beneath her hands; that was something she needed right now.

"You're a witch?" Niall asked.

Lexi hesitated before answering. If he believed she was a

witch, he might be less likely to try something. *Cole trusts him*, she reminded herself yet again.

And so far, he'd done nothing other than try to save his king. No, not just his king; he considered Cole a friend too. That much was obvious.

She had no one else to trust in this realm. She might as well give at least a little faith to this man, who'd earned it.

"No, but I know one," she said.

She took the towel away from Niall again and tossed the blood-soaked cloth onto the floor. Then she plucked a clean one from the bed and held it against Cole's back while she used her other hand to press down on the towel against his side. The blood didn't drench the towels as fast as before.

She wanted to take that as a good sign, but she was scared it was because Cole didn't have much blood left in him. When the cloths soaked through, she and Niall changed them out again.

Over the next hour, Cole's blood stopped flowing enough that they didn't require the towels, and the wounds to his shoulder, bicep, and forearm completely healed. When Niall helped her maneuver Cole to clean his injuries and examine them more closely, she saw his flesh was closing over all three of the awful holes in him.

She retrieved the water pitcher from a table in the main room, filled it with warm water, and returned it to Cole. She and Niall used the water to clean Cole.

Once they finished cleaning the wounds and Cole, Niall helped her dress his injuries with one of Sahira's salves before bandaging them. Then they removed the soiled bedding and, with tender care, remade the bed with sheets she found stored in a closet in the hallway.

She still wasn't entirely sure about Niall, but by the time they'd remade the bed and settled Cole onto it, she trusted him more.

"I should return to the hall," Niall said. "My presence there will deter anyone from trying to bother you."

Lexi followed him to the outer door. He moved the chair out of the way and stepped into the hall. He turned back toward her as she started to shut the door.

"I'm not going anywhere," he said. "If you need me for anything else, I'll be here. Anything at all."

"Thank you," she murmured before closing the door.

She put the chair against the door again and returned to Cole's room. Walking over, she brushed the hair back from his forehead and bent to kiss him. She still had two bottles of healing potion left and three-quarters of a jar of salve, but she'd wait a little bit before giving him more.

If she gave them all to him now, the pain-dulling properties would wear off, and she'd have nothing left to give him to help with it. If she kept them spaced out, then he shouldn't experience much discomfort as he healed.

Grabbing the chair beside the window in the corner of his room, Lexi carried it over to the bedroom doorway. She retrieved the sword they'd pulled from Cole and went into the bathroom to wash the blood from it.

She scowled as the blood ran down the drain of the luxurious steam shower. She was tempted to climb inside, sit on the bench, and let the hot water pound onto her aching muscles and filthy clothes, but she turned off the water and returned to the bedroom.

Rifling through Cole's things, she pulled out a clean shirt and pants. They were far too big for her, but she couldn't stand the stench of blood and death cleaving to her. She stripped out of her clothes and threw them near the door to the hallway.

Pulling Cole's clothes on, she rolled the waistband down and the bottom of the pants up. The shirt was short-sleeved and too big on her as the sleeves fell to nearly her wrists. She tucked the shirt into the pants to help keep them up.

Settling onto the chair, Lexi positioned herself to see the door to the hall and Cole. She placed the sword across her lap as she prepared to kill anyone who came through that door.

CHAPTER SEVENTEEN

"THAT DIDN'T GO AS PLANNED," Brokk muttered as he peeled himself off the ground and brushed the dirt from his ass.

Sahira's face scrunched, and her chin jutted out as she glared at the lodge like she was about to tear it apart with her bare hands.

"I am so sick of this shit," she muttered. "Being half vampire doesn't make me *lesser*."

Brokk agreed with her, but there weren't many witches who would. In their eyes, vamps would always be the scourge of the earth.

Sahira's hands fisted as she rose and stalked back toward the lodge. Brokk admired her determination, but he wasn't going anywhere near that pissed-off witch again.

When Sahira stopped outside the open flap, the phoenixes and pixies took flight. Brokk didn't blame them as the deadened fire beneath the cauldron blazed back to life.

The purple mixture within the cauldron boiled as it spewed out of the pot and splattered the ground. Despite not wanting to get any closer, Brokk stepped toward the lodge to stop Sahira.

"I said *no* vampires!" the woman inside snarled.

"I am half witch!" Sahira retorted.

"Not good enough."

Before Brokk could grasp Sahira's arm, another blast of wind rocked outward, blowing the flap out and knocking Sahira back a step. This time, they were better prepared for the attack and didn't go flying across the ground. It still took everything he had to withstand the tempest.

His hair blew back, and his clothes cleaved to his body as he leaned into the wind. Sahira's mahogany hair tore free of its bun to whip through the air, but she didn't back down. Though they fought it, it pushed them back a few feet as they leaned into the wind like climbers on Mount Everest.

When the fire beneath the cauldron increased, Brokk edged away as it nearly blistered his exposed flesh. The purple goo inside the pot shot everywhere. He jumped back to avoid being splattered by the witch's brew. It might turn him into a toad.

"I am one of you!" Sahira snapped.

The wind only increased as the ground became coated with purple slime. More witches emerged from their homes as the exchange started to draw their attention. As they drew closer, the hair on Brokk's nape rose.

None of them looked happy, and *all* of them could put a curse on them.

Sahira had said the journey to this realm wouldn't be dangerous. He doubted she'd expected the wrath of the irate witch they'd come to see or for the other witches to look like they wanted to kill them.

"Nothing with vampire blood is one of *us!*" the witch battering them with wind declared as she emerged from her lodge.

Her silvery blonde hair tumbled in thick waves to the backs of her knees. Translucent, pewter gray eyes shone with fury as they fixed on Sahira. For an ancient crone and a pretty *shitty* hostess, the woman was unbelievably beautiful.

A thin, white dress hugged her curvaceous figure and floated around her as she glided toward Sahira. The slight cleft in her chin gave her delicate appearance and oval face an air of stubborn strength.

A ball of fire hovered above the woman's hand. Sahira didn't back down or try to conjure something to use as a weapon against her. Brokk's fingers itched for the sword he left behind so as not to seem hostile to the witches.

Sahira had been certain they would not attack one of their own, even if she were half vampire. And now, he would give anything for a weapon.

He almost grabbed Sahira's arm to pull her away but stopped himself. Right now, this crone wasn't acknowledging him, but if he moved, he might draw her attention and her ire. And if she didn't like a vampire who was half witch, she certainly wasn't going to like *him*.

"We came for the harrow stone," Sahira said.

Brokk admired her calm as she continued to lean into the wind battering them.

"You'll never get it," the crone replied.

"I have an *extremely* important reason for it. One that could save countless lives," Sahira said.

The fire hovering over the witch's palm swelled. Brokk was certain she was about to launch those flames at Sahira.

Sahira must have suspected the same thing as her chin rose. "If you do not give it to us, you very well could be dooming countless others to death. We have come here to use it for good; we have come here in the hopes it will help us stop evil, and we need *your* help to do it."

When the woman stepped closer to Sahira, she had to tilt her head back to look up at the crone who stood a good four inches over her five-foot-five height. Brokk nervously eyed the women. He had no weapons, but if the crone tried to harm Sahira, he would take her down.

The crone studied Sahira before she closed her fingers around the fire, and the flames went out. Brokk nearly went tumbling forward when the wind abruptly cut off. He staggered a step before righting his balance.

The sudden hush after the berating wind was a welcome relief as he glanced around at the witches and other immortals who had crept closer throughout the exchange. He didn't look behind him to see what was there. Instead, he kept his attention focused on the woman before him, but at least he would hear any attacker coming from there if they came after him.

"You're telling the truth," the woman stated.

"Yes, Kaylia, I am," Sahira said.

"I will hear what you have to say."

The words looked like they were pulled involuntarily from her, and her face puckered like she'd sucked a lemon. The woman glanced at the other witches before turning to glower at him.

She could toast him, and she would enjoy doing it, but he couldn't stop himself from grinning at the stunning woman. He felt like Orin, but he enjoyed irritating her.

With a dismissive upturn of her slender nose, Kaylia turned away to speak to the other witches. "Go back to your homes," she commanded.

The witches hesitated before breaking up and walking away. Kaylia stood and stared after them for a minute before she flicked a disdainful glance at Sahira. As a half vampire, too, Brokk found the look infuriating, but Sahira remained docile.

If they didn't require this crone's help, he'd tell her to take the stone and shove it up her ass.

"I better find this worth my time, or I'm going to make you both pay for it," Kaylia vowed.

"It will be," Sahira promised.

Brokk didn't speak. He had no idea what this woman would find worth her time, and he wasn't about to make any promises to this witch when dozens of others surrounded them.

Besides, if he opened his mouth, Kaylia would not like what came out.

CHAPTER EIGHTEEN

COLE'S EYES cracked open before he closed them against the influx of light. It felt like someone was peeling away layers of his skull. White lights flashed against the backs of his eyelids.

He struggled against the wave of blackness trying to bury him as his stomach heaved. Sweat broke out on his forehead and slid down his back as he tried not to vomit.

He was in too much pain; if he threw up now, his head might explode and his insides would tear apart. At first, he couldn't recall why he ached so bad, and then memories of the battle started to return...

The blood, the death, the fae sword piercing his heart, and the agony erupting in his chest. And then, *Lexi!*

His eyes flew open again as he recalled her on that battlefield. *Where is she?*

Another knife stabbed into his eyes, but it wasn't as bad this time, and he ignored it to take in his surroundings. He was in his bedroom, lying on his bed, and surrounded by clean sheets. The chair he slept in when Lexi was here was gone, and his father's sword leaned against the wall near where the chair usually sat.

And then, he spotted it in the doorway with Lexi sitting in it.

Focused on the other room, she stared at what he assumed was the door. The same fae sword that once pierced his heart rested across her lap.

The regal way she sat reminded him of a warrior queen, and he recalled how the fire of the battlefield created a halo around her that set her hair ablaze. She'd been a warrior then, and she was one now.

But then, though she lacked the power of many immortals, she was a fighter. It was one of the things he loved most about her.

Pride encompassed him as he stared at the courageous woman who had stolen his heart. She was magnificent, and she was his.

As he recalled her on the battlefield, he remembered the silver marking on her hand from the dragon touching her. He'd touched a dragon before—he'd killed one—but his skin had never reacted like that.

His head pounded, but now that he remembered the marking on her hand, he also recalled the one on her forehead the night he attacked her. She'd fallen out of the bed after he woke from his nightmare and realized he was strangling her.

Cole still hated himself for that night; he always would, even if he hadn't meant to attack her.

At the time, he believed the silver on her forehead came from hitting her head on the bed frame when she fell, but now...

Now, he had no idea who or *what* the woman sitting across from him was. When Orin questioned her about it, Cole blew him off because Orin had just hurt her and Cole was infuriated with him.

Then word of the rebellion arrived, and they'd come here.

But now, after seeing her on the battlefield, he couldn't help questioning things. What were the silver marks? Who was this woman with no abilities that survived riding into a battle to save him?

And what did it all mean?

She didn't have the answers for him; he was certain of that.

She believed herself to be half human and half vampire. And how could she possibly be anything more?

He'd known her father before he died. Del was a vampire; Cole did not doubt that. He'd never known her mother, neither had Lexi, but if the woman were anything more than human, then Lexi would be more powerful than she was.

And while she possessed better senses and was stronger and faster than any human, she was nowhere near as strong as most immortals. In a short amount of time, she'd learned a lot while training with Brokk, but she hadn't exhibited anything beyond her capabilities.

Then he recalled his conversation with Orin after his brother burnt her hand…

"Sometimes the arach would get silver markings on them," Orin had said.

"So?" Cole asked.

"So, your mate had a silver marking on the back of her hand. Don't you find that a little strange?"

At the time, he hadn't, or at least he hadn't considered it, but Orin was right. The arach were said to have silver markings at times. Or at least that was the rumor.

However, there were plenty of rumors and legends about the long-dead race. No one knew what was true anymore.

But if Lexi were half arach, it would be impossible for her to hide those powers, even if she were only half. And how could that be possible?

It had been a thousand years since an arach, the rightful rulers of Dragonia and the dragons, had reigned. They were all supposed to have died centuries ago, but Lexi was only twenty-four.

What was going on here?

He'd like to figure that out, but the pounding in his head made thinking difficult.

CHAPTER NINETEEN

WHEN HE SHIFTED on the bed, Lexi's head twisted toward him. For a second, she simply stared at him. Then her face broke into a beautiful smile, her hunter green eyes lit with joy, and she jumped up.

Completely forgotten, the sword clattered against the stone as it hit the floor.

"Oh," she whispered.

He smiled when he saw she was wearing his clothes. They were far too big on her, rolled up too many times, and completely hid her lush figure. He'd never seen her look so adorable.

Lexi ran to him and was about to throw herself onto the bed when she caught herself and skidded to a halt beside the mattress. "You're awake!"

He managed to smile at her. "I'm awake. How long was I out?"

"A day."

"Have you slept?"

"I'm fine."

Which meant no, she hadn't, and it also explained the dark shadows under her eyes.

"Lexi—"

"I'm okay. I took a shower, and that was enough to keep me awake."

"You should have slept."

"I shouldn't have taken a shower, but—" She shrugged. "—I needed one."

"Lexi," he whispered.

Her eyes darted to his before she looked guiltily away. He grasped her hand resting on the mattress and rubbed it with his thumb.

"You pulled me off that field; you deserve a shower," he told her. "You deserve far more than that."

"I shouldn't have left you alone."

She was far too stubborn for her own good. "Have you eaten?"

"Niall had some food and coffee brought up to me."

"Where is Niall?"

"In the hallway. I thought it was better if he stayed out there."

"You can trust him."

"So you said, but I'm not trusting anyone else with your life." She lifted a bottle from the bedside table and carefully climbed onto the mattress. "I was so worried." She uncapped the bottle and held it to his lips. "I returned as fast as I could to the manor and gathered some of Sahira's healing potions. Drink."

He smiled as he obeyed her command and swallowed the sweet-tasting liquid. When he finished, she set the empty bottle on the nightstand and turned back to him. Her hands were tender as they ran over his face.

Sensing her continued anxiety, he clasped her hands and pulled them away. He kissed the backs of her knuckles before placing her hands in his lap.

"I'm fine," he assured her.

"You had a sword *through* your *heart*."

"But fae metal can't kill a werewolf."

Tears shimmered in her eyes.

"Lexi," he murmured.

A single tear slid down her cheek.

"Don't cry," he whispered as he brushed the tear away with his thumb.

He hated that tear. It tore into his heart more than the sword had.

"I'm not," she sniffled before thrusting her shoulders back. "Let's check your bandages."

He didn't say a word as she started to remove the wrappings. He studied her lovely face with its sun-kissed skin and smattering of freckles dotting the bridge of her nose. She'd twisted her deep auburn hair into a knot that rested against her slender nape.

Beneath the scent of his soap, her sweet, strawberry aroma drifted on the air. When he rested his hand against her cheek, her sweeping lashes rose, and her hunter green eyes, with their flecks of emerald, met his. Her rosebud lips parted.

She was so beautiful, and she was *his*.

Drawing her closer, he kissed her. When he deepened the kiss by running his tongue across her lips before nibbling at her bottom lip, she pulled away.

"You have to relax and heal," she scolded.

"I'm feeling much better," he assured her.

"Hmm," she grunted as she rested her hands on his chest and pushed him back. "Let me take a look."

The steely tone of her voice made him smile as she finished pulling off the bandages. He glanced at his healing wounds as she examined them. The one in his chest was still raw and red, while the one in his side was more of a pink color and nowhere near as irritated looking.

That one would mostly heal by tomorrow, and the one in his chest would be completely closed by then.

"They both look good," she said.

"They do."

"I'll clean them and wrap them again."

She washed them with tender care and pressed her hand against the hole in his chest when pink seeped out to stain the cloth. The bleeding soon stopped, and she finished dressing the wound.

As soon as she finished, he pushed aside the blankets and swung his legs out of bed. Before he could rise, she seized his arm and stepped in front of him.

"What are you doing?" she demanded.

"Getting up," he replied. "I've been in bed long enough, and the kingdom needs to see that I'm alive."

"You can't be serious. You were stabbed through the *heart*."

"And the sooner the dark fae see me walking around after that, the more they'll respect and follow me."

"Cole...." Her voice trailed off as he rose from the bed.

She scrambled back and grasped his arm when he swayed a little. The blood rushed from his head, and he nearly collapsed onto the bed. Gritting his teeth, he forced himself to remain standing while his healing heart raced.

He was doing a lot better, but there was a stutter in his heartbeat, and it lumbered harder than it used to. Unable to move, he stood and waited to see if he would have a heart attack. But then, the tension in it eased, and it gradually returned to normal.

Or the normal it was now as its beat was staccato at best. But it was still beating and far better than it should have been, given it had a sword through it yesterday.

Brokk had survived fae metal, he should have survived it too, and he had. But he shouldn't be healing this fast. It had taken Brokk more time to heal, even with Sahira's potions.

He'd always been stronger than his brothers, but this was different. This was a combination of the healing potions, finding his mate in Lexi, and the shadows he sensed all around him. The ones creeping through him now.

"Are you okay?" she demanded.

"I'm fine."

"You should rest for at least another day."

"I can't."

"Damn it, Cole."

"There are still rebels out there to hunt down."

"You are *not* going to do that today."

"Not today, but soon." He smiled when she stomped her foot. "I'm going to be fine."

Her glower was her only response.

CHAPTER TWENTY

LEXI BIT her tongue as Cole slowly dressed. His hair was still damp from the shower he'd taken, and he'd trimmed his rough stubble into a neat beard along his square jaw again. She'd helped him with the buttons on his tunic, but it was all he would let her do.

He slid his feet into soft leather boots and pulled a dark red cloak around his shoulders; he pinned it at his throat with a wolf broach. When he finished, the cloak fell forward to cover most of his tunic and chest. Lastly, he slipped his father's sword onto his back.

"You could get yourself killed," she said.

He lifted the last bottle of healing potion, removed the stopper, and downed the contents. He set the empty bottle down and crossed the room to stand before her. Tilting her head back, she took in all of his six-foot-seven frame as he towered over her.

Even having just risen from the dead, he was gorgeous with his black hair and Persian blue eyes. The tips of his pointed ears poking out through his hair made her recall how much he enjoyed having them touched.

His broad shoulders blocked out the sun shining through the

window behind him. She grasped his arms and squeezed as she tried not to think about every horrible thing that could happen to him outside this room. He would never admit it, but he was still weakened from what happened.

"You can't return to the fight," she said.

"Not today," he said. "But soon. The dark fae have to see me out there now, though. They have to know I survived when *no* purebred dark fae would have. And the sooner they see me, the sooner they'll know."

"Know what?"

"Not to *fuck* with me again. They're not going to take me down."

Lexi gulped, but she didn't know if she was afraid for him or what he was about to face. She retreated to the chair and lifted the short sword she wore onto the battlefield. She'd kept the larger sword in hand, but the smaller one had remained by her side. Unfortunately, she had no stars left.

"I'm coming with you," she said as she strapped the sword on and returned to his side.

He didn't argue as he held his arm out to her, and she slid her arm through his.

"When this is over, you're going to sleep," he said.

"So are you."

He smiled at her. Lexi tried not to let her apprehension show as he strode toward the door with far surer steps than she would have believed possible.

She hoped he could keep this portrayal of strength up as he unlocked the door and opened it. Niall turned toward them; he froze when he spotted Cole.

"Milord!" he blurted.

His eyes ran over Cole as if he couldn't believe what he was seeing. His mouth opened and then closed again.

"Niall," Cole greeted.

"You're... you're *up*."

"I am. Thank you for protecting her."

"Of course, milord."

Niall broke into a smile before bowing his head. He stepped aside as Cole exited the room. Lexi kept her arm locked through Cole's. She watched his every move and felt for every vibration as she searched for any sign he was weakening.

Lexi tried to imitate Cole's air of nonchalance as they strolled down the hall. Shocked by Cole's emergence and the fact he was walking after he'd been stabbed through the heart with fae metal just *yesterday*, Niall didn't follow them at first.

Then, he rushed to catch up.

"How many did we lose?" Cole inquired.

"I got the full report at sunrise. So far, we have lost twenty of the king's guards, but five more are still seriously injured. Ten citizens also perished as they tried to escape the approaching rebellion."

"Far too many," Cole murmured.

"Yes, milord."

"Did you send men to hunt down the rest of the rebels?"

"Yes. They went out this morning. I only sent ten of them. I thought you would prefer if most of the guards remained here. I can send more if you'd like."

"How many rebels do you think are left?"

"Best guess? I'd say thirty survived. The craz chased a lot of them across the field and took them down."

Lexi glanced up at Cole when he became quiet. She could practically see the wheels spinning in his mind as he considered Niall's words.

"Ten should suffice for now," Cole finally said. "I'll decide if there should be more after we go outside."

"Yes, milord."

"You've called me Cole for our whole lives, Niall. Please continue to do so."

"Yes, mil—Cole."

"How many displaced fae are in the courtyard?"

"The last report I received said there were a few hundred fae seeking safety within the courtyard."

Cole nodded, and Lexi tried not to glance nervously at him as they descended the stairs. He walked with confidence and grace, but he was still healing and weak from blood loss. He hadn't had the chance to feed or eat.

Her fingers tightened on his arm as they reached the bottom of the stairs and stepped into the hall. A few helots were in the hallway, and when they saw Cole, their mouths fell open. One of them let go of the supplies they held.

Glass shattered across the floor, and the woman who'd dropped the stuff jumped back to avoid the scattered debris. Amaris appeared in the hallway and froze when she saw them. Her hand flew to her mouth.

"Mi-mi-milord?" she stammered.

Cole bowed his head to her as he strolled past. Amaris looked like she was staring at a ghost, and maybe, in some ways, she was. She'd believed he was dead, so, to her, he did return to the land of the living.

"Was it not fae metal?" one of the women whispered after they passed.

"It was," another whispered. "You saw it. We *all* saw it."

Following Cole's lead, Lexi didn't look back at them as Cole opened the doors. The courtyard looked worse under the sun than it had beneath the moons' rays.

Dark fae were scattered everywhere. The injured lay sprawled across the ground as others tended to their injuries. Their moans and weeping intermingled with the barked commands of those trying to return order to the realm.

It was all so horrible, but they were alive and would hopefully remain that way.

Lexi searched the sky for the hideous birds but didn't see them anywhere. "Where are the craz?"

"When they finished with their meals, the fire eventually drove them off," Niall said.

Lexi gulped at the term "meals" and tried not to picture those birds pulling the flesh from their victims.

"Once they were gone, and we were able to regroup enough, the fae used their powers to smother the fires," Niall continued.

Lexi shifted her attention to the land beyond. It had once been so beautiful and vibrant, but now all the green grass and homes were gone. The scorched earth looked like something out of an apocalyptic movie as giant chunks of torn-up earth, ashes, and dead craz remained.

It would take a long time for this realm and its inhabitants to recover from this, and while she'd always been a little intimidated by the dark fae, her heart ached for them. Though, most of them would probably prefer to see her leave this realm and never return.

More bodies lay outside the gates, but no one tended them. It was far too late to save them.

CHAPTER TWENTY-ONE

COLE DESCENDED the stairs so swiftly Lexi almost had to run to keep up. She scowled at him before composing her face into something more neutral. He was trying to project an aura of strength and confidence, but he would weaken himself further if he didn't take it easy.

As they walked through the crowd of injured and displaced, they drew the attention of the fae helping with the wounded. They also attracted the attention of the ones huddled together, standing in doorways or in the middle of the courtyard with dazed expressions on their faces.

Etched onto all their dirt and blood-streaked faces was the trauma of losing their homes and land. Cole's presence broke through their disbelief, and though it took a couple of seconds to register on some of their faces, none of them could hide their astonishment once they saw him.

They stopped helping the wounded, they stood taller in the doorways, and they turned to follow him as he walked through the bailey. They rested their hands against their chests, pulled their children closer, and a couple openly wept.

And then they started going to one knee. At first, the movement was slow as they were too stunned, but eventually, they all started going down. They bowed their heads and pressed a fist to their foreheads in acknowledgment of their king.

She was so amazed by what she saw that it took a few minutes to realize they were also staring at her with open curiosity and admiration. Shifting uncomfortably, she inched closer to Cole before focusing straight ahead.

Cole bent and whispered in her ear, "You risked your life to save their king. You've earned their respect, and that is not an easy thing to earn from a dark fae."

Lexi gulped before she lifted her head to meet his twinkling, blue eyes. She didn't know what to say or how to react, so she remained silent as Cole spoke with his people.

He stopped to rest his hand on some of their shoulders. Others, he commanded to rise and spoke with them as he tried to learn more about what was needed to help the injured heal faster.

He promised to get them the supplies they required and ordered Niall to find someone who would go to the market in the human realm to purchase healing potions from the witches.

"We will start rebuilding at once," he promised a dark fae who had nowhere for his wife and children to live. "Until then, we have empty homes here in the bailey that you, and anyone else who needs them, can reside in."

The man bowed his head and stepped away. He was replaced by more who demanded Cole's time or simply sought to assure themselves he was alive.

Throughout it all, he remained strong and radiated an aura of confidence even as she felt his strength dwindling. He did nothing to reflect that growing weakness to them.

She didn't think he was aware of it, but his fingers dug into her arm as they made their way through the last of the survivors. Most of them were on one knee as they approached, and all had their heads bowed.

When Lexi looked behind them, she saw the reverence on the

faces of those who watched them after they passed. *Finally,* they finished greeting everyone and started toward the palace. Cole still maintained an air of strength, but sweat beaded his forehead, and his fingers had become painful against her flesh.

"I'd like to return to the palace," she blurted. "I'm tired, and I'd like to rest."

She was perfectly fine, but she wanted him back in bed.

"Of course," Cole murmured. He turned to Niall. "Please accompany us inside."

"Yes, mil—Cole."

They strolled back to the palace, climbed the stairs, and returned inside. Lexi clenched her jaw and glanced nervously around. If anyone saw him getting weaker, they might think it was a good time to attack.

She still had the short sword on her, but it might not be enough to destroy an attacker. Niall's eyes moved more constantly than hers; he would help keep Cole safe too.

Cole revealed no signs of weakness until they were back into the room and the door closed. Once Niall clicked the locks into place, he sank onto the chair she'd vacated earlier and, gripping the ends, took a deep breath.

Lexi knelt before him and started tugging at his tunic so she could examine his wounds. He tried to stop her, but she slapped his hands away.

"Don't," she commanded, and he relented to her.

She realized too late why he'd chosen the dark red cloak. The color hid the blood that had soaked through his tunic and into the cloak.

"You stupid, stubborn, foolish man," she muttered as his blood coated her fingers.

"I'm fine, love," he assured her as he clasped her hand. "It's only a little blood."

She pulled her hand away to scowl at him.

The annoying ass smiled in return. "It will be fine."

She didn't reply as she helped him remove his tunic and tossed it aside. She unwrapped the blood-soaked bandages to reveal the wounds beneath. Thankfully, the puncture through his lungs still looked good and hadn't bled, but he'd irritated the wounds in his chest and back.

"It's healing well," Niall remarked. When Lexi turned her glower on him, he hastily added. "But you need more rest."

"I know," Cole said. "But going out there today will buy me some time."

"And a lot of admiration," Niall agreed. Then he glanced pointedly at Lexi. "For both of you."

"Great. He reopened his injuries for admiration," she muttered.

"No," Cole said. "I did it to secure my throne and keep them in line. My father was a good, powerful leader, but they've never been led by a king as powerful as me, and now they all know it."

Those words must have cost him dearly to utter, as his father was his hero, but they were true. King Tove did a lot of good for this realm, and he was a powerful man; Cole was stronger.

Niall and Cole exchanged a smile that set Lexi's teeth on edge. Rising, she returned to Cole's bedroom and gathered the pitcher and some fresh towels to clean him again. She filled the pitcher with warm water and returned to find them talking about their strategy for the rebels.

"You're in no condition to go after them," Lexi said.

"Not yet," Cole replied. "But more than ten men will be required to hunt them. Unfortunately, with the injured and the fact we have to start rebuilding the homes here immediately, we cannot afford to send any more of the king's guard after them. They're needed here."

"So are you."

"They'll expect me to hunt down my enemies."

Lexi bit her tongue; he was right, but she still didn't like it. She knelt before him and gently started to clean the injury on his chest again.

"You don't have to do that," he said. "I'll take care of it."

With tender fingers, he brushed back a strand of her hair that had fallen free of its knot. He tucked it behind her ear, and Lexi melted a little beneath his touch.

Then she recalled she was annoyed with the stubborn ass and went back to scowling at him. He had the nerve to *chuckle*.

"If you weren't already hurt, I'd stab you myself," she told him.

Those words only caused him and Niall to laugh harder. Then Cole winced when it irritated his wounds, and his laughter faded.

"Serves you right, jackass," she muttered, and he laughed again but not as loudly.

"She will make a fine queen, milord," Niall said.

And she realized she'd earned more than the respect of the dark fae in the courtyard; she'd also earned his.

"That she will," Cole agreed as he caressed her cheek.

She desperately wanted to melt into his touch, but he was still bleeding, and she couldn't do it.

"You should rest," she said.

He cupped her cheek before focusing on Niall again. They continued to discuss their next move as she cleaned the blood from him and started to wrap a bandage around his chest and back again. She didn't bother to dress the wound in his side; it didn't need the attention.

As she worked, she tried not to let her apprehension show. She'd known being in a relationship with this stubborn, powerful man would be difficult, but she hadn't realized how difficult.

She tried to keep her hands from trembling as she cleaned wounds. These were going to be the first of the many injuries she'd clean of his in her lifetime.

CHAPTER TWENTY-TWO

BROKK STUDIED the beautiful woman who stood on the other side of the lodge as Sahira settled onto the ground and crossed her legs. Kaylia emanated disgust and hatred as she scanned them. Brokk considered giving her the finger.

Sahira looked at him and patted the space beside her. Brokk almost asked her if she was nuts. He'd rather play chicken with a dragon than sit cross-legged in this lodge with a witch who would gladly skewer them.

"Sit," Kaylia commanded.

Brokk bristled over the tone and the words, but the apprehension on Sahira's face silenced his response. Reluctantly, Brokk settled beside Sahira on the thick, fur rug. He remained on his knees with his toes tucked into the rug so he could jump up quickly if necessary.

Unable to look at them, Kaylia stared over their heads and at the canvas wall. For a second, her casual demeanor vanished as her nostrils flared. When she looked at them again, hatred simmered in her gray eyes.

Brokk kept his face impassive as he stared back at her, but it took everything he had not to give her the finger. He knew witches hated vampires, and he supposed they had a reason, but her hatred was a bit over the top and… annoying.

"Why are you here?" Kaylia asked.

He looked to Sahira and gave her a subtle nod. She was as much of a vampire as he was, but these were her people. Well, at the very least, she was half witch, but this woman made it clear she did *not* consider Sahira one of them.

It made him dislike Kaylia more. Despite the history between witches and vamps, Sahira had a kind heart, and the witches refused to see it because of her vamp blood.

If they weren't here to help save his brothers, he would have told Kaylia to go fuck herself and dragged Sahira from this realm. But they needed the harrow stone, and they couldn't make the crones an enemy of Cole, so he remained sitting.

"We need the harrow stone," Sahira stated. "It might help us to take down the Lord by saving some of his greatest enemies."

Some of Kaylia's loathing vanished as her eyebrows rose. She studied them before speaking. "Continue."

Sahira proceeded to fill her in on why they were here for the stone and how they intended to use it to clone his brothers. They planned to make the Lord believe Varo and Orin were dead so they could use their contacts to destroy the Lord while also getting the twisted prick to stop breathing down Cole's neck.

When Sahira finished, Kaylia stared at the wall. As he watched the emotions playing over Kaylia's face, Brokk worried Sahira had revealed too much about his brothers and Cole working together against the Lord.

He told himself to trust Sahira's instincts in this, but she put a lot of faith in a woman who clearly hated them.

"And how do you plan to destroy the Lord after that?" Kaylia asked.

"We're still working on that," Sahira said. "But we need time to form a plan, and the harrow stone is the best way to buy us this.

If Cole doesn't hand his brothers over soon, the Lord will make him, and the Gloaming, pay."

"I have little care for what happens to the dark fae."

Shit, she's a heartless bitch. Brokk couldn't decide if he admired that trait or not.

"He won't stop at the Gloaming, and you know it," Sahira countered. "If the dark fae fall or if he seizes control of their realm, he'll go for the witches or the lycan next. And he'll continue to take them all down until he's destroyed us all."

Kaylia didn't reply again for a while. "Why doesn't Cole just hand his brothers over? It's not like they haven't fought against each other throughout the war."

"They are still our brothers," Brokk said.

Kaylia didn't bother to look at him.

"Orin has followers who could help bring down the Lord if we all work together. We need his help," Sahira said.

"They're not vampires," Brokk said.

When she turned those pewter eyes on him, the chill in them could have iced the dead. She didn't bother to reply before focusing on the wall again.

"Why didn't they all work together in the first place? Why has Cole decided to go against the Lord now?" Kaylia asked.

Sahira gave Brokk a pointed look. "Tell her everything."

"I don't trust her," Brokk replied honestly.

"You don't have a choice."

Kaylia looked bored as she stifled a yawn and stared at the wall. He didn't want to give anything to this woman, but Orin and Varo—perhaps *all* of them—were screwed without that stone.

So, he told the miserable crone about how they'd secretly worked against the Lord the whole time. He didn't name any of the others on the Coalition, but he still felt like a traitor.

"And you think things will be different this time, if you all work together?" Kaylia asked.

"We don't have any other options. We tried to undermine him

and failed the first time. Orin tried to lead a rebellion against him and failed. All we can do now is hope to combine forces to go after him again."

"But many lives were lost during the war, and many armies were wiped out."

"Which is why he'll destroy all the realms one at a time, starting with the Gloaming. We need to join forces with all the realms and those who stand against the Lord, and we require Orin's help and resources to do so. We'll have to move slowly in the beginning, and this can give us time to do that."

She was quiet for so long that Brokk started to question if she'd fallen asleep with her eyes open. Finally, she blinked.

"I will think on it. Get out," she commanded.

Sahira rose, but Brokk remained where he was. That was all she had to say after all they'd revealed?

"If the Lord isn't stopped, he will kill thousands if not *millions* more, including witches," Brokk said.

Kaylia's eyes flicked over him before she turned away, lifted a flap in the back of the lodge, and started to duck out. "Do not leave this realm and get out of my home."

And then, she was gone.

Brokk looked to Sahira, who sighed before rising.

"Do you know her personally?" Brokk demanded.

"No," Sahira said. "I only know of her reputation and that she is the oldest living witch. I've only traveled into a witch realm a few times before, and I was not welcome to stay long."

That wasn't exactly the answer he was hoping to hear. "Then why did you trust her enough to reveal so much to her?"

Sahira gazed at the still-waving back flap as she replied. "Because the witches respect life and nature, all the things the Lord has *no* respect for. They hate the vampires—"

"She wasn't overly fond of the dark fae either."

"I sometimes think that when one lives for so many years, they lose track of what matters, and they harbor resentments they should let go. She will see reason and realize the Lord will destroy those she loves and cares about, including all the living creatures in this realm and beyond, and she *will* help us."

"You have a lot of faith in someone who threw us out on our asses when we first arrived."

"She didn't try to kill us."

"Are you sure?"

"Kaylia is old and powerful; we'd know it if she tried to kill us. She most likely would have succeeded."

"Wonderful," Brokk muttered.

"Is she going to tell anyone else what we revealed to her?"

"I don't know," Sahira admitted. "I prefer to think she'll keep it to herself, but I can't say for sure. If Kaylia gives us the harrow stone, she'll be as culpable in this as we are, so I think, for now, she'll keep it to herself or to those she trusts the most."

"So, if she gives us the stone, we'll know she'll keep our secrets. If she doesn't, then we know we might have condemned us all to life on the run from the Lord."

"Yes."

"Let's hope we get that stone."

Sahira twisted her clasped hands together before turning to leave. Brokk rose and started to follow her out of the lodge. His gaze returned to where he last saw Kaylia. Despite his dislike of the woman, he couldn't deny she also fascinated him.

He hoped Sahira was right and the stubborn witch decided to help them. She may have thrown him on his ass, but he didn't consider her an enemy. If she refused them, he would do everything in his power to bring her down before she destroyed them.

CHAPTER TWENTY-THREE

COLE SPENT the rest of the day and night in bed. Despite her protests, he got up once to shower before returning to bed. Once she had him settled in bed and sleeping again, she used the shower before returning to her guard post.

When he woke again, Lexi checked his wounds. The ones on his chest and back were healing well, and the one through his ribs only had a small red mark to show where the sword had gone through him.

They looked better than yesterday, but...

"I'm going to go home and see if Sahira is back," she said. "The wounds look good, but some more healing potion will help."

He clasped her hand and brought it to his mouth as he kissed her knuckles. Over the top of her hand, he gave her a suggestive smile. "I know something else that would help."

"You can't be serious," she huffed and tried to pull free of him. "You were stabbed through the heart."

"Very serious," he said as he refused to release her. "I'm a dark fae; we don't joke about sex."

"I didn't think the dark fae joked at all," she retorted.

He chuckled as he rubbed the back of her hand with his thumb. "It's very rare, but we can be rather amusing."

"Well, you're not amusing right now, and you're injured."

"You can strengthen me," he murmured as he clasped the back of her head.

"And I could hurt you more."

"Never."

"You're tempting me to do so right now."

When he laughed, she rolled her eyes.

"You can only hurt me in good ways," he told her.

Lexi glared at him, determined to ignore the sexy smile spreading across his lips. Despite the sparkling light in his eyes, she sensed his hunger as they raked over her. The lines around his mouth deepened when his lips compressed.

He'd been on death's door two days ago, but it was obvious he needed to feed and was more than happy to risk his health to do so.

"Cole—"

"It will be okay. *I* will be okay," he assured her.

She started to protest again, but he stopped it with a kiss. At first, she kept her mouth flattened into a line against the pressure of his full lips and their tantalizing taste. However, when his fingers threaded through her hair and his tongue teased her lips, her traitorous body eased into his.

She rested her hands on his shoulders, looking to push him away, but her hands remained frozen there.

He's injured!

That spurred her on a little bit. She tried not to be too rough as she pushed against him, but despite nearly dying recently, he was like trying to move a mountain.

"Easy," he whispered against her mouth. "You don't want to hurt me."

When she huffed and resisted the impulse to punch him, his laughter tickled her mouth. "You're depraved."

"I'm always depraved around you."

Lexi was not at all amused by his teasing tone or words. She turned her head away from him as she labored to catch her breath, but that meant his mouth had better access to her neck. He kissed his way down the side of it as he tasted her in leisurely, enticing caresses.

She was still concerned this was too soon and would only hurt him, but his kisses left her craving more. Before she knew what happened, she was on his lap as his lips made their way down to her collarbone.

His free hand pushed the bottom of her shirt up, and he rested his palm against her belly. Yearning speared through her, but he'd nearly died!

"Cole—"

"I need you, Lexi."

His desperate tone told her more than words how much he needed to feed and connect with her again. Feeding would help him heal, and she wanted this; they would just have to be careful.

Giving up on resisting him, she melted into his arms as he reclaimed her mouth. Suddenly, the fae clothes Amaris brought her to wear felt too abrasive against her skin. They'd been far more comfortable than Cole's clothes, but now she wanted them *off.*

He tried to clutch her back against him when she pulled away, but she kept her hands against his shoulders and broke their kiss. The normally vivid blue of his eyes was duller than usual, and shadows rimmed them.

His hair tickled her palm when she cupped his cheek. His eyes brightened a little, but his love for her wasn't enough to beat back his exhaustion.

Lowering her hand, she leaned further away from him. She grasped the bottom of her blue tunic and pulled it over her head. She'd thrown out her bra with the rest of her ruined clothes, so her breasts spilled free.

When his gaze fastened on her breasts, the blue of them faded, and silver bled through before they flickered back to blue. The fae and lycan parts of him competed for control; this time, she suspected the fae would win.

It was the hungrier of the two.

When she wiggled further back, he released her, and she swung her legs out of bed. Rising, she kept her back to him as she unbuttoned the brown pants before turning to face him. He ravenously drank in her movements as she slowly pushed them down her hips.

With tantalizing, seductive movements, she maneuvered them down her calves and kicked them off one foot. She then used the toes of her other foot to toss them aside. Standing before him, she felt sexy and alive as his gaze roamed over every inch of her.

His magnificent eyes turned silver, then blue and silver again before settling on blue. He shoved aside the blankets and looked about to rise, but when she held up her hand to stop him, he remained where he was.

"You're going to relax as much as possible," she told him.

"It's impossible to relax while looking at you."

She smiled as she shook her hair back from her shoulders. His shoulders tensed, and the muscles in his arms bulged as he gripped the edge of the mattress.

"If I can't touch you," he said, "then *you* have to do it."

His eyes remained blue, but the guttural way he spoke told her the lycan was close to the surface.

"Would you want me to do something like this?'

She ran her fingers between her breasts and down toward her belly. Cole watched her with the same intensity a hawk did a rabbit as she caressed herself. Beneath his unrelenting gaze, her excitement grew as her skin prickled.

She slid her hand further down her belly before bringing it up again. Though she relished this moment between them, she couldn't stop the small bit of shyness creeping in. She'd never done anything like this before.

I will not blush.

Despite her determination not to give in to the bodily function that got the best of her far too often, fire crept into her cheeks. She kept it suppressed as much as possible as she focused on him.

"Let me watch you," he said.

"Watch me do what?"

"Fuck yourself and push yourself to the brink of coming."

Lexi's breath came faster, and though she still felt a little uncertain, she couldn't help but do as he said. Her hand found her breast, and when she stroked her nipple until it hardened, he leaned back in the bed and rested his head against the headboard.

The movement caused the sheets to fall back from his erection. While he watched her hand slide down her belly and between her thighs, he stroked himself.

Lexi never could have imagined herself doing anything like this before Cole walked into her life. Now, she couldn't get enough of everything he did to her and all the new things she experienced with him.

"Are you wet?" he inquired.

"Yes," she whispered.

"Is your finger inside you?"

Lexi slipped a finger in and gasped as she moved it in and out while rubbing against her clit.

"That's it," he murmured. "Do you like the way it feels?"

At first, she couldn't find words as she struggled to remain standing on her increasingly rubbery legs.

"Lexi," he prodded.

"Yes," she admitted.

"But you like it more when it's me inside you, don't you?"

"Yes."

She whimpered, and her legs quivered as her body begged for release.

"Come here," Cole commanded.

Needing to sit down and desperate for release, she stopped

caressing herself. Her skin thrummed with electricity as she approached him.

"Sit in front of me," he commanded.

When she settled herself on the bed, he grasped her legs and pulled them apart to drape them over his thighs.

"Now, let me watch you," he commanded.

CHAPTER TWENTY-FOUR

COLE DIDN'T RECLAIM his cock as Lexi spread her legs wide to give him a good view of everything she did for him. And it was *all* for him. Every inch of her belonged to him, but then, she'd claimed every inch of him too.

When her hands slid between her legs again, his dick ached for release, but he still didn't reclaim it. No matter how badly he wanted to come, she would be the one to make him do so, but first, he would watch her fuck herself to completion.

Her finger moved in and out as she lifted her hips a little. Her head fell back, and her breath came faster as she pushed herself closer and closer to the edge.

When she cried out, the sound of her ecstasy was music to his ears even as she continued playing with herself. She wasn't done, but he would be inside her the next time she came.

Leaning forward, he clasped her wrist to cease her movements. Her head came down, and her dazed eyes met his before a sexy smile curved her mouth.

"It's my turn," he growled.

Seizing her hips, he pulled her further up his lap until the wet heat of her rubbed against his shaft. Her delicious scent filled his nostrils, and wrapping his hand around the back of her head, he brought her mouth down for another kiss.

Her arms slid around his neck as their tongues entwined, and he shifted until his erection prodded her entrance. She was so wet she easily slid down his shaft until he was buried deep inside her.

His wounds throbbed, but he ignored the twinge in them as Lexi moved up and down his rigid length. Their breaths mingled as the energy they produced filled the air around them.

He sensed an increase in the power she emitted before he started to draw on it. And as it filled him, he realized he was right; it was stronger and more potent as it helped ease his hunger while strengthening him.

Despite the influx of strength reducing the discomfort of his injuries and increasing his power, a tendril of unease crept through him. Why was the energy she emitted more powerful?

And then, he forgot all about the question as she moved her hips in a way that had him gritting his teeth to keep from coming. He lost himself to the feel of her as everything else around them faded away.

She cried out again, and her muscles contracted around him; he thrust into her once more before following her over the edge. He groaned as his semen filled her, and he shuddered from the wonder of her body and the way she made him feel.

Finally opening his eyes, he lifted his head to gaze up at her. Her head remained tipped back so the ends of her hair tickled his thighs. An influx of power flowed through his veins; she'd always made him stronger, but this...

This was something different. It was raw and vibrant. His veins thrummed with energy as his skin prickled with awareness. His gaze fell on his marks on her shoulder. They didn't glow in the sunlight, but they were vivid against her flesh.

Is this influx of power because she's my mate and it's been a while since I've fed, or is it something more?

Her head came back down, and she gave him a small, sultry smile before it vanished and her eyes flew to his chest.

"Are you okay?" she demanded.

He grinned at her. "I'm better than okay."

"Your wounds—"

"They feel better than before. I told you, you would help to heal me."

Her fingers rested against his chest. "It does look a little better."

"It is," he assured her.

When she continued to look worried, he clasped her hand and pressed it flat against his chest. It was time to reveal to her the one thing he still hadn't told her... that he'd never shown *anyone* before. It would help to ease her apprehension, or at least, he hoped it would.

"Do you remember when we were in the canoe on the lake by your manor?" he asked.

"I do."

"Do you remember when I said there was one more thing I had to tell you, but it would be easier to show you?"

She bit her bottom lip before replying. "Yes."

"It's time to show you."

∾

LEXI BRACED herself as Cole stared up at her from eyes that were once more a vibrant blue. She loved that striking color, but the tinge of uncertainty in them alarmed her. He was never uncertain about anything.

Then he grasped her hips and shifted her so she slid off him. She instantly missed the feel of him inside her and the connection between them, but he was already moving away. Before she could stop him, he swung his legs out of bed and rose.

"Cole—"

Her protest died when, as he rose, black ciphers materialized across his back, his ass, down his thighs, and to his calves. She forgot how to breathe as she leaned forward to discover more of them spreading across his feet.

She'd heard the dark fae concealed some of their ciphers and only allowed a certain amount to be visible to the outside world, but she'd never expected *this*. They covered his entire back.

When he turned toward her, the breath she'd forgotten about hitched into her burning lungs. Not only did they cover all of his backside, but they also covered his entire front too, including his face.

When her gaze fell lower, her jaw dropped at the flame-like markings encircling the head of his penis. They were *everywhere*. There wasn't one inch of his skin that didn't have some kind of marking on it.

It was amazing, and beautiful, and *terrifying*. How much power did he possess? What exactly could he do if pushed to the absolute edge of his control?

She hoped never to learn the answer to that question. If he hadn't lost complete control when the Lord killed his father, it would take something horrific to shove him over the edge.

He'd spent centuries keeping this power locked away and controlled. He'd already possessed more ciphers than any of the other dark fae, except maybe his father, but she hadn't seen much of his father's markings.

And she realized now she'd only seen the tip of the iceberg when it came to Cole's. Had it always been like this, or had the trials created this? Maybe he hadn't spent centuries learning to control himself; maybe, he'd only spent the short time they'd had between the trials and now.

CHAPTER TWENTY-FIVE

WHEN SHE TIPPED her head back, she discovered his eyes—which were an impossibly *brighter* blue against the black ciphers beneath his eyes—latched onto her.

"How…? I… I… This is amazing. Have these always been on you, or did the trials do this?"

"I've been this way since I stopped aging at twenty-eight. I've always had the ciphers you've seen, but when I reached maturity, more revealed themselves. It's how I knew I'd settled into my maturity. I have always kept them all hidden. *No* one else has ever seen all of them, not even my father. You're the only one who knows."

Lexi's hand went to her throat as she realized the depth of what he'd revealed here today. He trusted her with this secret and with something that could make the other dark fae and the Lord want to kill him even more.

They all respected power, but they didn't want that power turned on them. And they craved all the power for themselves; they wouldn't like the possibility that Cole could take many of them down.

She'd always known he was powerful, but seeing this, she realized she didn't have a clue as to how deep it ran. For the first time, she questioned if *he* knew.

"I'll never tell anyone," she vowed.

And she never would. She would take this secret to her grave.

"Has anyone ever possessed this many ciphers before?" she asked.

As Cole shrugged, she realized the ciphers were fading from view as swiftly as they appeared.

"I'll never know," he said. "If they did, they never revealed them, so it's not in our history."

"No fae has this many now, though," she said.

"No, they don't. I don't have to see their ciphers to know that; I simply know it's true."

And she had no doubt he was right. He would know if there was someone as powerful as him in the Gloaming.

No wonder he'd been so certain he would survive the trials.

"Do you think this is why you came back different after the trials? Why the shadows came out of you like they did with Orin?" she asked.

He stared over her head; his brow furrowed as he pondered this. "I don't know," he admitted. "I might never know."

Lexi was aware that never knowing was a possibility, but she didn't like it. The way those shadows came out of him in her kitchen, the way they attacked Orin and inflicted pain on him...

It wasn't normal, and she didn't like it. But this was Cole, and if anyone was strong enough to keep those shadows suppressed, it was him, especially after what he just revealed to her.

"But you can stop worrying about me so much," Cole said. "I'm stronger than I look."

"You look pretty strong to me," she muttered. "And as long as you keep putting yourself in danger, I'm going to worry about you."

"Then I will try to stop doing so."

"That's impossible with the Lord around."

He didn't argue, and as he moved toward her, the ciphers he'd revealed vanished until only the ones she'd always seen remained. With the markings gone, she could focus on his injuries again.

They looked better, but they still weren't as healed as she would like.

CHAPTER TWENTY-SIX

"I NEED to go back and see if Sahira has returned and can make more healing potions," Lexi said. "Your wounds do look better, but I'll be happier when they're gone."

"You're not going alone."

She shot him an irritated look as he settled onto the bed beside her. "Yes, because you should be traipsing around again. It worked so well for you yesterday."

He smiled as he clasped her hand and lifted it to kiss her knuckles. "It's only a trip through a portal, my love, and I'd prefer if you didn't go alone."

"I'd prefer if you weren't walking around, and I've already gone back once by myself."

"Only because I was too injured to stop you. Anyway, I doubt they're back," Cole continued. "If they were, Brokk would have come here to check on things by now."

"Maybe they're talking with Orin first. I should check, and you could use more potion."

Brokk and Sahira should have been back by now; Sahira had made it sound like the trip wouldn't take long and shouldn't be difficult.

But Cole was right; if they were back, Brokk would have come here. She chewed on her lip as her gaze went to his doorway and the portal in the room beyond. She couldn't see the portal from here, but it was there, and Sahira and Brokk would come if they could.

Concern for her friend and aunt gnawed at her gut.

∼

COLE UNDERSTOOD her need to protect him; he would have felt the same way about her, which was why he was going through the portal with her if she insisted on leaving. He knew she'd never slept with his brother, but after Orin hurt her, he wouldn't leave them alone together again.

And there was a good chance Orin was there, as he was living in the tunnels beneath her manor. There was also what Orin said about her and the markings.

Without thinking, he brushed the hair back from her temple. It was the same one he'd seen the marking on before, but there was nothing there now.

When she glanced at him, he buried his concern and smiled at her.

"If you leave, I'm going with you. You're not going to be anywhere near Orin on your own," he told her.

The two little lines that appeared between her eyes when she was angry became as deep as the Grand Canyon.

"I thought we were past this!" she snapped. "I did *not* have sex with your brother."

He went to cup her cheek, but she leaned away as she glared daggers into him.

"I know that," he assured her. "And I don't dislike the idea of the two of you being alone because I think that. The last time we saw him, he hurt you, and I won't let that happen again."

She relaxed a little but twisted her hands together as she

studied him. "I'm not a child. I can take care of myself around Orin, and he won't do that again. He was being an... an idiot."

Was he? Cole pondered as he studied her delicate features. *Does Sahira know something about the markings?*

He planned to have a talk with her aunt once he got the chance, which was another reason for him to return with her. Getting time alone with Sahira was probably going to prove difficult, but he would figure it out.

"We should probably clean and rebandage my wounds before we go," he said.

Her mouth pursed, but she rose from the bed and gathered what remained of the medical supplies and fresh water. He admired the elegant grace of her svelte body as she worked.

When she'd gathered everything she required, she returned to the bed and knelt beside him. She smelled of strawberries and sex, two scents that made it extremely difficult to keep from taking her again.

"We could always stay in bed," he murmured, and she flicked the pointed tip of his ear in response.

"Ow," he chuckled as he covered his ear with his hand. "Vicious woman."

"Hmm," she grunted as she taped a bandage to his back.

He applied a bandage and some tape to what remained of the hole in his chest. Feeding on her had improved his injury, but the sooner he completely healed, the better they would be.

He kissed her forehead. "Thank you, beautiful. Now, let's go check on them."

Lexi reluctantly rose and stepped away. He felt her eyes on him as he strode over to his armoire and removed a black tunic from inside. The healing edges of his wounds pulled as he slid the tunic over his head, but he kept his discomfort hidden.

When he finished, he pulled on a pair of loose-fitting brown pants and boots. He lifted his father's sword from the corner of the room, slid it into its sheath, and slung it over his back.

"It will be nice to get some of my clothes," Lexi murmured as she finished dressing.

"I like you in the fae attire." He stopped to admire the way the tunic fit her. "It's sexy."

She rolled her eyes but couldn't help the small smile tugging at her lips as a blush crept up her neck.

"Okay, then it will be good to have *clean* clothes," she said.

"Why didn't you have Amaris bring you more things?" he asked as he strolled toward her.

"I wanted to keep everyone away from this room as much as possible. Niall slept in the hall, but he assured me that he could hear a ghost piss and would awaken before anyone made it to the doorway."

"It's true; the man wakes at the smallest sound but passes out faster than anyone I've ever known."

"I was also hoping the palace would help keep us protected, especially you."

"It would."

Stopping before her, he rested his hands on her hips as pride swelled in his chest. She was weaker than most immortals, half human—probably—and one of the feistiest women he'd ever encountered.

"My protector," he murmured.

"Damn right."

She pulled away and, turning on her heel, stalked out of his room and toward the portal in the sitting room. When she crossed her arms over her chest and tapped her foot while she waited for him, Cole's amusement grew.

"I'm also eager to bring Torigon home," Cole said as they stepped into the portal and darkness enveloped them. He missed his horse.

CHAPTER TWENTY-SEVEN

By the end of the third day, Brokk had surpassed annoyed and entered the realm of *pissed off* as he and Sahira waited for the woman to stop being such a stubborn, judgmental ass.

That didn't seem to be happening anytime soon.

Since she walked away the other day, she hadn't returned to her lodge. They had no idea where she'd gone, but they'd spent the past three nights sleeping on the ground outside her home.

Sahira didn't complain, but the set of her jaw became tighter with each passing day. The phoenixes watched them with open curiosity, and he swore every creature in the realm passed by to study them.

Most of the crones and animals ignored them, except for the pixies. And how he wished the pixies would ignore them too. Even their music, which he'd always found beautiful and enchanting, was grating on his *last nerve*.

He'd forgotten how much the pixies could talk. It had never bothered him before because he was never subjected to it for endless hours, but now, it had been three days straight of their incessant gossip. He fell asleep listening to them prattling on and as soon they realized he was awake, they started all over again.

It was torture, and he was beginning to suspect Kaylia had decided to unleash a form of psychological warfare on them. That bitter, old crone had probably told the pixies to drive them crazy, and it was working, or at least it was for him.

Sahira barely acknowledged the pixies' existence as she drew runes in the dirt and cast stones that she'd received from the crones kind enough to offer them some food and water and to show them the restroom.

If this went on for much longer, he would have to find a way to feed. But, for now, normal fare was helping to keep his thirst for blood under control.

Brokk had no idea how Sahira could shut out the endless chatter of the pixies as they went on and on about the sasquatches' squabbles and the dwarves' arguments with the gnomes. They discussed how the pegasusses believed they were better than the unicorns and how the unicorns thought *they* were better.

And, of course, there were all kinds of goings-on in the pixie world. By the end of the first day, Brokk was contemplating puncturing his eardrums rather than listening to one more pixie chatter about another one.

By the end of the second day, it took everything he had not to smash his head off the ground. And by the end of the third day, he was trying not to break down and cry.

The newest pixie to bless him with her keen insights into the pixie world was prattling on and on about how her sister was boning her ex-boyfriend. The pixie kept one hand on her hip as she waved the other hand in the air while hovering before him.

"She should have known better!" the pixie declared in her sweet, tiny voice that had become nails on a chalkboard to his ears. "I told her that he was *bad* in bed."

Inwardly, Brokk heaved huge sobs of misery as he rested his head on his knees and covered his ears with his hands. He sang a Five Finger Death Punch song to himself until he felt a small tap on his shoulder.

Hoping that it was Sahira telling him that Ms. Queen Crone was back, he lifted his head to discover the pink pixie standing on his knee. Her head fell to the side, and her pink hair flowed around her shoulders as she studied him.

"Are you okay?" she asked.

Brokk lowered his hands from his ears. "I'm fine."

"Good." And then, without missing a beat, she plunged back into the daily soap opera of Pixie Land. "So, I told Mayflower she was being an idiot and would only be disappointed and that she had no idea how awful it was. But she knows now. Oh, she knows. And then *she* tried complaining to *me* about it."

Pink dust floated from the pixie as her hand flew to her chest, and she jutted one of her hips out. The tiny, pink dress she wore clung to her curvy figure.

"Then I told her, 'Mayflower, I warned you he was a two-pump chump.' And she was all, 'But he's so cute, Marigold. How can he be soooo bad?' And you know what? I have *no* idea how it's possible, but it's true."

Brokk started banging his forehead off his knees as he stifled a groan.

"Are you sure you're okay?" the pixie asked. "Because you're acting a little crazy."

He briefly contemplated splatting her like a fly, but he couldn't kill the tiny creature, even if she was driving him nuts. Besides, the sasquatches would probably rip his arms off afterward, and he was rather fond of his arms.

"I'm fine," he muttered.

"I'm Marigold, by the way. You can call me Mari."

He had about as much interest in calling her Mari as he did in continuing to talk to her. If they became that comfortable with each other, she would undoubtedly return, and no matter how annoying all the pixies were, she was the worst.

And then, the pixie stopped talking, the phoenix turned toward something, and a hush descended across the realm.

A few seconds later, Kaylia emerged from around the backside of her lodge. Sahira rose from where she'd been running her hand over the feathers of a baby phoenix. It squawked in protest but stopped when it spotted Kaylia.

"Come with me," Kaylia commanded and slipped into her lodge.

Brokk strained to keep his fraying patience under control. This woman had left them here in limbo while she wandered around trying to figure her shit out. And now she was *finally* back, commanding them around and expecting them to jump because she said so.

He almost told her to fuck off, but they needed her, and she knew it. He shot a look at Sahira, who stared at him like she was willing him to hold his tongue. Brokk shoved his festering ire aside as he started to rise.

Marigold giggled as she fluttered back from his knee. "Good luck!" she called before zipping away.

Brokk rose and trudged toward the lodge. Even if Kaylia had an attitude the size of a giant, at least they would get her decision, and he wouldn't have to listen to any more pixie drama.

One way or another, they were going to leave this place behind today… if the crones didn't decide to try to kill them first.

Sahira followed Kaylia into the lodge, and Brokk trailed her. The flap settled into place with a swish behind him. He remained standing by the exit with his arms crossed over his chest. Sahira sank onto the fluffy padding they sat on before; they both stared at him until he reluctantly did the same.

CHAPTER TWENTY-EIGHT

Kaylia stared down her aquiline nose at them before shifting her gaze to the wall again. He was growing tired of her inability to look at them. Half vampires or not, neither he nor Sahira was bad, and they didn't deserve to be treated as if they were lesser.

He didn't care how beautiful this woman was on the outside; there was something ugly and broken inside her.

"I have decided that to save lives, I will allow you to have the harrow stone," Kaylia said.

Brokk's heart lurched with excitement. This was the answer they'd hoped for, but as the days passed, and as he was again reminded how much she despised them, it was not the answer he expected.

"Thank you," Sahira murmured.

"Yes, thank you," Brokk said.

"There are, of course, rules to obey. If broken, at any time, you will both die. It won't be quick, but it *will* come with time, and it *will* be painful. You will pay for your disobedience. That is one of the curses of the harrow stone."

Brokk quirked an eyebrow over this declaration and glanced at

Sahira. His life was now entwined with hers and vice versa. Did he trust her enough for that?

He didn't have a choice if they were going to save his brothers and possibly bring down the Lord. Besides, Sahira wouldn't do anything to put Lexi at risk, and infuriating these crones could bring their wrath down on all of them.

"We will obey the rules," Brokk said.

"I know you will," Kaylia stated, and Brokk's teeth ground together as she looked dismissively away from him to Sahira. "*You* will be the only one allowed to use or touch the stone. If someone else touches the stone, they will die. Their death will be instantaneous. No one will be allowed to steal the stone."

"Understood," Sahira murmured.

"What are the names of the fae you intend to use it on?"

"Varo and Orin," Brokk said.

"You will *only* use it on those two fae. If it's used on anyone else, not only will *you* die, but so will they. You are to return it in three days, or you will both face the consequences. That should be plenty of time for you to gather the ingredients and perform the spell. Do you know how to do it?"

"There's a spell for it in the Book of Shadows my mother left me as a baby."

"She left you a very powerful book. Most have no record of the spell or the harrow stone. There aren't many witches who know it exists."

"It's the only thing she ever gave me."

Kaylia's gaze ran over Sahira before she lifted her nose into the air. "I can understand why."

The sorrow that flashed across Sahira's face sent a bolt of anger through Brokk. Yes, witches hated vampires, but Kaylia's intense loathing was the worst he'd ever encountered.

Sahira didn't deserve it, and neither did he, but especially not Sahira. From what he'd seen of her, she was good and kind.

However, Kaylia knew she had them at her mercy, and she enjoyed it.

Kaylia dipped her hand into the pocket of her ankle-length, white dress and removed something. She opened her hand to reveal a stone almost the size of her palm and more brilliant than a ruby, but the same red hue.

The dim rays of the sun shone off it as she bent to whisper a couple of words to it. He thought he caught his and Varo's name in the incantation but couldn't be sure. When she finished speaking, she blew on the stone.

It grew cloudy, and its color dimmed before she placed it on the ground in the center of the lodge. "You may take it now."

She withdrew in a way that made it clear she didn't want them touching her when they went for the stone. Brokk despised that she made him feel dirty. He was not lesser because he was a vampire, and neither was Sahira. He understood why the witches hated vampires, but Kaylia took it to a whole new level.

"Are you going to tell anyone what we revealed to you about going against the Lord?" Brokk asked.

Kaylia's eyes remained focused on the back wall as she spoke. "There are no secrets in the crone realm, but it will not go beyond us."

"How can you be sure?"

"Unlike vampires, we are loyal."

Brokk couldn't stop the snort of disgust that escaped him. He managed to stop himself from telling her where she could shove her stone, but just barely.

"There are many, in all the realms, who have been betrayed by someone they once considered loyal," he reminded her.

"No one here wants to see me dead."

He'd only talked to her for a combined total of five minutes, and he seriously doubted that, but before he could say something stupid, she kept speaking.

"We all rely on each other here. We are one here, and I have aligned us against the Lord by giving you the stone. *No* one will say anything."

Before they could respond, Kaylia ducked out the back and vanished again.

CHAPTER TWENTY-NINE

LEXI STEPPED into the manor's kitchen and immediately felt a sense of relief as calm stole through her. The familiar scents of Sahira's potions lingered in the air even though it had been days since she last brewed one.

For a second, Lexi had a surge of hope that perhaps Sahira had returned, but the scent was too faint. Sahira hadn't returned, but her essence remained. Lexi would give anything to hug her aunt again and worried it might not happen.

She couldn't lose Sahira too. She wouldn't be able to handle losing her aunt and her father. Swallowing back the lump in her throat, Lexi pushed aside her morose musings as Sahira's familiar, a black cat named Shade, twisted his way through Lexi's legs and meowed.

His food and water dishes were large containers that continuously fed and watered him. Both were still half full, which meant Shade was looking for companionship, which he *never* did from her.

Bending, she rubbed behind his ear and almost fell over when he rolled to let her pet his belly. She'd never been allowed to rub his belly before. Then he bit her, leapt up, and sauntered away.

"That's more like it," Lexi muttered as she rose. "Sahira and Brokk should be back by now."

"I'm sure they're fine," Cole replied.

He said the words, but she heard the concern in his voice, even if he was focused on something else. She rested her hand on the counter while Cole stared down at the piece of paper sitting on it.

She frowned at the paper, but from her angle, she couldn't see what was on it. Lexi didn't think it was here when she returned for the healing potions, but she was in such a rush that she probably wouldn't have noticed it.

Lexi glanced around the kitchen as if she could will her aunt and Brokk into being here. Anxiety gnawed at her gut as the house's emptiness became louder than the screech of the craz.

She shifted her attention back to Cole. "What is that?" she inquired.

He pushed the paper toward her, and she leaned over to read the words scrawled in a hasty hand on it.

We have to talk. You know where to find me. It's IMPORTANT.

She didn't recognize the handwriting, so Sahira didn't write it.

"It's from Orin," he said as if reading her mind.

"Oh," she murmured. "I'm assuming he means for us to find him in the tunnels."

"He can wait."

"Cole—"

"I still have rebels to hunt. Orin can wait."

She didn't particularly want to see Orin right now either—the man pissed her off—but if it kept Cole from a battle, she would talk to his brother.

"We should talk to him and find out if he's seen Brokk and Sahira. Maybe there's a chance they've already returned and we missed them, or they had to go somewhere else. Maybe *that's* what this note is about," she said.

"They would have left us one themselves if that was the case."

"He still might have seen them. We have to talk to him."

Cole shoved the piece of paper away from him. "Let's make this quick."

Lexi led the way to the fireplace and pushed the rock on it to open the tunnel. Ducking inside, she found the flashlight and clicked it on while the door slid shut behind them. Neither of them spoke as they made their way through the tunnels toward where the refugees hid.

Their shoes were silent against the concrete floor, and the familiar aroma of wet earth hung heavy on the air. She shone her light over the walls, but she'd memorized these catacombs years ago; her father made certain of it.

They were halfway there when Cole grasped her arm and pulled her to a stop. A second later, the shadows shifted and Orin emerged from the darkness. If Cole hadn't stopped her, she never would have known he was there.

She had no idea what he planned to talk to them about, but his stony face and the hardness of his black eyes was anything but welcoming. Cole's hand tightened on her arm as he pulled her back a step and moved to stand slightly in front of her.

Orin studied her before shifting his gaze to Cole. His eyes softened a little.

"We have to talk," Orin said.

"That's what the note said and why we're here," Cole replied.

"Have you seen Brokk or Sahira?" Lexi blurted.

Orin's attention remained riveted on Cole as he replied, "No."

A chill slid up her spine as an unsettling feeling knotted in her stomach. Something was *not* right here, and though Cole was doing a lot better, he was far from being ready to fight Orin.

But why would Orin want to fight him when things were fine with them before? They hadn't been great, but they were working together and tolerating each other. What happened to bring about this sudden change in Orin?

"I'll be back," Orin said.

He turned and disappeared into the shadows. A second later, his reemergence was followed by the clink of metal as something shifted behind him. Cole's shoulders hunched up in preparation for an attack, and his hand went to his sword's hilt.

She couldn't see what the darkness hid, but she felt the ripple of shock that ran through Cole as his hand fell from his sword.

A second later, the clanking of more metal was followed by her father's emergence from the shadows. Lexi's heart stopped beating before it lurched so forcefully it bruised her ribs when it knocked against them. Her breath caught, her hands started shaking, and something in her brain fractured.

It couldn't be her dad. He was dead; they'd received notice of his *death*. Cole was there when it happened, but it *was* him.

That was his pale blond hair and brilliant blue eyes twinkling with love as they landed on her. Except, they weren't as bright as she recalled. Now, shadows surrounded them, and they were filled with a sadness she'd never seen in them before.

Dirt streaked his face, a beard hid his jaw, and his hair was longer than ever before as it curled around his broad shoulders. He was thinner too, but not unbearably so.

He'd always been clean-shaven and had his hair neatly trimmed. She couldn't remember a time she'd ever seen him disheveled... until now.

"Dad?" she croaked.

Though he looked so different, the brilliant smile splitting his face was all his. It was *him*!

A sound somewhere between a laugh and a sob issued from her as she lunged forward. Cole's hand fell away from her arm as she staggered across the space separating them. She flung her arms around her father.

"Daddy," she breathed as she buried her face in his neck and sobbed.

CHAPTER THIRTY

COLE WATCHED in disbelief as the father and daughter embraced. Then warmth spread through him as Lexi's joy became palpable as she clung to her dad.

When Del lifted his hands to try to hug her back, the clinking metal drew Cole's attention to the thick, metal cuffs encasing Del's wrists. Another thick chain ran from the manacles to the shackles on his ankles.

Cole's gaze shot to his brother, and his hand returned to his sword. With his shock wearing off, he realized Orin had kept things from him. He didn't know exactly what was going on here, but he would find out.

"Step away from them," Cole growled as he fixed his murderous stare on Orin.

"Easy, brother," Orin murmured as he edged away from Lexi and Del.

It took a few more minutes, but Lexi finally released her dad and stepped back. Her hands fell to the chains on his wrists, and she frowned as tears continued to stream down her cheeks. With confusion marring her brow, she gazed from Del to the chains and back again.

"What's going on?" she whispered.

"That's what I'd like to know," Orin said. "Which is why Del is here."

Lexi blinked at Orin before understanding settled over her. "*You* did this? *You* brought him back? *How*?"

"I have my ways, Kitten," Orin said.

"*Move away*," Cole commanded as he pulled his sword free.

Resentment seethed in Orin's eyes as he inched further away from them. Cole kept his gaze on Orin as he walked over to them.

"Are you okay, Del?" he demanded.

He clasped his friend's hand and shook it as he kept his attention on Orin. He and Del clapped each other on the back before stepping apart.

"I'm fine."

"Where have you been?"

"Your brother decided I was better off behind bars. He imprisoned me on an outer realm."

Lexi's mouth parted as she stared at where Orin stood, half in and half out of the shadows. "You *jailed* my father?" she demanded.

Orin shrugged. "The consequences of war aren't pretty."

Lexi's hands fell away from the chains as rage clouded her face. "You imprisoned *my father* and hid it from *me*! I *saved* you. I brought you in here and took care of you. I've taken in refugees with you; I kept your secret and *protected* you, and throughout it all, you *knew* my father was alive and *kept* it from me!"

Before Cole knew what she intended, she flew across the distance separating them from Orin. Del's chains rattled as he lunged after his daughter, and Cole ran after her.

Before he could catch her, she kicked Orin in the shin. When his brother lifted his leg and grabbed it, she gave him an uppercut that caught him under his chin and snapped his head back. Standing on only one foot, the blow caused Orin to stagger into the wall.

When Lexi lunged for him again, Cole wrapped his arm around her waist and pulled her away. Orin's head came slowly back down, and he put his foot back on the ground. Malice shimmered in his eyes as he stared at Lexi, but when Cole turned her away and placed his body between them, some of the wrath eased from Orin's face.

"Put me down!" Lexi commanded.

When Cole set her down, she tugged her tunic back into place as she glowered at Orin. If he stepped out of the way, Cole had no doubt Lexi would go after Orin again.

And as irate as she was, she might take him down. But he wasn't going to take the chance Orin might hurt her in the process.

His brother rubbed the reddening spot under his chin as he looked from her to Del and back again. "I'm not the only one keeping secrets, Kitten."

"Fuck you!" she spat.

She may have been too mad to catch Orin's words and the direction of his gaze, but Cole did.

"What secrets?" Cole inquired as he stared between Del and Orin.

"I don't know, brother. Your general will not share what he knows with me, but he said he would with *you*. That's the only reason he's here."

The hair on Cole's nape rose as his attention shifted to Del. Lexi had made her way back to her father and was examining the manacles. She was still too emotional to really pay attention to the conversation.

"Take these off," she commanded.

"Not until he talks," Orin replied. "And then *I'll* decide if they come off."

"They're coming off," Cole said.

He had no idea what secrets Del held, but he wouldn't let his friend and Lexi's father remain chained.

Orin didn't move. "Not until he speaks."

When Cole stepped toward him to beat his brother into submission, injuries or not, Del's words stopped him.

"The chains are fine… for now."

"Has he had you imprisoned this whole time?" Cole asked Del.

"I have," Orin replied.

"How could you?" Lexi whispered.

Orin rolled his eyes. "It's called the spoils of war, Kitten. I captured one of my brother's most powerful generals and strategists. I wasn't going to let him go to plan against me again. I'm not a fool."

"But you are a dick."

"Oh, relax, it's not like I killed him. I found him injured on the battlefield and took him."

When Lexi looked about to fly at him again, Cole rested his hand on her arm. Like a leaf in a hurricane, she trembled beneath his touch.

"Unchain him," she commanded again.

"Not until he talks," Orin replied.

"Talks about *what*?" Lexi exploded.

"Andi," Del said kindly, calling her by the childhood nickname he'd given her. It worked at defusing her a little as her shoulders softened and tears filled her eyes again. "It's okay."

"See, he's perfectly fine with being chained. Stop making such a big deal about it," Orin said flippantly.

"Watch it," Cole warned.

For a second, Orin maintained his air of aloof indifference, but he wilted a little beneath Cole's glare.

"Let the man speak," Orin said with a little less bravado.

"Not in front of you," Del said.

"I'm not going anywhere," Orin retorted. "I brought you here to hear what you have to say, and I *will* hear it."

"Not if I decide that you won't," Cole told him.

Orin's eyes flashed with fury when they met his, and the set of his brother's jaw told him he would fight over this. Cole was still weak from his wounds, but he would tear Orin apart.

CHAPTER THIRTY-ONE

WHEN ORIN STEPPED from the shadows, Lexi lurched forward, and Cole grasped her arm to keep her from getting too close to Orin again.

"No!" she shouted. "There will be *no* fighting!"

Cole's hand tightened on her arm. "Lexi—"

Her eyes were full of fire when she spun on him. "*You* are in no condition to fight right now, and if this is about *me,* then I will decide who gets to hear it." She turned to her father. "This is my decision to make. And as much as I'm beginning to loathe him—" She thrust a finger at Orin. "—he is an ally in this."

"He also has no qualms about using anything and *anyone* to achieve his goal," Del said. "I won't have that be you."

"It's too late for that," Lexi said. "If it comes to it, and we decide it's better he didn't hear what you have to say, then we'll kill him before he leaves here."

Her father's eyebrows shot up, and Cole chuckled while Orin did a double take at her declaration.

"It seems Kitten is becoming a tiger," Orin murmured.

"Shut up," Cole told him.

"Tell us what it is that you have to tell us," Lexi said to her dad.

"Did you teach her to fight?" Del asked Cole.

"Brokk did," Cole answered, "while I was going through the trials."

"Your father is dead," Del stated.

"He is."

Del released a small breath. "That one—" He waved a hand at Orin. "—said you were now king of the dark fae, but I wasn't sure what to believe from him."

"I do not lie," Orin said.

When they all shot him an irritated look, he shrugged. "I may embellish, but I don't lie. Well, not unless it benefits me."

Deciding to ignore Orin, Del focused on Cole. "I'm sorry to hear about King Tove. Your father was a good man."

"He was." Cole pulled Lexi closer. "What is it you have to say?"

Instead of answering, Del looked between the two of them before his gaze settled on Cole. "Is it true? Is she your mate?"

"Yes." Cole's eyes narrowed on Del. He'd always considered Del a friend, but if anyone could get between them, it would be her long-lost father, and he would *not* allow that to happen. "She is."

Del closed his eyes, and his shoulders slumped forward. "Good, because you might be the only one strong enough to keep her safe."

Lexi glanced at him in confusion as Cole slid his arm around her waist, and Lexi grasped his hand. Whatever her father was about to reveal, she would not like it; he doubted he would either.

He could still feel the power of their sexual encounter thrumming through his veins in a way it never had before. Orin had brought Del here for a reason. And then there were those markings.

He'd risked Cole and Lexi's wrath because this was important, and Del obviously had *something* to say. He looked too distraught not to have something, which meant he hadn't made it up to escape Orin's prison.

When Del looked at Lexi again, sadness and regret radiated in his eyes. He reached for her, but his jaw clenched when the chains rattled, and he lowered his hands.

"You know that I love you," he said.

"Of course I do," Lexi said. "I've never doubted it."

"There are things I haven't told you. Things that will only put you in danger."

Lexi's fingers crushed his, but Cole was already starting to put the pieces together. He didn't have the complete puzzle yet, and they formed a picture he didn't like.

"What things?" Lexi whispered.

Del took a deep breath before plunging on. "You're not half human and half vampire; you're arach."

"I knew it," Orin muttered, but no one acknowledged him.

Cole had figured out enough that this revelation didn't come as a complete surprise to him. However, it still rocked him a little as he swayed back on his heels.

He still didn't see how it was possible, but he had no doubt it was true. Lexi stopped breathing for a good thirty seconds before she inhaled sharply and started to laugh.

When she looked up at him and he simply stared back at her, she stopped laughing. Her brow furrowed, her mouth pursed, and confusion filled her eyes as she started to shake her head.

"Lexi," Cole said gently.

"That can't be possible," she stated as she turned her attention back to her father.

"It is," Del said.

"*You* said my mother was a human."

"I was there when your mother gave birth to you; she was arach."

Lexi opened and closed her mouth a few times as she tried to form some response. All through the tunnels, the shadows twisted and twined as they crept closer. He sensed they were responding to his distress and coming because they believed he required help.

When he refused to draw them any closer, they hovered at the edges of the light, building a force no one else could see. Not even Orin noticed them, and the dark fae had a special affinity for the shadows that could cloak them.

What would happen if he did unleash them? A thrill of excitement and dread ran through him at the possibility.

Between the influx of power from the trials and Lexi, things were shifting and changing inside him. He didn't know what those changes would do to him if he ever unleashed them or lost control.

His gaze settled on Lexi; he would never find out either. He would always be there to protect her, and if he lost control, he wasn't so sure he'd be able to do such a thing.

Finally, Lexi found her voice again. "The arach were extremely powerful beings. I have *no* abilities or anything special about me. *Nothing.*"

Cole could argue that point for hours; she may not have other immortals' physical or psychic abilities, but she was definitely special. He kept his mouth shut as he had no idea how she could be arach and *not* have any powers.

"That's not true," Del said. "You do have abilities. You've possessed them since birth. Even then, you were so small and *so* powerful."

Lexi's fingers clenched Cole's until his bones ground together. She didn't realize she was doing it, and he didn't try to extricate himself from her grip. A tremor worked its way through her as she shook her head.

"And what happened to them?" she demanded. "Did I lose them over the years?"

"No." Sadness and a plea for understanding shone in Del's eyes as they held Lexi's. "We took them from you."

CHAPTER THIRTY-TWO

It took everything Lexi had not to slump to the ground. Her mind screamed denials at her, but her father wouldn't lie to her about this.

Are you kidding me? Are you seriously thinking he wouldn't lie to you? He's telling you that he's lied to you your whole life!

Lexi's mind spun, and she had to brace her legs apart as she leaned against Cole's side or else she might sink. And she could not do that in front of Orin.

Cole helped to keep her up as she leaned against him. Everything she'd always known was falling apart around her, but he was still solid; she could still count on him.

"Who is *we*?" Cole inquired.

It was then Lexi realized that all of what her father said hadn't entirely sunk into her scattered brain. He had said *we* took them from you, not *I*.

Acid burned in her belly at who that *we* was. There was only one other immortal he would have trusted with this.

Her father gave her a sympathetic look as he responded. "Me and Sahira. We did what we believed was best to keep you safe. You were so young you couldn't control your abilities, and if the

Lord *ever* learned of your existence, he would have killed you. I couldn't let that happen, so we bound your powers."

"And you planned to keep them like that... forever?" Lexi croaked.

"Oh no," Del said ruefully. "We never could have kept them suppressed for that long. You were growing stronger with each passing year. We had planned to tell you, but then the war started, and I was captured.

"The two of you believed I was dead, and I'm sure Sahira didn't know what to do about it after that, but it would have only been a matter of time before she *had* to tell you because your powers would have eventually broken free. Neither of us knew how we were going to keep you protected once we stopped binding your powers. The arachs were powerful beings, but neither of us was sure what they were capable of or how their powers worked."

"I don't know either," Cole said. "I'm not sure anyone does."

Lexi gulped as she tried to process this information. She might possess these powerful abilities but have no idea how to control them, and losing control of them would only paint a giant bull's-eye on her back for the Lord.

"*How* did you bind them? With a spell?" Lexi asked.

"Not just a spell. We learned real fast a spell alone wasn't enough. We had to give you a daily potion, too," Del said.

"A daily...." Her voice trailed off as the blood drained from her head. It took everything she had not to stagger into the tunnel to vomit. "My daily tea with Sahira. She wasn't drinking tea with me because she wanted to... it was... it was to make me into something I wasn't."

"It was to *protect* you," Del said. "We also put it in your bottle, and I do *not* regret it. It kept you alive."

"Why didn't you tell me what I was?"

"At first, you were too young, and then, as the years slipped by, it became easier to keep it a secret."

"Easier for *you.*"

Del flinched a little at her words. "Yes," he admitted. "We knew you'd be angry and upset, and we kept putting it off because of that. But we were also trying to keep you from having to deal with that burden. We wanted you to live as normal a life as possible for as long as possible. We truly believed we were doing the right thing."

She could tell he had believed this, and maybe they were right, or perhaps they'd been completely wrong. She'd never know because she was never given that chance by the two people who had loved her for her entire life.

Lexi released Cole's hand and stepped out of his embrace. She couldn't stand still right now; she had to move.

Pacing into the shadows, she stopped when she came to a wall. Standing there, she recalled all the times as a toddler, child, teen, and adult she shared her daily tea with Sahira.

At the time, she assumed her aunt wanted to play and be around her. But it had all been an excuse to get her to drink the potion that was suppressing who she really was.

How many of those teas had she consumed over the years? She tried to do the math in her head, but her brain was too frazzled to add two and two, never mind years and days and whatnot.

As a child, she'd laughed over those tea times while they sat at her little table in their pink dresses and tiaras. She'd layered bracelets and necklaces onto herself and Sahira, and they would sometimes do their makeup and hair.

She recalled all the times she'd prattled on about dragons and palaces and faraway realms, all while drinking that tea. And it had all been *lies*.

The betrayal of it twisted deep in her gut and tore at her heart.

And then she realized something else. Turning, she walked back toward her father and stopped next to Cole.

"How often do I have to drink this potion?" she demanded of her dad.

"Every day, without fail. We tried doing it more rarely while you were still young, but your powers would slip through after a couple of days."

"Things have been so crazy lately that I can't remember the last time Sahira and I had tea together."

"Then she must be giving the potion to you in some other way, but it has to be consumed daily. The potion can go in anything; we put it in your bottle when you were a baby and in your tea later. Whatever the potion is in would probably still be effective for its intended use."

"No, there's nothing else… except… oh," she breathed as that sickness returned, and much to her horror, a blush crept up her neck toward her cheeks.

CHAPTER THIRTY-THREE

"How is she doing it?" Orin demanded.

"Lexi?" Cole inquired.

When she looked helplessly toward him and the blush started burning her cheeks, he stared at her before nodding. He had come to the same realization as her...

The potion was in the birth control Sahira made for her. No wonder her aunt was so adamant she take it.

"I see," Cole said.

"What is it?" Orin demanded.

Lexi refused to answer him.

"So you *are* taking something from her every day?" her father asked.

"Yes," Lexi murmured.

"If you were to stop...." Her father's voice trailed off.

"What would happen?" she asked.

"I'm not sure. Your powers have been bound for most of your life. Sahira has continuously had to increase the dosage to keep them that way. The arach were *extremely* powerful beings, and if you were to stop taking the potion, there's no telling what might happen."

Lexi really wanted to sit somewhere and think, but she was acutely aware of Orin's attention on her, judging her. That treacherous, manipulative bastard would not find her lacking.

So instead, in her head, she tried to remember the last time she took her birth control. "It's ah… it's been two or three days since I last took it. Things were so crazy in the Gloaming with the rebellion that I completely forgot." She glanced anxiously at Cole. "I'm sorry."

"For what?"

Was her face on fire? It took everything she had not to press her hand against it as her cheeks burned. She glanced at her father and Orin, but she couldn't bring herself to air their sex life in front of them.

"You have *no* reason to apologize. Things were crazy, you were doing your best to keep me alive and safe, and you barely slept. You also have nothing to worry about," Cole assured her.

She was aware he took birth control too, but she still should have paid better attention. The last thing they needed was a baby right now.

And now she also knew why Cole could take a monthly dose of birth control while hers was daily. She felt like such an idiot.

"If it's been that long, then your powers are going to start coming through," Del said.

"They already are," Cole said.

"They are?" she asked in confusion.

"Yes," he said but didn't explain further.

"You mean the mark from the dragon," Orin said.

"No," Cole said.

"I was still taking the potion regularly then," Lexi said.

"That mark appeared because your ability broke through the binding potion in reaction to touching a dragon," Cole said. "The night you woke me from my nightmare, you also had a mark on your forehead."

"I did?"

"Yes. I thought it was because you hit your head on the bedframe when you fell out of bed, but now I think your powers were trying to break through the binding powers of the potion to protect you. The potion is highly effective, but your powers are seeping through."

"Fascinating," Orin murmured as he rubbed his chin and studied her raptly.

When Lexi gave him the finger, he smiled. Torn between hitting him again and ignoring him, Lexi opted for the second option. She didn't want Cole to have to intervene again.

"Okay, so no one knows much about the arachs, but they could control the dragons?" she asked.

"They had a special affinity with the dragons for sure," Cole said.

"The arach lived among the dragons and withstood all fire, including that of a dragon's. Some say they possessed sun and moon magic, but it's all rumors and myth," her dad said.

"And a lot of it was probably started by the arach. They guarded their magic and abilities closely," Cole said. "They were also rumored to make things grow as well as kill them."

"So, there's no knowing what could happen to me or what I can do once the potion completely wears off?" she asked.

"You can take control of the dragons and take them away from the Lord," Orin said.

Everyone ignored him.

Lexi rubbed at her temples as she tried to process all of this. She decided talking it out would help her. "Okay, so I'm not half human and half vampire. Instead, I'm half vampire and half arach. So—"

"No," her father interrupted. "You're not half arach."

When she lifted her head, the sadness in his eyes caused her to brace for a punch because whatever he was about to say was going to be another blow.

He took a deep breath before letting it out. "You're *full* arach. I'm not your birth father, Andi."

CHAPTER THIRTY-FOUR

WHEN LEXI SWAYED, Cole slipped his arm around her waist again and pulled her close. He'd never seen anyone go from so red from embarrassment to that pale so fast.

Cole had no idea what to say, and Del looked as helpless as a newborn. Unfortunately, Orin didn't have the same issue.

"That's even better," Orin murmured.

"Better for what?" Lexi snapped before anyone else could react.

"For us."

"For us *who*?" Lexi demanded. "None of this makes anything better for *you*! And I'm so glad that me learning *everything* I've ever known is a lie is so wonderful for you."

"Not just for me, for *all* the realms," Orin replied. "We have a better chance of taking the Lord down with you. You're our secret weapon. All we have to do is—"

"Enough!" Cole interrupted harshly.

"She has to understand that she's a game changer," Orin insisted.

"That's enough!" Cole shouted.

His words rebounded down the tunnels before fading into the

darkness. The shadows behind Orin rose like cobras from baskets. They hovered behind Orin, preparing to strike if Cole allowed it.

He kept them restrained, but it was so tempting to have them knock Orin on his ass. He'd never see it coming, and it would take him down a peg or two.

Orin's jaw clenched, but he remained silent as he stared sullenly at them.

"She needs time to adjust to all of this," Cole continued. "And she *will* have it."

Lexi wasn't the only one who needed time; he did too. She was a game changer. She might be able to take the dragons from the Lord, which would weaken him considerably, but she was also his *mate,* and this could put her at the forefront of a battle he'd meant for her to mostly avoid.

"How… how is that possible?" Lexi whispered in a tremulous voice.

And then he realized that future possibilities didn't matter. What mattered were the tears in her eyes as she gazed at Del with a look of such utter betrayal, it damn near broke his heart.

Tears shone in Del's eyes too. He took a step toward her, but Del spun on his brother when Orin pulled back on his chains.

"Don't," Cole ordered. "Not here and not now. This is *not* the time."

Del glowered at Orin before turning back to Lexi.

"You're supposed to be my dad," Lexi whispered.

"I *am* your dad," Del said. "But I'm not your father. Your birth father died before you were born."

When Lexi trembled against him, he kissed her forehead before looking to Del.

"I think you should explain how Lexi came to be in your care," Cole said.

"Yes, please do," Orin drawled.

"Honestly, it was luck," Del said to Lexi. "Not your parents' luck, but *I* got lucky when you came to me."

The earnestness in his tone and eyes was undeniable, as was the love and hope that this would be okay in the end and that Lexi would forgive him.

"What happened?" Lexi asked.

"I found your mother under the willow tree," Del said.

When Lexi stiffened against him, Cole recalled her saying she found Orin there after lycans attacked him.

"She was badly injured and already in labor when I discovered her. She and your father were ambushed by a pack of the Lord's lycan. Your father didn't survive the battle, but the two of them took down the pack, which is why *no* one else ever heard about arach bodies being discovered in the human realm.

"I managed to get your mom inside and into bed without anyone seeing us, but things were a lot quieter then. I had no idea how I would deliver a baby, and Sahira was living in Europe at the time, so I didn't have her help or healing potions. I cleaned your mother's wounds and wrapped them the best I could, but they were really bad.

"I wasn't sure she was going to live to deliver you, but she did. When I finished, it was still early in her labor, so I went to find your father's body and the lycans and buried them before anyone else could discover them."

"Where?" Lexi asked.

"Your father is on the other side of the lake, in the woods. I kept him separate from the lycan bodies. I had no idea why I did at the time. It would have been easier to dig a mass grave, but I decided to keep him apart from his murderers.

"When I returned to your mom, her labor had progressed, and she'd grown weaker. I don't know why she trusted me; maybe because there was no other choice, maybe because I'd saved her, maybe she sensed something in me, or maybe because she was dying and wanted to leave her legacy for her child, but she told me about herself and your father.

"Her name was Galeah. She and your father were the last two

surviving arach. She was once a princess in her realm, but shortly after she married your father, they were driven from Dragonia when civil war broke out a thousand years before.

"They'd been trying to hide by traveling through all the realms and keeping a low profile. It was simply bad luck when they ran into a pack of lycan that day."

"Why didn't they return to Dragonia once the civil war was over and all the arach were dead?" Lexi asked.

"Because, by then, the first Lord had seized the throne and the land. They were both tired of fighting and only wanted to live a simple life with each other."

"Isn't that what we all want?" she whispered so low the others didn't hear her.

"It is," Cole whispered back as he hugged her closer.

But it was something he never considered for himself until meeting her. He'd never wanted the endless war and death the last two years of his life had become. But he *had* craved adventure and women as he traveled the realms.

Now, all he wanted was peace, a home, and a family with her. And they were going to have to fight tooth and nail to get it.

"What happened next?" Lexi asked.

"As the day progressed into night, she weakened more and more. No matter what I did for her, it wasn't enough to stop the blood from flowing, and her injuries weren't healing at all. The attack had weakened her too much, and her injuries were so *bad*."

"And the labor weakened her further," Lexi stated.

Del hesitated before replying. "Yes, but she would *not* give up. She so badly wanted you in this world. She'd never met you, but her love for you was so obvious as she rubbed her belly and coaxed you to come out."

The scent of Lexi's tears on the air drew Cole's attention. She kept her head bowed as she wiped them away.

"You were born shortly before midnight," Del continued. "She wept when I gave you to her. I tried to stop the bleeding, but I... I was clueless, and she'd endured too much. Even if I'd gone for Sahira, I wouldn't have gotten back in time to save her. She begged me to keep you safe, and I promised her I would.

"I have no idea what compelled me to make such a promise. I'd always been a rather selfish, carefree immortal, like most vampires, but looking at the two of you and seeing the vast amount of love she had for you, I knew I would *never* let anything happen to you.

"She whispered your name to me and died while still cradling you in her arms. I took you from her, and the second I held you, I was *certain* I'd done the right thing in vowing to protect you.

"After a few hours of holding you and reassuring you that we would somehow get through this, I cleaned up the mess, went to the store to buy you some formula, which was thankfully enough to keep you alive when mixed with my blood, and called Sahira to ask her to come home.

"I didn't want to carry you through a portal or bring you around other immortals. She was the only one I trusted completely with my secret, and she's never failed you or me. I didn't tell Sahira why I needed her, but she arrived less than an hour later and never left again.

"After I buried your mom beside your father, Sahira and I came up with the story that one of my human mistresses arrived on my doorstep while nine months pregnant. She died while giving birth. No one questioned it. Once we bound your powers, there was no reason for anyone to question your heritage."

When Lexi finally looked at him again, tears streamed down her face, but she didn't speak. Del stared helplessly at her as he held out his manacled wrists.

"I'm not your father, Andi, but I am your dad."

She released a hitching breath but didn't move toward him.

"*This* is the reason you built these tunnels," she said.

"Yes," Del confirmed. "I always knew there was a chance our secret would get out and I would have to get you away from here as quickly and quietly as possible. Or I would have to keep you hidden away for a while."

"We have to figure out how we're going to use this information to our advantage," Orin said.

Cole envisioned ripping Orin's head off, but he wouldn't release Lexi to go after him, and death was the last thing she needed right now.

"No one is going to use *anything* until she's had time to process all this, and even then, our number one priority is to keep her safe and *alive*," Cole said.

"We can use her to take down the Lord," Orin said.

"*No* one is using her for anything," Cole snarled.

"*No* one is going to fight over me either," Lexi interjected in a voice far steadier than her tear-filled eyes would have indicated.

Before he could reply, a footstep from further down the tunnel drew his attention. The hair on his nape rose, and his upper lip curled. If someone had overheard Del's revelation, he'd kill them, and he didn't care who it was.

The shadows shifted around the tunnel, and some turned in the direction of the footstep. For a second, he sensed a shimmer of a connection. It was faint, barely more than the strand of a single spiderweb on a dewy morning, but it was there.

And then it was gone.

Am I connected to all these shadows and not just the ones inside me?

The possibility made his throat go dry at the same time it filled him with a rush of excitement. If that was true, and he learned how to utilize it, there were endless possibilities in this new power. And if he wasn't careful, endless pitfalls.

He was about to go after whoever was in the tunnel when he caught a familiar scent. He relaxed, and a few seconds later, Sahira and Brokk emerged from the shadows. They both stopped when they spotted Del.

"Holy shit," Brokk breathed.

CHAPTER THIRTY-FIVE

LEXI DIDN'T KNOW how to take the arrival of Sahira and Brokk. She wasn't sure how to react to any of this. *What am I going to do? Who am I?*

She felt like she'd lost her entire identity. Just half an hour ago, she'd been so sure of who she was and her place in this world. And even if it was difficult, she was perfectly happy with it.

But now, things were a lot more difficult, and she wasn't sure who she could trust or who she *was*. She certainly wasn't a powerless half human anymore, or at least she wouldn't be powerless for much longer... if she continued not to drink the potion.

She took a deep breath and looked to her aunt, but Sahira's attention was riveted on her brother.

"Del," Sahira whispered.

And then she let out a small cry and raced across the space separating them. She laughed and cried as they embraced each other. Del hugged her back the best he could as she started talking at a hundred miles an hour, firing off questions as his face started to turn red from the strength of her embrace.

Despite her lingering confusion and distrust, Lexi's heart

melted as she watched them. The love and joy on their faces were evident. They were half-siblings, but they loved each other dearly.

"What is going on here?" Brokk asked as he cautiously approached them.

It wasn't until he came closer that Lexi noticed Cole's eyes were a brilliant silver color. Not only did she need to get away, but so did he.

"Orin captured Del and has been keeping him prisoner," Cole said.

"What?" Brokk blurted before looking to Orin.

Orin smiled. "He was good leverage if I ever required it."

"Then why is he here if he's good leverage?" Brokk demanded.

"That's a long story," Cole replied. "Did you get the stone?"

"Yeah, and that was no easy feat. The crones dislike vampires a lot more than Sahira believed."

"Are you okay?"

"Yeah. The head crone was a little bit pissy when we arrived, but after some time to think about it, she gave us the stone."

"Is that what took so long?"

"Yep."

"How did you know we were here?" Lexi asked.

"The note on the counter," Brokk replied.

"Oh," she muttered as Del and Sahira broke apart.

"Where have you been?" Sahira demanded.

"First," Lexi interjected, "unchain my father."

Orin waved his index finger at her. "Quid pro quo, Kitten."

"What do you *want* from me?" she demanded.

"Your word you'll stand with us against the Lord."

"I already made a stand against the Lord when I brought you in here."

She could no longer say it was a mistake to do so, even if Orin infuriated her. Bringing him here had also brought her dad back to her, and no matter how angry she was at him and Sahira, she would never change that.

"You're going to get close to a dragon again," Orin said.

"Why would she do that?" Brokk demanded as the color drained from Sahira's face.

When her aunt looked to her dad, he closed his eyes and gave a small nod. Sahira gripped his arm and sent Lexi a sympathetic look that made her want to run from this tunnel. *No* one was going to feel sorry for her.

"She's not giving you anything or doing anything she isn't willing to do," Cole said. "Unlock him, Orin."

"That's not part of the deal," Orin said.

"*Unlock him*!" Cole's roar, caused everyone to jump as it rebounded off the walls and down the tunnels.

She wasn't sure if it would make its way to the refugees, but she glanced nervously toward the tunnel they resided in.

"Are you still taking care of the refugees?" she asked Orin.

"Of course I am," he retorted. "They are safe and well-fed. We are going to have to move them soon, though; they can't keep living in the darkness like this."

Lexi really disliked him right now, but she believed he was taking care of them and was right about not keeping them in the dark anymore. He wouldn't leave them down here to suffer or starve.

Then she looked to Cole and discovered the shadows around him were darker than they were around the others.

But that couldn't be right, could it? She'd seen what the shadows could do to Orin in the kitchen, and she doubted that was the worst of it, but to be darker?

She gulped and tried to convince herself she was seeing things as Orin and Cole glowered at each other. Lexi tensed as she waited for them to start fighting. Cole's wounds still weren't completely healed, and she couldn't handle him getting hurt again on top of everything else.

"Cole, please don't," she whispered as his silver eyes burned.

Her dad and aunt edged away from Orin as Cole's mounting

fury vibrated the walls. She swore the shadows shifted even though her light was focused away from them and no one else moved.

"Unlock. Him," Cole ordered.

Orin's eyes didn't leave Cole's as he stepped closer to her dad. He dipped a hand into his pocket and removed a key. A second later, the shackles clinked as they landed on the floor.

Cole relaxed only a little and, torn between her heart and head, Lexi stared at her dad and aunt before crossing over to hug them. Despite her resentment, she still loved them, but the hugs she gave them were brisk.

"Where are my parents buried?" she asked as she stepped away.

"On the other side of the lake, beneath two maples. I can take you there," her dad offered.

"No, I want to go alone."

"Okay."

After he told her how to find the graves, she turned and left the tunnel without saying another word.

Behind her, she heard Cole command, "Tell Brokk what happened here," before his footsteps followed her.

~

COLE WALKED beside Lexi and around the lake. When they arrived at the other side, he remained in the shadows as Lexi strolled around two large maples located about twenty feet from the water. Del had told her they would be recognizable because they were the only two red maples in a sea of green ones.

Lexi walked closer to the shore. She was all fluid grace and beauty as she moved, but the sad slope of her shoulders and the circles shadowing her eyes revealed the ordeal she'd been through over the past few days.

When she was about ten feet away from the tree trunks, she

turned to stare at them. She clasped her hands before her as she bowed her head.

After a few minutes, she lifted her hand and walked forward to kneel between the two trees. Reaching each hand out at her sides, she rested her palms against the ground.

Minutes passed, and she whispered something before rising and strolling toward the lake. When she stopped at the shore, with the water barely touching the toes of her boots, he slipped from the shadows to join her.

The sun shining off the pristine surface of the lake turned the water a brighter blue. Around them, the birds sang as a single fish jumped from the water. It ate a bug before plunging beneath the surface again. The ripples it created were the only imperfections on the lake.

"I spent my entire life playing along this lakeshore and running through these woods. I've climbed those maples before, swung from their branches, and stomped across the ground all while never knowing my parents were beneath me," she said.

"Del and Sahira were trying to protect you."

"I know, and I understand that, but how do I get past all the *lies*?"

Enveloping her in his arms, he pulled her against his chest and cradled her there. Her fingers dug into his back as she rested her head over his heart.

He held her as they stared at the glimmering water. He believed they both knew this would be the last moment of peace they'd have for a while.

He waited for her to speak again, and after a while, she did.

"What will happen to me if I don't return to taking Sahira's potion?"

"There's no way to know. Your abilities were suppressed for years, and they'll most likely be volatile and difficult to contain until you learn to control them. It will be overwhelming and hard, but we'll get through it together."

CHAPTER THIRTY-SIX

LEXI'S HEART warmed at Cole's words. They would get through this together. It would be frightening, it would be difficult, but he would be by her side.

"Do you want to stop taking it?" Cole asked.

"I think it's been two days since I took it. I'm pretty sure I took it the morning we returned to the Gloaming. I didn't mean to forget it; I got so sidetracked with the battle, your wounds, and making sure you survived that—"

"Stop," he said as he brushed the hair back from her forehead. "It's okay."

"We can't have a baby, Cole, especially not with everything we just learned."

"And we won't," he assured her. "Don't forget, I am also taking something."

"I know, I just... I should have been more responsible."

"Even if we did have a baby now, we would figure it out, we would protect it, and we *would* get through all this, but it's not something you have to worry about, okay?"

"Yes," she murmured.

"Do you want to stop taking the potion or go back to doing so? This is your choice, Lexi. *No one* will force you into anything."

"It won't matter after a while. According to my dad, my powers will eventually break through, and you believe they already are."

"I do."

"Why?"

"Because the last time we had sex, what you fed me was a *lot* stronger. Our connection has always been deeper and more powerful; this was more so."

She considered this before replying. "I never wanted to be the queen of the dark fae, but I would be for you."

"I know."

"Orin thinks I can help take the throne from the Lord."

"You're only going to do what *you* want to do."

"The Lord is a monster."

"He is."

"He won't be happy until he destroys everything, including us," she said.

"Especially *you*, if he ever learns the truth."

"And right now, *you're* one of his favorite targets."

Cole's arms squeezed briefly around her before relaxing a little.

"We have to fight him," she murmured. "I can't return to taking the potion."

~

A PART of him had hoped she would refuse to do this. That she would keep her powers trapped until they figured out a way to destroy the Lord, but he'd always known this was the choice she'd make.

She'd never expected this, but she never backed down.

"If that's what you feel is best," he said.

When she tilted her head to look up at him, her green eyes shone with fear. "You don't?"

"All I want is to keep you safe and to make sure you're not feeling pressured into this. This is your decision to make, and Orin can fuck off if he doesn't like your choice."

He studied the stubborn set of her delicate profile as she turned back to the lake. "I have no idea how to get the dragons away from the Lord."

A hand clenched around his heart at the idea of her going anywhere near those beasts again. They'd taken his father from him; he could *not* lose her to them.

But he wouldn't stand in her way, no matter how badly he wanted to. Whatever choice she made in this, it was *her* destiny, and he would make sure she stayed alive to fulfill it.

"Let's worry about that after we discover what your powers are like without the potion," he said. "And after you have more training."

"What about the rebellion?"

"I have to return to make sure it's ended and the Gloaming is free of the remaining rebels."

"I can help with that now. I'm not as useless as—"

"You were *never* useless, Lexi. Don't ever think that."

She took a deep breath before continuing. "But I'll be able to fight better now, and I'll eventually have abilities. I can help instead of staying in the palace."

"It will probably take some time for your powers to emerge fully and even *more* time for you to learn how to use them. Besides, we need to keep the Lord from learning about you until you have better control over them and we learn what you can do. You cannot ride into battle right now."

And he *would* put his foot down on that. "If this is to be your path, then so be it, but you are going to take it slow because your path will not end in death, Lexi. I *will* make sure of that. You can return to the Gloaming with me and stay with me while your powers remain mostly suppressed. Once they start to emerge more, we will have to return here."

She removed her hands from around his waist and threw them around his neck. Despite the fact he would much prefer to keep her locked away, and the lycan part of him protested allowing her to do this, he lifted her off the ground and crushed her against him.

He would have to destroy anything that tried to harm her.

CHAPTER THIRTY-SEVEN

"Dɪᴅ someone fill you in on everything?" Cole asked Brokk when they rejoined the others an hour later.

"Yes," Brokk answered as his gaze ran over Lexi. "Quite an interesting turn of events."

He set aside the Harry Potter book he was reading when they entered and rose to lean against the wall. Cole missed reading those books. Maybe, one day, he would get the chance to return to them, but he doubted it.

"That it is," Cole muttered before shifting his attention to Sahira. "How long will it take you to cast the spell with the harrow stone?"

Someone had closed all the curtains in the manor, and they'd all gathered in the library. Sahira sat on one of the chairs with Shade on her lap. She had yet to look at Lexi as she ran her hand along the cat's back and its loud purr filled the air.

Del sat in the other chair with his hands clasped before him and his head bowed. Orin stood near the fireplace with his arm draped across the mantle. His attention had been on the wall, but it shifted to Sahira after Cole asked the question.

"A few hours, at least," Sahira answered.

"We have to get Varo here," Cole said.

"I'll get him," Orin said.

"You're taking someone with you."

"I don't need a babysitter."

"You've been living a double life and keeping things from us. That is *not* going to happen anymore. You either take Brokk with you willingly, or Sahira will track you. Who else do you have imprisoned?"

"No one of use to you."

"I will decide that," Cole growled. "Who else and where are they?"

Orin turned to stare at the wall again. "At a prison on an outer realm."

"Brokk, go with him to get Varo and learn who else is imprisoned there. I have to return to the Gloaming to check in and see how the hunt for the rebels is going. Lexi is going to come with me. If we're not back by the time you're ready to start the spell, begin it without us."

"I'll come with you to the Gloaming," Del volunteered.

"That's not a good idea," Cole told him. "*No one* else can know you're alive. It will create too many questions about where you were and how you got free."

"Then I'll go with Brokk. I'd like to see my cell from the other side," he said with a pointed look at Orin. "I can stay out of view of those imprisoned there."

Cole was aware Del would only play nice with Orin for so long. But he would play nice as long as he believed that Orin could help keep Lexi safe. And Orin would do that, not only because she could be the key to bringing down the Lord, but also because it would destroy Cole to lose her.

"Do you think that's a good idea?" Cole asked Del.

A small smile curved Del's mouth. "I'm not going to kill him... yet."

Orin smirked back at him and held out his hands to wiggle his fingers before him. "I'm so scared."

"Don't," Lexi said.

"Don't worry, Andi," Del said. "There won't be any fighting here."

"Or anywhere anytime soon," Cole said, but it would happen, and he wouldn't try to stop it. He didn't think Del would really try to kill Orin, but he deserved a little justice after what his brother did to him.

"Just out of curiosity," Orin said as he shifted his attention to Sahira. "Did you ever plan to tell Lexi and utilize her in the war against the Lord?"

Sahira's hand stilled on the cat as she stared at Orin with a look of such loathing that Cole wondered if she might be the one to kill his brother. Then her hand started moving on the cat again, and its purring resumed.

"I planned to tell her when we returned from the ball in the Gloaming," Sahira said. "It had been long enough since news of Del's death arrived and we'd had time to grieve. I kept increasing the dosage, and it was only a matter of time before the potion stopped working, but I *never* planned to utilize her for anything. I'm not like *you*."

Orin rolled his eyes. "Yes, we all know I'm the devil. Blah blah blah blah blah. Let's move on to something new, shall we? Like, why *didn't* you tell her after the ball?"

Sahira looked to Cole. "Cole arrived, and then there was so much going on, and it was all happening so fast that I couldn't dump it on her then. When he disappeared for two weeks and she was so heartbroken, I couldn't bring myself to do it. I had no idea when I would tell her; I was running out of time, but I... I..." Sahira's words trailed off as her head bowed and she focused on the cat. "I was a coward, and I didn't want to hurt her."

Del leaned across the space separating them and rested his hand on her shoulder. "It should have been me. I should have told her when the war broke out. We all knew there was a chance I wouldn't come home, and it never should have been left to you, but I couldn't bring myself to do it either. You're not a coward; I am."

"Neither of you are cowards," Lexi whispered.

And they both looked to her, but Orin cut into the touching moment.

"Are you going to continue taking the potion?" Orin asked Lexi.

CHAPTER THIRTY-EIGHT

SAHIRA'S HAND stilled on the cat as everyone in the room focused on Lexi. Cole chose not to acknowledge him.

"You stopped taking it?" Sahira asked.

"Not on purpose. I forgot with everything going on in the Gloaming. Cole was injured, and…." She shrugged.

"Are you okay?" Brokk demanded when Lexi's voice trailed off.

"I'm fine," Cole assured him. "Just a couple of stab wounds."

"You took a fae sword to the heart," Lexi said irritably. "And another to the ribs."

"How the *fuck* are you still alive?" Orin blurted.

"It seems that not being a purebred dark fae has its advantages," Brokk said with a smile. "But it hurts like a bitch."

"That it does," Cole agreed. "But Sahira's potions took care of that."

"Holy shit," Orin muttered as he ran a hand through his hair and glanced between him and Lexi. "We have to be able to bring the Lord down."

"We shall see, and we will take our time in getting to that point. We're *not* rushing into this," Cole said.

"Of course not, but we can take him. I *know* we can."

Cole hoped Orin was right, because something had to stop that monster before he destroyed them all.

"The sooner we get the duplicates of my brothers to the Lord, the sooner he'll stop breathing down my neck. After that, we can start really planning." He shifted his attention to Del. "Before you disappeared, you told me you were working on something that might change things and get us to the Lord; was it Lexi?"

"No," Del said. "I never wanted her involved in any of this. Even if we took him out, I wouldn't have revealed her true identity. Someone else wouldn't have cared about the consequences of what that throne brings with it and would have tried to seize it for themselves. They would have tried to take her out to get it. I was afraid I wouldn't be enough to protect her from that."

"Now, she'll have an army behind her," Orin said.

"*No one* else, other than Varo, is to know what she is until we have her abilities under control and are capable of protecting her," Cole told him.

"What about the coalition?" Del asked.

Cole thought about the group formed between some of the most powerful immortals from each realm to secretly plot against the Lord. They hadn't done much good to stop the Lord so far, but they were his allies.

"Not yet," he finally said. "Maybe Maverick when we know more about Lexi's abilities, but, for now, this is to remain between us."

He could trust his uncle with this; he just didn't want to draw Maverick into something this dangerous until they had a better idea of what was going on.

He focused on Del. "What was your plan back then?"

"It was a battle strategy to get some of us into Dragonia. Even though he believed we were on his side, the Lord never trusted us enough to allow too many of us into that realm. I was working on a way around that. It wouldn't work now. We don't have enough men—"

"We will get them," Orin interjected.

Del ignored him as he continued. "And it wasn't complete. I still have many details to hammer out."

"You work on that," Cole said, and Del nodded.

"How long do you think the Lord will back off after you give him your brothers?" Lexi asked.

"Not long."

"And then what?" Brokk asked.

"By then, Lexi should be experiencing her powers. We'll have to figure out how to get her around a dragon," Orin said.

"What?" Lexi blurted.

"We have to see how they'll react to you once you have your powers," Orin said.

"That's not going to happen," Cole said.

Orin lowered his arm from the mantle. "It has to happen. Without them, the Lord only has the power of the throne, and that's not enough for him to keep control of the realm."

"That throne is what helps him control the dragons."

"Is it? Or do they follow him because he sits on it and they haven't encountered an arach in a thousand years? How will the dragons react when they feel an arach in their presence? Will they still follow him, or will they follow *her*? We have to figure out how to catch one, and then we'll send her in to introduce herself."

"Have you lost your *fucking* mind?" Cole demanded. "That's *not* going to happen."

"Why not? Once her powers are active, she'll be immune to their fire."

"They could still *eat* her," Del said.

"What are the odds of that happening?" Orin inquired.

"One. Ate. Your. *Father*," Sahira said slowly.

"Eh, Tomato, Tomahto."

"You're an asshole," Brokk said.

"You know you're curious about what would happen too," Orin retorted.

"So am I," Lexi said. "He's right. It's something I have to know; we all do."

CHAPTER THIRTY-NINE

LEXI COULDN'T BELIEVE she'd said that. Was she really talking about putting herself in the path of a *dragon*?

Though the dragons had always fascinated her, they also petrified her when she saw them in Dragonia. They were amazing, but so was life, and she was not in the mood to be some dragon's meal.

However, there was no other choice. When the potion wore off, if she possessed powers that would help them defeat the Lord, she had to figure them out.

And if it took throwing herself into the path of a dragon to do so, then so be it.

"I don't like this," Cole said.

"Relax, brother, it won't be until she's more powerful," Orin said.

"You are about one sentence away from losing your tongue! Do not test me!" Cole roared.

Lexi flinched at the rage in his tone. The surge of his power against her skin sent an electric current racing up and down her arm and caused her hair to stand on end as the air between them crackled.

When Cole looked down at her, she knew he felt it too. He slid his fingers into hers, and she held him as his eyes burned a beautiful silver that touched her soul. This handsome, powerful man was *hers,* and while he would die to keep her safe, he wouldn't stand in her way when it came to any of this.

Instead, he would walk by her side. And together, they would find a way to right all the wrongs the Lord had created... if they didn't die first.

When she looked to the others again, Orin was staring at them with his mouth firmly closed. She could practically see the wheels in his mind churning as his gaze fell to their joined hands. Her father watched them with a mixture of awe and sadness while Sahira stared at them with raised eyebrows, and Brokk studied the wall behind their heads.

"There is a lot of power between the two of you," Sahira murmured.

"Get Varo, and if we're not back by then, start the spell," Cole said.

"I'll gather everything I'll need for the spell while they're gone," Sahira said.

"Do you have any more healing potions?" Lexi asked her.

"I'll make some more before you go," Sahira said. "It won't take long."

～

SHADE WAS SITTING on the counter, tail twitching as he watched Sahira stirring the pot on the stove. Lexi hovered in the doorway while her aunt worked. Different bottles, ingredients, and a mishmash of stones and plants she'd seen countless times over the years covered the counter.

"Would you like me to make you a new birth control?" Sahira asked.

"No," Lexi said.

"I wouldn't put the suppressing potion in it again."

"Is that what it's called? A suppressing potion?"

"Suppressing, binding, quenching, smothering, stifling; it has lots of different names from different people, but they all mean the same thing."

Lexi stared at the wall behind her aunt's head as she tried not to lose her temper. She understood why her dad and Sahira did what they did, but she couldn't deny the pain and anger festering inside her.

However, she couldn't keep beating them up about it; she loved them too much to lose them. She couldn't ignore the knife twisting into her chest either.

"When I revealed to you that I was hiding Orin in the tunnels, I promised there would be no more secrets between us," Lexi said. "But you had this *big* one."

"I did, and I'm sorry about that, but I did what I believed was best," Sahira said. "As did your father."

"I know." But it still hurt.

"You need birth control."

"Cole is on it."

"You can't trust a man to take care of you in that way."

"Maybe I couldn't trust another man, but I trust Cole. He'll keep me safe no matter what."

Sahira stopped stirring and lifted her head to meet Lexi's eyes for the first time. "You can't stay mad at me forever."

"I'm not mad... or at least, I don't think I am. Not anymore anyway."

"Then what are you?"

"Hurt, betrayed, lost, confused about everything I thought I knew, and terrified of a future I never imagined," she said honestly. "I understand why you both kept it from me, I do, but you should have told me. I'm not a child anymore, even if you both still see me that way."

Sahira's amber eyes swam with tears. "But to me, you'll

always be that vulnerable baby who needed protection and who I love very much."

When Sahira's voice broke, Lexi crossed the room and embraced her. They clung to each other before Lexi pulled away.

She'd needed to hug her aunt, and now, she also required her space.

"It's going to take me some time," she whispered.

"You have to forgive me one day," Sahira said.

"I already do."

"You'll have to trust me again."

Lexi stared at the floor before lifting her eyes to her aunt. "I trust you... but I don't. If that makes any sense."

"It does."

Sahira set her spoon down, turned off the fire, and with tender care, she moved the pot to another burner. She spooned some of its contents into a bowl and put it in the fridge.

Lexi wasn't sure how to respond or what would become of them, but she was at a complete loss. Instead, she stood there as Sahira worked.

She used to find watching her aunt make her potions one of the most relaxing, fascinating things to do, but now there was something almost sinister in it. She could be putting anything into those bottles, and Lexi would never know.

She gulped at the possibility and glanced around the room as she sought to think about something, *anything*, else. Her gaze settled on the window; she should see the horses. It had been far too long, and they were once her refuge.

Then she recalled Malakai's attack on her in the barn. "Did you ever cast a spell to revoke Malakai's invitation to our home?" she asked Sahira.

"The day he attacked you," Sahira said. "I should have done it before then, but I was afraid of enraging him if he found out. But he can't come in here again without a new invite, and since he's not getting one, he's permanently banned."

"Good."

"Lexi."

She turned to find Cole standing in the doorway with his hand resting against the frame.

"Are you okay?" he asked.

"Yes."

He studied her before his attention shifted to Sahira. "I knew a dark fae named Sindri. My father had his powers bound after he tried to start a rebellion. It took a coven of witches to do so, and it weakened them considerably, but you alone were able to bind hers. How?"

"He was probably a full immortal who was well aware of his powers. Lexi was young, not fully matured, and taking the potion from the time she was a babe," Sahira replied. "It also sounds like his was a permanent binding."

"It was."

"Hers was never meant to be permanent. I could *never* do that on my own. I'm not sure a coven of witches would succeed in doing it either. She's too powerful for that."

"I see," Cole murmured before looking to Lexi and smiling. "We have to go."

Lexi started walking toward him.

"Wait," Sahira said.

She opened the fridge, removed the bowl, and, using a small funnel, she poured the potion into two different bottles. She capped them both and rounded the island with them in hand. When she held them out to Lexi, she found herself unable to take them from her aunt.

"It's the healing potion," Sahira said.

Lexi still didn't move.

"Lexi, I would never do anything to harm you or Cole," Sahira said.

She believed that; she truly did, but still, her arms didn't move.

Maybe her sense of betrayal and distrust ran a lot deeper than she'd realized.

"Thank you," Cole said as he lowered his hand from the doorway and crossed the kitchen. He took the bottles from Sahira.

"Yes, thank you," Lexi murmured.

The sorrow in Sahira's eyes clogged Lexi's throat with tears, but she still didn't move. Time would help her get over this, but she wasn't sure things would ever be the same. With a sigh, Lexi decided to focus on the bigger issue at hand... returning to the Gloaming.

"We'll be back soon," Cole said.

"I'll be here," Sahira murmured.

"See you soon," Lexi whispered.

She walked with him from the room as her dad descended the stairs. Lexi stopped and smiled when she saw him. He was still too thin, but he'd trimmed his hair and shaved the beard from his face. He was much like the man she remembered, and the sight of him warmed her heart.

"What do you think?" he asked as he stopped at the bottom.

"Much better."

His grin lit up his face and caused his eyes to twinkle. Then he glanced between her and Cole, and his smile faded. "Are you leaving already?"

"I have to get back, but we'll return soon," Cole said.

Her dad nodded and opened his arms to her. Lexi hesitated for the briefest of seconds before hugging him. She was still upset, yes, but he was *alive*. She'd been granted a miracle, and she couldn't turn away from that.

"I'm so glad you're home," she whispered.

"Me too," he said and squeezed her. "Be careful."

"You too."

She released him and stepped back to take Cole's hand. Her dad glanced between the two of them before walking into the library to rejoin Brokk and Orin. They would be leaving soon too.

"Come on, let's go get Torigon," Cole said.

She followed him outside and to the barn. George, the man they'd hired to help with caring for the horses, had gone home already. Even though George recently fed them, all the horses stuck their heads out and nickered when the barn door opened.

"I know, I know," Lexi said as she released Cole. "You're all starving."

She walked into the feed room as Cole closed the door. Gathering carrots, she gave one to each horse and took the time to talk to and pet them. She'd been away from her friends far too often lately.

"I have to figure out a way to keep paying George to care for them," she said as Darby took the carrot she offered him. "We don't have much money left."

"I will pay him," Cole said.

"I can't let you do that."

"You're not *letting* me do anything. I'm *offering* to do it. You're my mate, Lexi, and I'm not going to let you worry about this. You never have to worry about money again."

She stared at Darby as he nudged her hand for more treats. Finally, she turned to look at Cole. "Thank you," she whispered.

"Don't thank me for this. I love you, and I'm *always* going to be here for you."

Tears burned Lexi's eyes as she walked over to hug him. His strong arms swept her off her feet, and he crushed her against him.

"You don't have to worry about the horses or anything else," he told her as he kissed her temple. When one of the horses kneed their stall door and nickered impatiently, he set her down again. "Go give them some more treats before they break out."

Lexi chuckled before returning to give an impatient Cricket a carrot. Cole removed Torigon from his stall and stood patiently by until she finished.

He'd closed the portal in their kitchen, but when she finished, he opened a new one in the barn. She walked through with him and Torigon as they returned to the Gloaming.

CHAPTER FORTY

BROKK COULDN'T STOP GLARING at the back of Orin's head as he led them through the prison on the outer realm. If he could bash his brother's head into a few of these walls, he'd probably feel a lot better, but fighting with Orin wasn't an option right now.

Because if they started fighting, they'd beat each other into bloody pulps… if they didn't kill each other in the process. And with the way he was feeling, it would be a fight to the death.

Instead, he concentrated on learning who was imprisoned in this place. He and Del stayed out of view as Orin opened each window on the steel doors, looked inside, and called the prisoner's name.

The ones who wept behind the doors were the worst. They would gladly hand them all over to the Lord if they ever learned they were working with Orin, but he'd have far preferred death to this perpetual state of unknowing and suffering. The scent of despair choked the air.

These were immortals facing a prison sentence with no end in sight. "Why not kill them?" Brokk inquired.

"For some, that is too kind a fate," Orin replied.

"No, it's not."

So far, none of them would be useful as they were all loyal to the Lord and the Lord only, but to see so many here, and how much Orin kept from them, was disturbing. He'd always known Orin was ruthless and determined, but he'd never expected this.

"Stop glaring at me, little brother," Orin said.

Brokk didn't respond.

"Just exactly what did I do to you?" Orin asked.

"What have you ever done *for* me?"

"I brought Del back."

Beside him, Del grunted. The vampire's anger was another reason not to start fighting with Orin; it would only fuel Del's animosity, and while Brokk despised Orin right now, he couldn't let someone else kill him. However, it was very, *very* tempting.

"You did that for you," Brokk said.

"I did it for *all* of us. Because of Lexi, we finally have a chance against the Lord now."

"None of us are going to let you sacrifice Lexi for your own desires," Brokk warned. "It's not just Cole you're going to have to watch out for when it comes to her."

"Oh, joy, more threats," Orin muttered.

Brokk couldn't see his face, but he knew Orin's eyes were rolling. Beside him, Del's hands fisted. Brokk rested his hand on Del's arm and shook his head. A muscle twitched in Del's locked jaw, and his arm vibrated beneath Brokk's touch.

It would take only one small thing to push Del over the edge when it came to Orin. They probably should have left Del behind, but he didn't think the vamp would have agreed to it.

When they rounded a corner, a couple of lycan and a dark fae came into view. They stood outside a steel door. When they saw Orin, they stood away from the wall they'd slumped against.

"General," one of the lycan greeted, and this time, Brokk rolled his eyes.

"At ease, men," Orin replied.

Brokk was sure his eyes were going to roll out of his head. He could almost feel the power trip oozing from Orin's pores. When they relaxed again, his men's eyes went past him and widened on Del.

"What's he doing out of his cage?" one of the lycan demanded.

"He's going to help us take down the Lord," Orin replied.

"He fought *for* the Lord."

"Things change."

"You're going to trust him?" the dark fae demanded.

Brokk thought he looked familiar, but he couldn't quite place him.

"Not at all," Orin said with a chuckle. "But I know something that will keep him a good boy for a while."

When Del stepped toward Orin, Brokk stepped in front of him to keep him from killing his arrogant prick of a brother.

"What are you doing with your brother?" the other lycan demanded. "He was on the Lord's side too."

"Don't worry, fellas. I have a plan," Orin assured them as he clapped the lycan on the shoulder. "Things are looking up for our side."

It was a testament to how loyal these men were to Orin when the lycan didn't rip off his arm. It *almost* made Brokk respect his brother a little more, but the days of respecting Orin were gone.

"Where's Varo?" Orin asked.

"The last I saw him, he was at the lookout," the dark fae replied.

"Let's go," Orin said and jerked his head to the right.

Brokk scowled at him, and Orin grinned back as he started down the hall again. They took a left, and Orin's men vanished.

"We have many guards from all over the realms," Orin said with a wave back at his men.

"I know," Del growled.

Orin had the nerve to chuckle.

"Remember Lexi," Brokk cautioned Del.

"That's the only reason he's still alive," Del said.

"Do you think you could take me, vamp? You were the one in *my* cell after all," Orin taunted.

"I was knocked out and half dead when you took me," Del retorted.

"Exactly. You were weak enough to get captured," Orin said.

Right then, Brokk knew Orin was itching for a fight. He didn't know why; maybe it was because Orin enjoyed the fight, or maybe it was guilt for what he'd done to Del and Lexi.

Orin was not one for guilt and wouldn't know how to handle it. This could be his way of reacting to it.

The more Brokk considered it, the more likely *that* was the reason for Orin's abrasiveness. His brother was always unlikeable, but this was a bit much, even for him.

Del seemed to realize this too as, instead of going for Orin, he relaxed and started to laugh. Orin shot a look over his shoulder, but Del wasn't paying attention to him as he examined the prison walls.

When they got to the end of the hall, Orin opened another steel door to reveal a set of stairs stretching into the darkness above. The thick, gray walls enclosed around them, and their steps were silent on the rocky steps. The airflow became stifled as they climbed and climbed until sweat beaded Brokk's brow, his lungs burned, and his legs ached.

He wiped away his sweat with the back of his forearm as he cursed this place and his brother. Then the scent of fresh air finally drifted to him. A cooling breeze carried it; he relished it as it dried the sweat coating him.

He had no idea how far they'd climbed until they stepped onto a balcony overlooking the rocky, barren, outer realm. They towered over the world below, and he imagined this was what it was like to look into the Grand Canyon.

He'd enjoyed the breeze in the hallway, but he loathed this howling wind whipping around him as it drowned out any other sounds, blew back his hair, and plastered his clothes to him. He glanced behind him at the open doorway, but it remained empty.

The balcony towered over the craggy, black rocks and deep, gray canyons of the outer realm. And at the far end of the balcony stood his brother Varo.

CHAPTER FORTY-ONE

FOR A SECOND, Brokk's heart leapt, and joy filled him at the sight of his brother's familiar black hair and slender frame. That frame was a lot thinner now than the last time he saw him, but that didn't surprise him.

None of the light fae were doing well since the war... or at least that was the rumor. No one had seen much of the immortals who opted out of the war. In doing so, they incurred the wrath of those who fought it.

Varo was only half light fae, but he'd always been the more caring and tender of his brothers. He'd chosen to fight and endure the consequences of that fight, but then, they all had.

Varo stood with his head bowed and his hands around the banister. Brokk sensed the pain radiating from him, but whether it was from the world, those imprisoned below them, or from lack of feeding, Brokk didn't know.

When Orin started toward him, Brokk and Del followed. They were only a few feet away, and Varo still hadn't realized they approached.

Brokk didn't know if it was the wind or if lack of feeding had weakened him, but something hid their approach from Varo, and he didn't like it. Varo should have sensed them by now.

"Varo!" Orin shouted over the wailing wind, and it still didn't carry. Cupping his hands to his mouth, Orin yelled. "Varo!"

Varo's shoulders stiffened before relaxing a little. He took a deep breath and turned to face them. His mouth was open as if he were about to speak, but whatever he was going to say died on his lips as he froze. Sorrow and joy flickered through the depths of Varo's white-blue eyes.

"Brokk," Varo said, and the wind barely carried the word to him.

Brokk heard the yearning in that one word and felt an answering tug at his heart. Varo wasn't like the rest of them; he never had been. The war would have ravaged him almost as much as it did the human realm.

But he'd sided with Orin, probably because he hoped to stop the misery spreading across the land. He'd failed; they all had, and now more than half their brothers were dead, and the remaining ones were on the verge of killing each other.

Not Varo, though. He had chosen his side, but if he'd ever encountered one of his brothers on the battlefield, he wouldn't have drawn his sword against them, and he wouldn't fight them now, either.

"Varo," Brokk greeted.

He wanted to embrace his brother but couldn't find it in himself to move. Varo stared at him for a minute before bowing his head. When the silence spread and Varo's sadness deepened, Brokk knew he had to end it.

"We might have a way to save you and Orin," he said. "We need you to come with us."

CHAPTER FORTY-TWO

"ARE YOU SURE ABOUT DRINKING THAT?" Lexi asked as Cole
uncorked the bottle of healing potion Sahira gave him.

He paused with the bottle halfway to his mouth before drinking
the contents down. The anxiety on her face kept him from telling
her that his chest was on fire. It would only distress her more.

He recorked the bottle and set it on the table to the left of the
portal they'd emerged from. Torigon's ears twitched as he
surveyed Cole's room with the same aplomb that he surveyed a
battlefield.

"She's not going to do anything to hurt us," Cole assured Lexi
as he cupped her cheek and drew her closer. "She did what she did
to protect you; she won't do anything to stifle me as it wouldn't do
you any good."

If she did, she'd regret it.

But Sahira wasn't that foolish.

"I have to talk to Niall, and I'm sure the council, or what
remains of them, will descend on the palace soon. They're going to
be thrilled to learn I'm putting Brokk in Durin's place on the council, but they will *not* be picking his replacement."

She didn't say anything as she rested her hands against his

chest. With tender hands, she lifted his tunic. He didn't stop her; the potion was already taking the edge of the ache in his chest, but if he didn't let her look, it would only upset her more.

Carefully, she peeled away the bandage. "Oh, Cole," she breathed.

"They're healing."

She put the bandage back in place before walking around him to examine the one on his back. With a sigh, she taped that bandage back into place too. "They're swollen and red; you've irritated them."

He clasped her hands against his chest and looked down at the wound. "And the potion is already helping them."

She grunted in response, and he slipped the remaining potion into his pocket.

"Come on," he said and tugged his tunic back down. "Let's get this taken care of so we can return to the others."

She looked about to protest more but instead said, "Stubborn ass."

He clasped her chin, lifted her face, and kissed her again. "And so are you. I'm going to take Torigon to the courtyard; I'll be right back."

Lexi stepped away as he opened a portal and led his horse through. A startled stable boy jumped back when Cole emerged with Torigon, but he rushed forward to take the horse from him.

"Take good care of him," Cole commanded.

"Of course, milord," the boy murmured before bowing and hurrying away.

Cole returned to find Lexi staring out the window overlooking the courtyard. She turned to him and smiled when he emerged.

"Are you ready?" he asked.

She walked over and hooked her arm through his extended one. "I am."

Together, they made their way to the door. He slid the locks free and opened the door to reveal Niall standing on the other side. His guard turned to look at him over his shoulder.

"You didn't have to keep watch," Cole said.

"Yes, I did," Niall replied. "How are you feeling?"

"Much better," Cole said. "Have there been any changes?"

"Most of the rebels have been hunted down and killed, but some fled the realm. Those who have been caught are locked in the dungeon."

"They'll stay there for now." Only the king could open a portal into the palace so they wouldn't be opening a portal out of the dungeon.

"I didn't know if you wanted the king's guard to follow the ones who are still on the run."

"No," Cole said. "Do we know who they are?"

"Yes. Some of their *allies*"—Niall spit the word out—"have given them up."

"Then we will send men after them once things here have settled and we've rebuilt more homes. We'll put out the word that they have a bounty on their heads. More than likely, someone will turn them in. If not, we'll send men after them then, but the dark fae of this realm are more important right now, and we need all the help we can get to rebuild."

"I agree," Niall said. "We've brought more displaced fae into the courtyard and have secured them homes. A few craz returned for some carrion, but they were chased away or destroyed."

"Good," Cole said.

He hated that he would have to leave here again so soon, but someone was going to have to take the duplicate bodies of Varo and Orin to the Lord. He also had to get Lexi out of the Gloaming before her powers started to emerge fully.

They had no way of knowing what would happen when they did, and no one here could learn what she was. Someone had already gone back and reported her existence and that she was his mate to the Lord; if they noticed anything odd about her, they would turn her in, and he could *not* have that.

The three of them descended to the first floor together. They were approaching the main doors when they swung open and what remained of the council strode inside. He'd known he would have to deal with them soon, but he was not in the mood for them right now.

However, he was going to have to speak with them.

"You are alive." Finn couldn't keep his disappointment hidden.

Cole didn't bother to reply. "What do you want?"

"What do we *want?*" Becca asked incredulously. "The Gloaming is in complete disarray and—"

"And I am taking care of it."

Cole's eyes narrowed on Becca as she swung her glare from him to Lexi and back again. If he had to put money on it, *she's* the one he would bet told the Lord about Lexi being his mate. And if he discovered that it was, council member or not, he would make Becca pay for it.

"May we speak with you, milord?" Elvin inquired.

No was on the tip of his tongue, but part of regaining control of the Gloaming was dealing with them.

"Yes," Cole replied.

Becca's eyes flicked to Lexi. "Alone," she said pointedly.

"My future queen will hear what you have to say," he stated.

A flicker of annoyance crossed all their faces, but it was Lexi who spoke. "I'd like to go to the moon room," she said.

His chest constricted at the idea of allowing her to wander around the palace without him. It had been a couple of days since she last drank her potion; who knew what was going to happen and when it would start.

But then his attention shifted to what remained of the council. Unfortunately, he had to deal with them, and it would be better if it didn't start with all of them fighting. And Lexi would be much happier in the moon room than listening to the council bitch.

"I'll stay with her and keep her safe," Niall offered.

Niall would keep her safe, but that potion was wearing off.

"I'll be fine," Lexi assured him.

"I won't be long," he grated through his teeth. "And it's best if you stay in that room."

"I will," she promised.

When she started to walk away, he caught her and, clasping her elbow, drew her a few steps away. Casting his voice low, he bent his head to whisper in her ear. "If you feel anything different, tell Niall to bring you back to me immediately."

She rested her hand over his. "I'll be fine."

He reluctantly released her and looked to Niall.

"I'll defend her with my life," Niall vowed.

"I have no doubt," Cole said.

While the council stalked into the main hall, Cole watched as Lexi strolled away with Niall close at her side. His guard and friend had his hand resting on the hilt of his sword as they walked.

He almost went after her, then realized that if she was determined to embrace what she was, this was the first of *many* times where he would have to let her do something he'd prefer she didn't.

She was right; if she was going to be his queen and fight in this war, then he couldn't keep her sheltered.

Fighting the lycan that wanted to track its mate, he followed the council into the main hall. He shut the door behind them; no one else would overhear this conversation.

CHAPTER FORTY-THREE

By the time he finished with the council, they weren't happy, but they had accepted that Brokk would claim a seat at the table. They were still infuriated about his choices, but they wouldn't try to start another rebellion.

They weren't foolish enough to do that after Aelfdane's siblings and Durin failed to take the throne from him. No one else on the council could rally the same number of troops as those two families, and after what they'd witnessed, they didn't have the balls to rise against him.

If they had joined with Durin, Fiadh, and Nissa, they might have stood a chance against him, but it was too late for that. He didn't know if they'd been too cowardly to join with them, biding their time, or were actually loyal to *him*. And he'd probably never know.

In the distance, the clock chimed, and he realized this meeting was taking longer than he would have liked.

"I think that's enough for now," Cole said. "I must check on my people again."

And my mate.

They weren't at all thrilled about being dismissed, but he didn't care. Becca, Elvin, Alston, and Finn were all that remained of the council. They were hesitant to leave, but once he rose, they all did too.

As they filed toward the door, Elvin hung back and turned toward Cole as he followed them to the door Alston opened before exiting. Becca, who was just ahead, cast a suspicious glance back at them.

"Milord," Elvin said in a demure tone as he kept his head bowed. "May I speak to you privately for a minute?"

Elvin glanced at Becca, who didn't try to pretend like she wasn't listening. Cole was eager to return to Lexi, but Elvin was the only fae on the council he trusted a little.

Cole didn't say a word as he stared at Becca. Eventually, she took the hint and slithered out of the room.

"What is it?" he asked Elvin when he was certain Becca was gone.

Elvin hesitated before lifting his eyes to him. "Milord, I know you have found your mate, and I understand how important that is to a lycan, but I think you should consider something."

"And that is?" Cole inquired when Elvin stopped speaking.

Elvin's dark skin paled a little, but he continued. "That since there has been an uprising, you should marry someone from a powerful *fae* family who would help unite the Gloaming. Someone such as Becca."

Cole inwardly recoiled at the suggestion while outwardly he managed to retain a calm façade. "Absolutely not."

Elvin's chin rose a little, and steely resolve shone in his black eyes. The man knew he was playing with fire, but he wasn't going to back down. As much as his suggestion irritated Cole, he admired the man's determination to see this through.

"A marriage between the two of you would help unite the Gloaming, milord, which should be your priority," Elvin said.

"My priority is to make sure the Lord doesn't destroy us all," Cole replied. "Do not question my loyalty to the dark fae or my right to sit on the throne. I *earned* the crown by surviving the trials. I put my life on the line for *all* of you throughout those trials and the rebellion. I will *not* tolerate less than complete loyalty from *all* the fae whether I marry one of them or not. Those who do not provide it, will die."

Elvin gulped, but Cole's warning didn't deter him. "I understand, milord. I do not question your devotion to our realm or your right to the throne, but it might bring peace to the land sooner and reassure those who are nervous about your half-fae status if you marry a woman from our realm. If not Becca, then there are plenty of other beautiful, powerful women from good families who would make a fine wife."

"A better wife than a half vampire half human?" Cole asked, but he wasn't upset or offended by this truth.

The dark fae coveted power, he did too, and he understood they saw Lexi as weak, even though she'd raced across a battlefield to save him. What would Elvin think or say if he knew Lexi's true heritage?

Would he and the others be more accepting of her once they learned she was one of the most powerful beings to ever walk the realms?

It was probably only a matter of time before that happened, but it wouldn't be today.

"The fae in the courtyard bowed to her after she saved me," Cole said.

"We were all very impressed by her bravery." Elvin looked to the wall again before focusing on Cole. "But those in the courtyard are peasants, milord. To unite the more powerful families in the land, a powerful union would be best. Your mate is a strong, beautiful woman and obviously courageous, but she is not one of us."

"Neither am I, not fully. That's also part of the problem, isn't it?"

Elvin's chin jutted out. "You know how the dark fae are."

"Are you the same way?"

"It doesn't matter how *I* am. All that matters is the safety of the realm and those residing in it."

And that was the truth, and probably why Cole wasn't more annoyed by this conversation. Elvin wasn't discussing this because he doubted Cole or disliked Lexi.

He was doing it because the Gloaming and its residents' safety were the most important thing to him. He would do whatever it took to protect the realm.

That was what made him loyal... it also made him dangerous. But since he couldn't force Cole into marriage, and he would never get close enough to try anything against Lexi, Cole wasn't concerned about Elvin doing something foolish to exert his will.

"That is important to me too," Cole told him.

"I know, milord. But I think you should consider marrying another."

"Lexi is more than my mate; I love her."

Elvin closed his eyes as if this pained him. "I am not asking you to give her up. You could marry another and keep her on the side."

That infuriated him. "You are well aware marriage does *not* work that way for immortals. Amongst us, marriage is a permanent, powerful bond that no one takes lightly."

"I am aware, milord, but this is a special circumstance. I'm sure if you explain that to your dark fae wife before you marry, she will understand. Some women would be happy to have the throne, and status that comes with it. They would agree to a marriage in name only."

"I am aware of that. I'm also aware Lexi is not one of those women."

Elvin's eyes darted away from him. "Milord—"

"I understand your priority is the Gloaming, and that is the *only* reason I've allowed this conversation to continue, but I will not hear any more of this, and I will *not* talk about it again. Lexi is going to be my wife. *She* is the one who will be your future queen, and I can assure you, Elvin, no one deserves it more than her. We will not talk of this again."

Elvin opened his mouth before closing it and bowing his head. "Of course, milord."

"I do hope for your counsel on other matters in the future."

"Of course."

Cole grasped his shoulder and squeezed it to show he held no hard feelings; he hoped Elvin felt the same. "If you'll excuse me, I must find my mate."

He didn't wait for Elvin's reply before leaving the room.

CHAPTER FORTY-FOUR

COLE WAS NEARLY to the moon room when he spotted Niall standing in the doorway. His hand rested on the hilt of his sword while his attention remained on the moon room.

Hearing Cole's approach, Niall turned toward him. Cole's step faltered when he saw Niall's parted mouth and the paleness of his friend's skin.

Drawing his father's sword from its sheath, he stalked forward, but even as he was moving, he knew there couldn't be a threat. Niall would have gone after it if there was one.

Instead, he remained frozen in the doorway as he seemed to try to decide if he should attack or not. Cole arrived at his side in mere seconds and froze in the doorway.

When Lexi laughed, Cole suddenly understood Niall's uncertainty. Part of him wanted to hack his way through the wall of green vines and colorful flowers encircling her. The other part was so riveted in amazement that he barely breathed.

He'd been with the council for so long that night had fallen. The four moons of the Gloaming were out, and the luna flowers...

Well, the luna flowers were in love. They'd always reacted to her, but not like *this*. The potion must be wearing off faster than they'd realized if the arach truly did possess sun *and* moon magic.

The luna flowers were lycan plants that reacted to the moonlight and lycans. But he'd *never* seen anything like this.

After his mother died, these flowers encased him in a warm, protective cocoon, but they'd never played with him like this. He originally believed the flowers reacted to her because they somehow knew she was his mate before he did, but now he thought they responded to her because she was an arach.

She was a powerful, beautiful, vibrant being who exuded life, and these plants loved her for it.

When her hand rose out of the center of the vines, the moonlight filling the room spilled across her sun-kissed skin before the vines enveloped it.

"I... I didn't know what to do," Niall said. "I've never seen anything like this, and she's *laughing,* so I... I just...." His voice trailed off when Lexi laughed again. "What is going on?"

"The luna flowers like her."

"No shit," Niall snorted.

"Lexi!" Cole called.

The vines and flowers shifted, and Lexi's flushed face popped out from between them. Despite the radiant smile on her face, his heart slammed against his ribs. She was so beautiful, so *alive*, and soon, so many would want her dead.

He *had* to be enough to protect her.

"Hey," she said breathlessly.

The vines and flowers started to unravel as she slipped out from between them. They followed her across the room as she practically skipped over to him. When she stopped before him, a couple of the vines brushed his arms as he hugged her.

Cradling her against his chest, he watched as the flowers turned their faces to the moonlight streaming into the room. His hand slid up her back and into her hair; he ran the silken strands through his fingers as he pondered how much time they'd have before he would have to keep her sheltered.

He was about to tell Niall to leave them when the thud of running feet drew his attention to the hall. Releasing Lexi, he stepped in front of her as a breathless, dark fae teenager rounded the corner.

"Milord! Milord!" he called.

"Now what?" Cole muttered.

The young fae skidded to a halt and bent over to rest his hands on his knees as he panted heavily. "Milord! There is a dragon in the Gloaming!"

Cole's blood turned to ice in his veins. Had it come for Lexi?

CHAPTER FORTY-FIVE

COLE RAN AHEAD of the boy and the others as he raced down the corridors to the main doors. Before he could get to them, the doors swung open, even though no one stood near them. He stopped at the stairs and looked to the sky as Lexi and Niall skidded to a halt beside him.

Lexi's heart thundered in her chest, and she was trying to catch her breath when Cole turned toward her and nudged her back inside.

"Don't come out here," he commanded.

"Cole—"

Before she could say anything more, a thunderous roar erupted across the land. It shook the windows in the palace, vibrated the ground, and quaked the earth beneath her feet. She didn't see it yet, but she knew what creature made that sound.

She almost ducked back into the palace, but that roar caused something like a tuning fork to vibrate inside her. Since the end of the war, she'd heard the dragons bellow often in the human realm, but she'd never had such a visceral reaction to it before.

She opened her mouth to say something, but no words came

out as she gazed up at Cole. Whatever he saw on her face caused silver to flash through his eyes as a muscle twitched in his jaw.

"Get inside," he told her.

Lexi almost did that, but when the screams of the dark fae pierced her shock, she knew she couldn't run from this. Everyone in this realm had been through so much. They were injured, broken, beaten, and trying to flee from the beast now haunting their kingdom.

She couldn't retreat when there might be something she could do. She had no idea what that was, but she *couldn't* retreat.

"Cole," she whispered.

Whatever else she might have said was drowned out by another loud bellow. And then, a red dragon rose over the top of the charred hills of the Gloaming. It swooped across the burnt-out land and toward them.

Lexi gaped as the magnificent, terrifying beast soared through the sky. In the moonlight, its red scales shimmered with silver. The flecks of yellow decorating it underneath reminded her of the sun even as it became a part of the moonlight encompassing it.

She'd never seen a dragon so large before. Its lethal, three-foot-long talons were held curved against its belly as it twisted to the side and arced toward the palace.

The screams of those in the courtyard grew louder as they ran around, looking for somewhere to hide. They dashed into the stables, ran into the homes of the soldiers, and hid where they could.

On the fence surrounding the palace, the head of the dragon Cole killed remained staked to a spike. It was rotting but clearly the head of a dragon; Lexi doubted that would make this giant beast any happier.

Had it come here to destroy Cole for killing one of them? Though it was a warm night in the Gloaming, she suddenly felt encased in ice.

Its next roar kicked up a breeze that blew the tendrils of her hair back from her face. Dirt and ashes billowed across the land as the dragon swooped toward them before soaring high again.

It wasn't until it was swooping over the top of the palace that she realized it wasn't releasing its fire. This creature could cause so much destruction, but it wasn't unleashing its wrath upon the realm.

She had no idea why or what it was doing here, but after the battle and the craz, she was grateful for this small reprieve. That didn't mean it wasn't going to start destroying at any second.

She craned her head to see where it went, but the palace blocked her view.

"We have to find out where it's going. It can't stay in the realm," Cole said.

"We told Sahira we'd be back soon," Lexi said.

She didn't dare say anyone else's names. Cole trusted Niall to protect her, but she didn't know how far that trust ran.

"I'll send a crow back to let her know we're going to be here for longer than planned," Cole said.

Lexi didn't like that, but he was right. The dragon couldn't remain in the Gloaming.

~

BROKK OPENED the letter the crow had brought to the kitchen window earlier. As soon as Sahira announced she had everything she required for the spell, he'd been in a rush to return to the tunnels where Orin and Varo had already retreated.

He'd returned with Sahira and Del and hadn't taken the time to read it beforehand. He wanted this spell over and the stone *out* of their possession.

In the dim glow of the flashlight Sahira held, he scanned the note. His eyebrows rose when he saw the word dragon, and an uneasy feeling settled into the pit of his stomach. Had the Lord sent the dragon or had it just flown into the realm as they sometimes did?

The arrival of a dragon in the Gloaming was a lot less common than it used to be; they had the human realm to explore and torment now.

Was it seeking revenge against Cole for killing one of its brethren? But it had been a while since then, and they hadn't eaten him yet; the Lord ensured that. He didn't see one of those beasts breaking the Lord's control to go after Cole now when they could have easily killed him in Dragonia.

What if Lexi somehow drew it there?

He hoped not, because the longer they kept what she was a secret, the better they would all be. And having a dragon following her around was *not* going to help them keep that cat in the bag.

And for all he knew, the dragon might eat her first. He had no idea how the creatures were going to react to her. Some of them had probably never met an arach.

It had been a thousand years since they last ruled, and while dragons weren't known to be prolific breeders—they would have invaded all the realms by now if they were—they'd certainly produced new dragons over those thousand years.

And the ones who *did* remember the arachs might prefer to have nothing to do with another one. The arachs destroyed each other and nearly their realm with their greed and petty infighting. The dragons might have grown sick of their shit before the arachs all killed each other.

He could only hope not. Lexi's true heritage might be their only chance of surviving this whole mess. He had no doubt the Lord meant to destroy them all and anyone else who possessed any amount of power.

Now that the Lord had won his battle against the rebels, he would turn his attention to better prizes than the human realm. And the Gloaming, being one of the stronger realms, would make a fantastic prize.

"What does it say?" Sahira asked.

Brokk crumpled the paper and shoved it in his pocket. "There's a dragon in the Gloaming. They're going to be gone longer than they anticipated and want us to start without them."

"Is Lexi okay?" Del demanded.

"I'm sure she's fine," Orin replied. "We should do what Cole said and get this started. What do Varo and I have to do?"

"My daughter—"

"Your daughter is in the Gloaming with its king and a dragon her people once ruled. She's perfectly fine."

Del's hands fisted, and while Orin deserved a beatdown, Brokk wasn't in the mood for this.

"Enough," Brokk interjected. "Orin, stop being an asshole."

"I think you forget your place, little brother," Orin said.

"No," Brokk retorted. "I think you forget *yours*. Sahira doesn't have to help you."

Orin glanced at Sahira, who smirked in return. "I'd prefer not to," she said.

"Perhaps we should do this at another time, when Cole is here, and we are all more relaxed," Varo said in his cool, soothing voice.

Brokk had forgotten how much Varo could calm a room with his gentle presence and levelheaded approach to everything. Of course, his pacifying nature hadn't stopped their family from splitting apart, but he wasn't a miracle worker, and they were all stubborn asses.

"We can't," Brokk said. "We only have the stone for three days—"

"Less than that now," Sahira said. "And the spell takes hours to complete."

"Then let's get started," Orin stated. "What do you need from us?"

Sahira hesitated before reluctantly replying. "You both have to lie down in the center of the floor."

She waved her hand toward the bare space on the ground. Once they had all the supplies they needed, they'd closed off two of the gates and locked themselves into a small section of the tunnel. It wasn't a large section, but Sahira said it was big enough for what she had to do. Orin and Varo could lie side by side and still have almost two feet of room on each side of them.

Varo walked over and laid down; he'd always been the most trusting of his brothers. Brokk always believed it was the trait that would get him killed, but he'd survived when their far less trusting brothers were dead.

For the first time, Brokk speculated if Varo's trust might have a basis in something more than the naivete he always wrote it off as.

Orin didn't move. "How do I know you're not going to do something to me?" he asked Sahira.

"You don't," she replied dismissively. "I guess you'll have to trust me."

"Maybe if you take the tracking spell off, I could trust you a little more."

Sahira laughed but didn't bother to reply as she pulled the harrow stone out from the pocket of her red skirt. The hem of the dress brushed the ground as she walked over to Varo and knelt at his side.

"That's not going to happen," Sahira said as she started to remove crystals from her pockets. "And I wouldn't wait too long. I'll only have enough power to perform this spell once, and then the stone will have to be returned."

Next, she removed vials of potions and set them out. Then came satchels full of herbs. When she finished, she looked to Orin. "Aren't you going to take part in this?"

Orin scowled as he looked from her to the circle of stones and herbs. The potions remained in their bottles.

"I'm about to start," she said.

When Sahira uncorked the first bottle, Orin walked over to lie beside his brother.

"Get as close as you can to each other," Sahira instructed.

Their shoulders and fingers touched as they inched closer together on the floor. Sahira grinned at Orin. "Wise choice."

With mesmerizing grace, she poured the potion out around them. The scent of lavender, ashwagandha, clove, peppermint, eucalyptus, myrrh, nasturtiums, lemon balm, and many other aromas he couldn't name blended with the earthy odor of the tunnels.

The odors on their own weren't unpleasant, but mixed all together and trapped in these small confines, they soon became overwhelming.

It wasn't until Sahira poured the last bottle that Brokk saw she'd created the shape of a squished pentagram with his brothers and the harrow stone in the center.

CHAPTER FORTY-SIX

IT WAS WELL past midnight when Cole called a halt to their pursuit of the dragon. He pulled Torigon to a stop outside an inn. They'd been riding for hours, the horses were exhausted, and though she'd never admit it, he knew Lexi was too.

The dragon had landed on one of the mountains miles away and folded its wings as it surveyed the land. Not only would it take them days to get to it, but the horses would never make the journey, and neither could they.

He had no idea what the thing was doing in the Gloaming. It had eaten a couple of horses when it arrived in this area, but for now, it was content to sit there.

When Cole grasped Lexi's waist, she rested her hands on his shoulders, and he plucked her from the saddle. He held her close to him as he set her on the ground.

Her legs wobbled a little before she locked them into place. He understood how she felt; even after all his experience on a horse, his legs felt rubbery too.

When she was steady on her feet, he turned to Niall and the three other men who'd come with them.

"Assign one of the men to keep watch for the next two hours.

After that, have them switch out with another man," Cole told Niall. "I will get us all rooms."

Niall nodded, and Cole took Lexi's hand as he led her to the inn. He didn't often come to this area of the Gloaming; it was a remote section full of farmland and horses who roamed the open pastures and rolling hills.

Most of those horses scattered the second the dragon flew into view, but a couple weren't lucky enough to escape its wrath. The surviving horses fled into the foothills and numerous caves that abounded in this area of the Gloaming. The locals often explored those caves, but many of them remained mysteries.

"Where are we?" Lexi asked around a yawn that she covered with her hand.

"This area of the Gloaming is known as Underhill," Cole replied. "It consists mostly of farmers and horsemen."

When Lexi turned to survey the verdant land and rolling hills, so did he. He didn't get the chance to visit here often, but it was one of his favorite places in the Gloaming, especially when the horses weren't hiding. They normally spotted the land for as far as the eyes could see.

"They're all hiding now, but usually, the fields are full of wild horses who make excellent mounts once broken. The best warhorses come from Underhill. It's where Torigon hails from," he told her. "Come, let's get some rooms."

"Is the inn open?" she asked.

Before she finished asking her question, a young boy darted out of the stable and ran for the horses. Another young lad, still tugging on his pants, followed him out the door.

"Underhill is always open," Cole told her. "They're known for their hospitality."

They didn't reach the door to the inn before it opened to reveal a pretty fae woman with her breasts pushed up by her formfitting dress. Piled into a loose knot on top of her head, curly tendrils of black hair had worked themselves free to frame her brown skin—the glow from the moons reflected in her black eyes.

Her inviting smile faltered when she spotted him. "Mi-milord. Your Highness!" she stammered, and a chair scraped against the floor behind her.

Cole bowed his head to the woman; he'd met her before, when he stayed here a few years ago, but that was a war, and what seemed like a lifetime, ago.

"Your Highness, you bless us with your presence," the woman said.

She regained her composure and stepped aside to beckon them to enter with a graceful curtsey and a swooping wave of her arm. She glanced curiously at Lexi before turning her full attention back to him.

"Please, come in and make yourself at home," she said. "We still have warm stew in the pot and fresh bread as well as ale, wine, and water, if you would like some. If not, we can make you some tea."

The warm, inviting inn was much as he remembered it from his previous visit. Bronze sconces hung on the wooden walls; four of them held lit torches that cast shadows around the large, open room.

Six, round, dark wood tables filled the room. Each of them had six chairs surrounding them. Cards and a chessboard sat out on two of the tables, but a chest against the far wall stored the rest of the games. To his right was the swinging door to the kitchen; despite the time, delicious aromas of cooking food wafted out.

"Are you hungry?" Cole asked Lexi.

"No," she said and hid another yawn.

A tall man with broad shoulders and the build of a lycan stood near the fire crackling in the gray, stone hearth. The flames nearly matched the man's orange hair. His gray eyes were full of curiosity as he stared at them, and Cole was just as curious; what was a lycan doing in the Gloaming?

CHAPTER FORTY-SEVEN

"MILORD," the woman murmured. "This is my husband, Bledig. He was not here the last time you visited. We wed last year."

"Congratulations to you both. It is nice to meet you, Bledig," Cole greeted.

The man bowed his head. "You also, Your Highness. Your uncle is my alpha."

"Maverick is a good man."

"Yes, he is. He and your father gave me permission to reside in the Gloaming with my mate."

And he was afraid Cole would revoke that permission. He hadn't been aware his father had granted it, but there were plenty of things his father did that he never knew about.

"I wish you both a lifetime of happiness in the Gloaming," Cole told him.

Bledig visibly relaxed. "Thank you, milord."

Cole turned back to the woman. He didn't see any marks on her, but then, Lexi's clothes also covered his bite.

"I'm sorry, but I forgot your name," Cole said to her.

"I am Dora," she replied with a warm smile.

"It's nice to meet you both," Lexi murmured.

Exhaustion made her words thicker than normal.

"We require some rooms for my men and us," Cole said. "Though they may wish to eat."

"Of course, milord. Our best room is taken, but I can wake the occupants and have it readied for you."

"There's no need," Cole assured her. "A bed, any bed, is all we require."

Besides, he wasn't sure Lexi would stay awake long enough to wait for a room to be readied for them. When a bellow pierced the air, Dora jumped. Her eyes widened as they flew past him and to the open door.

"What was that?" she whispered.

"A dragon," Cole said. "That is why we are here."

"In the Gloaming?" she blurted. "In *Underhill?*"

Cole didn't reply as she rushed toward the door, but her husband shoved a chair aside and, leaping over the table, wrapped his arm around her waist to hold her back.

"The horses!" Dora cried.

"It ate a couple of them, but the rest have gone into hiding," Cole assured her.

"The dragon is on a mountain," Lexi said. "It seemed quite happy to be there, and I don't think it's coming down anytime soon."

When Dora relaxed in her husband's hold, he released her. Remembering she had guests, Dora straightened her skirt and smoothed it down as she turned toward them. She plastered on a smile as she edged closer to the door.

A low grumble made its way up Bledig's chest and throat, but Dora waved her hand at him as she poked her head out the door. "I'm only going to take a peek. My goodness," she whispered.

"We've been tracking it," Lexi said.

"What's it doing here?" Bledig inquired.

Cole had far too many guesses than answers to that question.

His best guess as to what drew the dragon was standing in his arms, and she needed sleep.

"They occasionally come into the Gloaming," Cole replied. "It's not often, but they do make their way here."

"I've never seen one in Underhill," Dora murmured. "It's terrifying."

It was many things, and dead would be one of them if it came off that mountain.

"We require rooms," Cole reminded her when Lexi yawned again.

"Oh, of course!" Dora exclaimed as she turned away from the door. "My apologies, milord. I have just… I've never—"

"It's okay," Cole interrupted as the dragon released another bellow.

From what he could see of it through the window, it spread its wings before taking flight. Dora staggered away from the door as Cole stepped toward it.

The dragon swooped down the mountain, heading directly for the inn. Beside him, Lexi stiffened as if she were bracing for an attack, Dora released a small squeak, and the stable boys ran for the stables with the last two horses.

His men pulled their swords. Cole was reaching for his to go out there when the dragon opened its own portal and vanished into it. Lexi remained rigid against him as Cole relaxed.

It wasn't the first time a dragon had entered the Gloaming, and it wouldn't be the last. None of the others ever traveled this far, but then again, the land around the palace had never been a burnt-out wasteland when they arrived before.

The dragons had always managed to scrounge some food from there, but not this time. The creature's disappearance eased the tension in his chest. It hadn't come here for Lexi; it had come for food and, after a short pause to digest, decided to go home.

The only problem was, it would recall where it filled its belly. The residents of Underhill were *not* prepared to defend themselves against dragons. This was a peaceful village; a dragon would tear it apart.

He would have to send men here, at least for a little while. It was not the best option so soon after the attack on the palace, but he couldn't leave Underhill unprotected.

Right now, he had to get Lexi a room and some sleep.

CHAPTER FORTY-EIGHT

SHADOWS SLITHERED across the ground and crept across the sky until they blanketed out the day. The sun blackened and shriveled until it resembled nothing more than a desiccated heart in the sky. And while the sun never pulsed like a real heart, it always had a rhythm and life all its own.

That rhythm was gone. An incessant screaming rose from the shadows until the sound encompassed the land they'd claimed. And then Cole realized it was not the shadows screaming...

The screams were coming from those trapped *within* the shadows.

Those lost souls being devoured by the shadows emitted sounds he knew well from his time spent on countless battlefields. They were the sounds of the dying and the damned. They wailed incessantly until those wails cut off, but silence never descended.

As soon as one scream cut off, new ones rose as the shadows moved across the land, eating everything in their way.

And then the shadows found him.

They rose from the ground like cobras preparing to strike as they hovered over him. He'd never expected the Grim Reaper to dance or sway, but this one did in such a rhythmic, beautiful way that he found himself fascinated by the thing about to destroy him.

But no, they wouldn't destroy him. They wanted something more from him than death.

He didn't try to fight them or flee as the striking shadows latched onto his skin, pierced through his flesh, and crept into his veins.

They coiled around his heart and filled his body until they replaced the air filling his lungs. He jerked as they seeped into his soul. While all around him, screams ruled the unnatural night, he didn't scream as the shadows consumed him.

~

A SMALL THUD pulled Lexi from her sleep. She blinked against the darkness as she tried to recall where she was. In the dim light of the lantern on the bedside table, she studied the unfamiliar room until her groggy brain fit the pieces together.

She was at the inn, and Cole was...

When she rolled over, she expected to discover Cole where she last saw him, lying beside her on the bed. She recalled the warmth and strength of his arms enveloping her while she drifted to sleep.

But, of course, he wasn't still there; she should have known better.

Edging closer to the edge of the bed, she looked down to discover him on the floor. The stubborn fool hadn't even taken one of the blankets; he'd left her with them.

While she understood his fear that he would attack her while he slept, she was so tired of it. He should not be sleeping on a cold, hard floor while she had this big bed to herself. He was scared he'd hurt her, but she was positive he wouldn't.

He'd removed his pants and tunic last night, so the corded muscles in his arms and thighs stood starkly out, and the contours of his chiseled body were visible. His wounds from the battle had completely healed; she couldn't see any mark on him from them anymore.

Last night, she was too exhausted to appreciate how amazing he was. But today, with the early light of dawn starting to brighten the night, she couldn't stop herself from admiring him as she tried to ascertain what was happening.

She was pretty sure he was having a nightmare as his hands clenched and his body tensed, but he wasn't moving or thrashing like the other times she saw him having one. She knew better than to try to wake him during a nightmare, but she couldn't let him suffer either.

Slipping from the bed, she padded closer to him. The tunic she wore when they left the palace brushed against her thighs as she walked.

Before they left the palace, Amaris brought her the emerald-green tunic with silver piping and a pair of formfitting, brown pants. The pants were the most comfortable pair of riding pants she'd ever worn.

She'd meant to take the tunic off before climbing into bed, but she must have forgotten. Most of the night was an exhausted blur. She recalled the door to this room opening and stumbling toward the welcoming, queen-sized bed with all the fluffy pillows on top of it.

After that, she only remembered Cole holding her, and then... nothing. Despite not getting much sleep, she felt a *lot* more rested.

Kneeling beside Cole, she didn't bother trying to wake him. He would only react violently if she did.

Instead, she lay beside him, rested her head on his shoulder and her hand on his chest. Beneath her palm, his heart raced, but as she lay there, its wild beat slowed and his body steadily relaxed.

She smiled when his breathing returned to normal and the horror haunting him faded away.

~

THE SHADOWS POURED from his mouth, out of his nose, and filled the air around him. They were everywhere; not a single piece of him, or the world, was spared their coldness and wrath.

But through the icy tendrils of their grasp, a trickle of warmth started to fill a heart he hadn't realized had gone cold. The beams of light piercing the darkness reminded him of the sun peeking through the black clouds of a thunderstorm.

Little shafts of light danced across the ground, chasing away the shadows there. The shadows hissed as they recoiled from those rays. The blackened ground turned green once more, and when he tipped his face toward the light, the heat melted the icy chill encompassing him.

The warmth spreading out from his heart pulsed through his veins with every beat. It seeped into his arms and legs as it pushed the shadows out from his veins. When the light forced the shadows to retreat, the sun became exposed once more.

It was still black, but brilliant gold light illuminated its shriveled edges.

Cole flexed his fingers as he gazed at the field spread around him. The shadows retreated, and life was returning to the land, but the dead didn't rise. Their bodies remained strewn across the rolling green fields.

The sight of them was as unnerving as the realization that, though warmth flowed through him once more, a small ball of coldness remained deep inside his soul.

CHAPTER FORTY-NINE

Cole woke to discover he wasn't in a land filled with darkness and death but one of warmth and temptation. A lush body, one he would have recognized anywhere, pressed against his side.

A strawberry aroma teased his senses, and though the strangeness of his all-too-realistic dream lingered, his cock stirred. But then, he could plunge into an icy lake, and Lexi would still entice him. She always would.

"What are you doing here?" he asked as he ran his fingers down her arm to her hip. He loved seeing her in the clothes of the dark fae. The color of the tunic brought out the emerald flecks in her hunter green eyes and hugged her body in all the right ways. "I left you in bed."

"That's funny because that's where I left *you* too."

"There's a reason for that," he reminded her.

"I think it's beyond time we both moved past that reason. I helped pull you off that battlefield; I'm not the weak half human we believed me to be, and I'm sick of waking up to find you on the floor or in a chair. We can't spend the rest of our lives sleeping like this; I won't allow it."

Cole's hand stilled on her hip, and he almost chuckled over her commanding declaration. But there was nothing to laugh about, given that he nearly killed her before.

"All those things may be true, but what happens if I attack you again and you're not so lucky, or—" He gulped because the possibility of losing her terrified him, and if it happened at his hand—no, he would *not* allow it. "—I kill you?"

"I wasn't lucky last time; I punched you in the face and woke you up."

"That you did. It was a good, solid punch too."

"Damn right it was, and that was before Brokk started training me. Now, I have more skill, and I will have more strength soon."

"You still have a long way to go on both fronts before you get there."

"I know, and I'm determined to get better trained, stronger, and to learn all the things I might be capable of doing; I'm also determined to sleep beside you. I'm not sure if you were having a nightmare or not, but something was clearly bothering you when I laid down beside you this time. And guess what? You didn't hurt me. In fact, you calmed down."

"I wasn't dreaming about being back in the war this time. Things might have been different if I was."

"What were you dreaming about then?"

He recalled the darkness, the ice, the feeling of suffocating as the shadows filled him, and then the warmth and light. That light had been Lexi; he was sure of it. Somehow, she chased the shadows away, but that didn't mean she'd chase away the dreams of war.

And since she would only worry if he told her about this dream, he simply said, "It was a normal, run-of-the-mill, bad dream. So, since I wasn't dreaming about killing someone, there's no way to know how I'd react with you sleeping beside me."

"I don't care," Lexi said. "I don't want to keep doing this, Cole. We at least need to know what would happen. If you go to sleep knowing I'm beside you, and I don't try to wake you from a nightmare, things could be completely different."

He sighed and caressed her hip. The feel of her silken skin shoved away the remnants of his strange dream. As his fingers trailed up to her rib cage, he pushed the tunic with them until his hand settled on her waist.

Lexi's fingers tapped his chest. "What are you doing?"

"Nothing," he replied innocently.

"You're not getting out of this conversation that easily."

"If you think it's easy to resist rolling you over and taking you right now, then you are sadly mistaken."

The hint of a smile tugged at her lips before she composed her face into a serious mask again.

"So, what are we going to do about our sleeping arrangement?" she inquired.

He slid his fingers up higher, pushing the tunic with him until he reached the soft swell of the side of her breast. He didn't miss the way her eyes darkened or the quick inhalation of her breath.

She was determined to see this through, but she couldn't deny her growing arousal.

"I don't know; what are we going to do?" he murmured.

"Tonight, we *will* spend the whole night together. You will remain in the bed with me, and you *will* sleep."

"Bossy little thing, aren't you?" he murmured.

When his knuckles skimmed her nipple, it hardened against his hand.

"Cole," Lexi whispered, "this means a lot to me."

His hand stilled on her as she gazed up at him with pleading eyes. He didn't like it, but he couldn't deny something so important to her.

"I'll stay in bed with you all night," he said.

"And you're going to sleep."

He hesitated before replying, "If I'm going to sleep, then you're going to have to tire me out."

Lexi gasped and then laughed when he rolled, so she was on top of him. He settled her core against the rigid evidence of his lust. She bit her bottom lip as her hands settled on his chest and her auburn hair fell forward to tickle his skin.

The sensation of her hair brushing against him, and her warm body on his, was almost too much to bear. No matter how often it happened, he would never get used to how right she felt in his arms or how beautiful she was.

Releasing her hips, he grasped the tunic that had fallen back down and pulled it up to expose her taut belly. And then, he edged it higher to reveal more and more of her supple body.

When it made it to her breasts, Lexi gripped the edge of it and pulled it over her head to reveal her breasts and pert nipples. His mouth watered, and his dick jumped as his gaze settled on his bite marks on her. They weren't fading yet, but his fangs pricked with his compulsion to mark her again.

"How should I start on tiring you out?" she asked as she leisurely moved back and forth along his cock.

He grinned at her. "Never ask a dark fae what they want from you in bed."

"I'll keep that in mind if I ever find myself in the bed of another dark fae."

His amusement vanished as a low growl issued from him. The lycan part of him didn't find this teasing banter anywhere near as amusing as his dark fae side.

"Now, now," she murmured as she leaned toward him. Her breasts flattened against his chest, and her lips nearly brushed his as she spoke. "No reason to get all grumpy when I plan on making you very, *very* happy."

CHAPTER FIFTY

HER LIPS TEASED his as her hips rose and fell in a slow, undulating movement that made him groan. Just as the kiss between them was starting to deepen, she pulled her mouth away and rested it against his ear.

"Let me see your ciphers again," she whispered.

More than happy to let go of his ever-constant restraint, Cole released the magic keeping them hidden. As that magic slipped away, he felt them spreading across his skin to cover his body.

Leaning back, Lexi placed one palm on the center of his chest. She used her other hand to trace the markings on his chest, down his torso, and toward his dick. Sitting further back on him, she pulled his shaft forward and ran her fingers across the ciphers enveloping it.

The awe on her face was almost as riveting as her tender, teasing touch. He resisted his desperate need to be inside her while he watched her explore. It was torture, but it was *exquisite* torture.

"Amazing," she murmured.

He considered her the amazing one, but he didn't say that as she marveled over his body with her fingers and eyes. Releasing

236 BRENDA K DAVIES

her hips, he propped his hands behind his head to watch as she explored him.

He'd never seen anyone do this before. But then, she was the only one who'd ever seen all of him and the only one who ever would. She'd inspected him the first time she saw all his ciphers, but not with this intense an interest as she traced all of them from his face, down his collarbone, stomach, and hips.

Beneath her touch, his skin rippled as it begged for more, and she was happy to give it to him. The increased scent of strawberries on the air told him that she also took delight in exploring him.

Her hands settled on his shaft again before she bent to run her tongue along the ciphers encompassing his head. He sucked in a breath as his hips rose off the floor.

He almost grabbed her waist again as his first reaction was to bury himself inside her, but he kept himself restrained. Instead, he gave himself over to the wondrous things her mouth and tongue could do.

~

LEXI COULDN'T GET ENOUGH of the taste and feel of him. His allspice aroma mixed with the musky scent he emitted only turned her on more. She wasn't sure what was happening to her. Her skin tingled as if little electrical currents were running through her, and her body begged for more.

She was always aroused by him; being with him was one of the greatest pleasures of her life, but this was different somehow. She felt more alive and more... powerful?

She wasn't quite sure if that was the right way to describe it, and she didn't care as her entire body begged for more of him. Releasing his cock, she made her way further down as she used her hands to explore all the ciphers covering the rest of his body to his toes.

The amount of power he exuded caused the air to crackle

between them. It hadn't done this when he first revealed his ciphers to her. But he hadn't uncovered all his ciphers until after they made love before, and he'd covered them quickly again afterward.

Now, they were on full display, his barriers were down, and power pulsated out of him.

Her mouth watered as the hair on her arms rose. The power in the air intensified until it caused strands of her hair to float around her face. When Cole growled, her attention shifted to his striking face and silver eyes.

The thud of her heart was so fast and loud, she was certain he could hear it. Then his hands settled on her hips, and he lifted her. Lexi started to protest, but as he rose, he turned and set her on the bed in a move so fluid and effortless she could have been a pixie for all her size mattered to him.

When his weight came down on top of her, she reacted like a bolt of lightning hit her soul. The heat of their connection sizzled between them as she lay staring up at him while his gaze remained locked on hers.

When she reached for him, he caught her wrists and brought them down to pin them on either side of her head.

"You'll be the death of me, and I'll welcome it with open arms," he said.

Then he claimed her mouth in a kiss that not only left her breathless and aching for more but it touched her to the very center of her being. In that kiss, she felt all his love and desire for her.

With his kiss, he made it clear he would never let her go.

And she welcomed his claim and possession of her because he was hers too, and nothing would ever change that. She hoped she was conveying that to him as her fingers threaded into his hair to pull him closer.

His hands slid down her body, tracing her curves before one of them slid between her legs. She arched into his touch as he fucked her with his fingers until she was panting and on the verge of begging for more, but she couldn't break their kiss.

When he finally entered her, every one of her nerve endings begged for release. But he wasn't going to give it to her as they touched and explored each other.

She felt the tug of his power when he started feeding on her. Felt him drawing strength from the energy they created as they remained entwined. She sought to give him more and offered it to him as she locked her legs around his waist and urged him faster.

When she came, it was with her fingers entwined in his hair and their mouths still joined as she cried out. With one final thrust, he buried himself deep inside her.

His body shuddered against hers, and his cock pulsed deep inside her. She felt every single pulsation as his seed filled her.

Her heart swelled, and she cleaved to him as their kiss eased before finally ending. She ran her hands over the carved muscles of his back as she sought to catch her breath and return to reality. It was difficult to do when her body was still hungry for more.

When he buried his face in the hollow of her shoulder, she felt the scrape of his fangs a second before he bit deep, renewing his claim on his mate. And when he started moving inside her again, she eagerly welcomed it.

When he released his bite, she turned her mouth into his neck and rested her lips against his vein. Closing her eyes, she bit deep, and his blood filled her mouth. It had been too long, and she hadn't realized how much she'd needed to feed until it started to sate her hunger.

She'd always thought it was the vampire half of her that thirsted for blood, but it never was. Instead, it was the arach who craved blood and sighed with pleasure.

CHAPTER FIFTY-ONE

"I'LL GET US SOME FOOD," Cole said sometime later when they finally parted. "Why don't you run a hot bath for yourself while I'm gone."

Lexi could only nod in agreement. She was far too sated after the events of earlier to speak right now. A bath sounded good, but she also wouldn't mind going back to sleep.

Unfortunately, she couldn't do that. They had far too much to do for that to be an option.

Sunlight streamed around the edges of the drawn curtains as dawn gave way to early morning. Outside, the jingle of horse harnesses and bridles filled the air as travelers left the inn in a cart. The wheels of the cart rattled over the dirt road.

Along the hall, a door opened and closed. The thudding footsteps of guests heading toward the stairs followed it.

As quiet descended, so did all the responsibilities she and Cole had to handle. They had to return to the human realm and the manor soon to learn how everything was going with Sahira and the others. Had her aunt already cast the spell?

She was both eager to see how it would go and dreaded it. If the spell worked, then Cole would have to face the Lord again soon. She suppressed a shiver.

Cole kissed her forehead before sliding out from under her. Since she wasn't going to find the sleep she so desperately craved anytime soon, Lexi pushed herself up on the bed.

She stifled a yawn as he gathered his clothes from where he'd left them on the wooden rocking chair in the corner. As he walked, the ciphers he'd revealed to her vanished until all that remained were the ones he allowed the world to see.

She missed seeing them but understood why he hid them. He was already a big enough target without all their countless enemies realizing how much power he truly contained. Many would find taking him down to be an enticing challenge.

The thick muscles in his thighs flexed as he pulled on his brown pants. He tugged on his socks before shoving his feet into his boots.

When he pulled the tunic over his head, she sighed in disappointment and hugged her legs to her chest. The smile tugging at the corner of his lips revealed he'd heard her as he slipped his father's sword onto his back.

He walked over to the bed, planted his hands on the mattress, and leaned down to kiss her. "I have to talk to the men, but I'll be back with some food soon."

"I'll be here."

When he opened the door, voices and the clattering of dishes and pans drifted into the room. The closing of the door drowned out most of the noise, but some still seeped through the thick wood.

The key clicked as it turned in the lock, but another one sat on top of the dresser. Her gaze traveled over the empty dark, wood walls. Besides the bed and the chair, a dresser was the only other piece of furniture in the room.

Despite its barren appearance, the comfort of the mattress, the fluffy pillows, the baby blue curtains surrounding the windows, and the periwinkle blue comforter made the room cozy. Tossing aside the blanket, she revealed the white sheets beneath. They were the softest she'd ever slept on.

They may not be much for decorating in Underhill, but they were all about comfort, as emphasized by the bathroom she padded into. She'd used it briefly last night, but her eyes hadn't been open enough to notice the gold faucets in the sink and shower, the gleaming white surfaces, and the large tub that might be big enough for her *and* Cole.

She turned on the water in the tub and added some of the deliciously scented bubble bath. Bubbles rose to fill the surface as she returned to the sink. She studied her reflection in the mirror, searching for any sign the potion was wearing off and she was changing.

She looked the same as yesterday, except the shadows under her eyes were a little darker. Her fangs were the same, as was her eye color and everything else about her.

Still, she leaned closer and turned her head back and forth as she searched for something... *anything* that may prove what her dad and Sahira said was true.

If she was different, then she couldn't tell. She wasn't sure if this relieved or disappointed her.

She lifted one of the two toothbrushes from the sink, opened the silver wrapping around it, and put on a small dab of toothpaste from the bottle beside it. The toothbrush was made of smooth wood, and she wasn't sure what the bristles were, but it felt fantastic to scrub her teeth.

When she finished, she turned off the water in the tub and climbed into it. The warm water helped ease some of the lingering soreness from her muscles, and she was sure that whatever was in the bubble bath helped too. She used a small, yellow, unbelievably soft cloth to clean her skin before washing her hair and shaving.

The water was starting to cool by the time she climbed out, enveloped herself in a plush towel, and left the bathroom. Her feet were noiseless against the wooden floor as she strode over to the window. She pulled aside a corner of a curtain to peer at the yard below.

Saddled horses were tied to the posts in front of the inn. They munched on the lush grass beneath their feet while wild horses grazed on the land in the meadow beyond. She was glad to see they'd returned after hiding from the dragon.

She heard voices outside but didn't see anyone. Lexi was about to let the curtain fall back into place but froze when she saw her fingertips.

In the rays of the sun spilling across them, little currents of what looked like golden electricity danced across her fingers. The breath she didn't realize she was holding started to burn in her lungs, and she released it on a loud "puh."

That golden light illuminated the curtain, and she managed to react enough to release it before she set it on fire. Lifting her hand before her, she studied it as the rays fell over her hand and down her forearm.

The golden light continued to emanate from her fingers, but she realized it wasn't like electricity; instead, it was an actual light radiating *out* of her. When she touched the tips of her fingers to her other arm, she didn't get a zap as she would from electricity.

It didn't hurt at all.

But the movement drew her attention to her forearms and the silver markings on them. Her mouth went so dry her tongue stuck to the roof of it.

The marks ran from her fingertips almost to her elbows, and they emerged everywhere the sun touched her skin. As she examined them more closely, she realized they looked like...

Dragon scales!

The knowledge hit her so hard that she felt like someone had hammered a fist into her gut. She labored to breathe as she twisted her arm before her.

The light on her fingers grew brighter. She glanced down at her other arm, the one still hidden in the shadows, to discover it remained normal.

Taking a deep breath, she tried to steady the tremor in her fingers as she lifted her other arm toward the light. The second the sun touched her skin, that light flared to life at the ends of her fingers, and the scale-like pattern emerged on her flesh.

Breath coming faster, Lexi was nearly panting as she twisted her arms before her in awe. She may not have seen any changes in the bathroom mirror, but she couldn't deny them now.

And she couldn't deny what she was.

It wasn't until then she realized that she hadn't quite believed her dad or Sahira. Or not so much as she didn't believe them; it was more like she was sure they had to be *wrong* somehow. But they weren't wrong, and she couldn't live in denial.

She was *not* what she'd always believed herself to be.

And her already complicated life was about to get a whole lot more so.

CHAPTER FIFTY-TWO

COLE SHIFTED his hold on the tray to slip the key into the lock and turn it. He opened the door and froze when he spotted Lexi with her hands raised in front of her.

The golden glow emanating from her hands highlighted the dark spill of wet hair tumbling down her back, as well as the sun-kissed hue of her skin.

It also revealed the markings on her arms and the golden aura radiating from her fingertips. He'd never seen anything so beautiful, but even as he stood there, admiring the power she emanated, terror crept into his bones.

The potion was wearing off, her arach powers were starting to reveal themselves, and no one was entirely sure what that would bring. He was certain what was happening to her would put the biggest target on her back.

Fuck!

He'd known this was coming after what Del revealed—well, not this exactly, as he never could have imagined the glow or what looked like scales on her arms—but he'd expected more time.

Although, he hadn't expected to chase a dragon through the Gloaming or for her abilities to break through so soon. Now that they were, Lexi would have to go into hiding until she could get her powers under control.

And then, he realized she was standing in front of the window and the door was still open. With a muttered curse, he stepped into the room and kicked the door shut behind him.

Lexi's head turned toward him as he set the food tray down on the dresser and crossed to her. His step faltered when he saw her eyes. Those beautiful, magnificent, and, he had to admit, a little eerie, eyes gazed up at him in awe.

For a second, he forgot that anyone could look up and see her as his eyes searched hers. Gone was the lovely green he'd come to know and love so well.

In its place was a shade of gold so deep it rivaled any metal pulled from this or any other land. And in the center of all that gold was a slitted pupil...

Just like those of the dragons.

That pupil told him more about the arach powers than anything he'd ever heard before. Turning away from her, he pulled the curtain from her hand and tugged it snuggly into place.

"Get away from the window," he commanded.

Lexi kept her hands up as she backed away from the window. He pulled the curtain back a little bit to peer outside. Thankfully, he didn't see anyone out there. That didn't mean someone hadn't seen her.

Gritting his teeth, he turned toward her. He wanted to yell at her, *"What were you thinking? What were you doing?"* But the words clogged in his throat.

Those questions would only be his panic talking, and that was not what she needed. She needed to be protected and given time to grow into what she would become; yelling at her wouldn't help with that.

The lycan part of him didn't agree, but thankfully, the more logical, dark fae part of him was in charge right now.

She'd been standing there, absorbing the sun's rays, with the curtain *open*, because she was fascinated by what was happening to her. She wasn't doing it to put herself in danger purposely; she'd just never seen anything like it before.

Neither had he, and he couldn't deny he'd wanted to do the same thing as her.

But if anyone saw her, the Lord would unleash hell on them. They weren't prepared for a battle against him yet. They had to learn what she could do first and if she could bring the dragons to their side.

And no matter what, she had to be ready because he would *not* lose her.

"No one was down there," she whispered. "That's why I was at the window. I was looking to see what was going on, but... I... I... got distracted."

"Someone could have walked by and seen you."

"No. I wasn't there for long, and if someone had seen me, *this* would have made them stop. They would have still been there when you got to the window."

He couldn't argue that point because it was true.

"My arms," she whispered as her attention shifted to her arms.

Without the sun on them, the glow was starting to fade from her fingers and the scales were vanishing.

"Your eyes," Cole said.

Her fingers flew up to her eyes. "What about them?"

Before the gold could fade from her eyes, he clasped her elbow and hurried her into the bathroom. When he flipped on the light switch, she followed him into the room.

He clasped her shoulders and turned her toward the glass. She gasped, but as she leaned closer to peer more intently at them, they shifted back to their normal, vibrant green color.

"What's happening to me?" she whispered as she inspected her fangs, but they remained unchanged.

"Your powers are waking up. Until you learn how to control

them, and can keep these changes hidden, we're going to have to keep you somewhere safe."

She leaned away from the mirror and lowered her hands to her sides. "What if I can't keep them hidden? What if, from now on, this is what happens to me every time I'm in sunlight... or moonlight? What if any kind of natural light turns me into this glowing... glowing *thing*?"

"I don't know much about the arach, but I'm sure *all* immortals would have heard and passed it down through the years if *every* time an arach stepped outside, they started to glow and resembled a dragon. I think that with time, like with my ciphers, you'll be able to control this and keep it hidden."

"And if I can't learn to control it? There are no other arach around to teach me how to navigate these abilities or even *what* my abilities are. I can't spend the rest of my life locked away. And what exactly can I do? Glow like I'm some sort of... sort of... glowworm. That's not helpful."

"This is only the beginning, Lexi, and maybe it is the end of your abilities, but I doubt it. The arach *definitely* had a connection to the dragons; whether that will translate into something more than resembling the creatures when in sunlight, I don't know. There is also the fire thing; I bet this time, you won't burn if you stick your hand in a fire, and they were also supposed to be able to throw fire from their hands.

"It's been centuries since the arach walked the realms, and they were too secretive of their powers for anyone to know everything they could do. But at one time, they could control the dragons, and there's no reason to think you can't."

Taking a deep breath, she lowered her fingers from where they rested beneath her eyes. "What do we do now?"

"Now we have to get you out of here. We can't have you out in the Gloaming if you can light up like a glowworm," he teased as he poked the end of her nose.

His teasing didn't lighten his mood, but it did cause her mouth to quirk in a little smile before it slid away.

"It's time to return to the others," he said.

"But you still have so much to handle here."

"And I will. For now, I'll tell Niall that I'll meet him at the palace later. While I'm gone, stay away from the window."

"I will," she muttered.

But as she spoke, a wistful look crossed her face, and she glanced back at the curtains.

CHAPTER FIFTY-THREE

"IT'S DONE," Sahira whispered. "The spell… it's… it is complete."

Sahira leaned back and, with her forearm, wiped the sweat from her forehead. When she went to rise, her knees wobbled before giving out. Brokk lunged forward and caught her before she hit the ground. He helped ease her down again.

"Are you okay?" Del demanded as he knelt on her other side.

"I'm fine," Sahira muttered.

But she didn't look fine. Her skin was paler than normal, and her amber eyes were dull. They didn't seem to be focusing as she tipped her head back to blink at Brokk.

"I think you should sit here for a little bit," he said.

"Ye-yes. I think you might be right."

Her head dropped, and her chin rested against her chest. Brokk shifted his attention to the pentacle in the center of the tunnel.

Beside both of his brothers lay an identical clone. They both looked so perfectly like his brothers that Brokk couldn't tell them apart until Orin and Varo sat up and the clones didn't move.

Orin's lip curled in distaste as he studied his doppelgänger. With the tip of his index finger, he poked at the clone. Brokk almost told him to stop, but he was morbidly fascinated by the clone's chin pushing in before resuming its previous state.

It almost looked like a wax doll, but it reacted like a dead immortal's flesh would. It was too creepy, and it *had* to work.

"So weird," Orin muttered.

"Very impressive," Varo said as he poked his clone's cheek. Then he turned toward Sahira. "Are you okay?"

"Yes," Sahira said. "It just took more out of me than I was expecting."

"Well, that's because you did a fantastic job," Orin said.

"Did something *nice* just come out of your mouth?" Sahira asked.

"I'm not a complete dick," Orin retorted. "I appreciate it when others help me."

It's always about you, Brokk thought but kept the words to himself. There was no point in bickering with his brother when Sahira had pulled *this* off.

"That's good to know," Sahira muttered as she rubbed at her temples.

"Thank you," Varo said. "Even if this doesn't work, you did all you could to help us survive. It's very appreciated."

"Thank you," Sahira said.

"Now what do we do?" Del asked.

"We wait for Cole and Lexi to return," Brokk said. "And then I'll help him take the clones to the Lord."

"I have to put the harrow stone somewhere safe until we can return it," Sahira said.

When she tried to rise again, Brokk clasped her elbow. She swayed a little, but this time, she was far steadier on her feet.

"Thank you," she murmured as she pulled her arm free of his grasp. "Some fresh air will do me good. I'm tired of these tunnels."

"You must be starving," Del said.

The spell had taken hours to complete, far longer than he'd anticipated. And he didn't think Sahira was expecting the grind it became either. He didn't know if it was her half-witch status, the fact it was for two immortals, or if Sahira had underestimated the spell's difficulty, but he wasn't sure what time of day or even *what* day it was anymore.

"I am," Sahira said. When she swayed again, Del steadied her. "I have to gather my things."

"We'll bring them up for you," Varo offered.

"No!" Sahira shouted when he bent to pick up the harrow stone. "Don't touch it!"

"It will kill you," Brokk said.

Varo snatched his hand back and eyed the stone like it was an alien monstrosity about to eat him. Taking a deep breath, Sahira threw back her shoulders and stepped over Orin's clone to retrieve the stone.

"Everything else is safe to pick up," she told Varo as she lifted the harrow stone and slipped it into her pocket. "But not this."

"What do we do with our duplicates?" Orin asked.

"Leave them here for now. We'll keep the gates closed, so no one accidentally stumbles across them," Del said.

Brokk helped to gather the remainder of Sahira's supplies and, with the others, made his way out of the cordoned off section of the tunnel. Del closed the gate behind them.

No one spoke as they trudged behind Sahira and Del toward the exit in the fireplace. They emerged into the library, and though the curtains remained closed over the large windows, Brokk was surprised to see sunlight filtering around their edges.

Had they really been down there all night?

He yawned as he ran a hand through his hair. The dirt and sweat from being underground and away from a shower for far longer than he would have liked caused it to stand on end. He gave a halfhearted attempt to flatten it before giving up.

Orin strolled over and sat on one of the oversized, brown chairs. He turned sideways to drape his legs over the arm and yawned.

Brokk resisted the urge to kick his foot as it swung in the air. All he'd done was lie there all night, and Brokk was sure he'd fallen asleep a time or two.

Granted, *he* hadn't done anything more than watch the whole time either, but the tension of it all was exhausting. He couldn't imagine how Sahira felt. But he didn't have to, as her shoulders hunched forward while she shuffled toward the doorway.

Orin frowned at her and lowered his leg to sit up. "Are you okay?"

Brokk's eyebrows rose at this; it was rare to see Orin voicing concern over anyone. Sahira may have helped give him a chance at a longer life, but he still wasn't one for concern.

"Yeah," she muttered. "I have to get this stone somewhere safe. Then a drink and some food, and I'll be fine."

Before any of them could respond, she shuffled out the door.

"Where are we?" Varo asked as he gazed around the room with open curiosity.

Del settled onto the other chair and leaned forward to rest his elbows on his knees. "My home."

Varo clasped his hands behind his back as he studied the shelves. "It's a beautiful home."

"Thank you," Del murmured.

Varo tilted his head to the side and looked about to say something more, but before he could speak, a portal opened in the middle of the room. Orin rose, and Del stiffened, but since most immortals, if not all of them, had protective spells around their homes to keep unwanted visitors out, Brokk didn't think anyone coming through that portal was a threat.

Just in case, his hand fell to the dagger at his side. He released its hilt when Cole emerged with Lexi tucked securely against his side.

At least, he assumed it was Lexi, as a thick cloak hid her face and body, but it was her build. Besides, Cole wouldn't hold anyone else in such a protective way.

Cole's eyes immediately went to the windows as they emerged, and some of his tension eased. "Keep those curtains closed," he commanded.

"Oh shucks, Varo and I were about to throw them open and have a party in front of them," Orin retorted.

"Don't," Cole snarled.

Brokk never saw Cole move; he wasn't sure he *did* move before a thwack sounded, and Orin stumbled back. He managed to catch his balance before crashing into one of the bookshelves.

His hand flew to his nose as Cole's settled at his side. Brokk blinked and blinked again, but he still wasn't sure what had happened.

He didn't think Cole had punched Orin but had he backhanded him across the face somehow? How had Cole moved liked that? Brokk should have seen him, but there hadn't even been a *blur*.

Rubbing his nose, Orin looked as stunned as he stared at Cole. When his hand fell away, it revealed the red and swollen tip of it.

What. The. Fuck? Brokk wondered, but he had no answer for what just transpired.

Cole looked unphased by the interaction as he hugged Lexi closer. Brokk didn't know what to say, and Orin remained silent as he eyed Cole not with anger but with the same uncertainty as Brokk.

Varo's gaze was riveted on Cole as he edged away from the bookcases. On his face was an expression of hope and dread that reminded Brokk of a dog in a pound.

Before anyone could say anything, Varo spoke. "Cole."

CHAPTER FIFTY-FOUR

COLE HAD BEEN ABOUT to pull Lexi's hood back when Varo spoke. Twisting his head, he spotted his younger brother standing near the doorway to the library.

Seeing his youngest brother again was like a punch to the gut. For a second, Cole's hands hovered in the air near Lexi's hood before falling back to his side.

Orin had said that Varo survived the war, but until now, a part of Cole had feared it was another one of Orin's games. He hadn't dared let himself hope Varo had survived.

They'd never been the closest. With him being the oldest and Varo the youngest, nearly two hundred years separated them, but Cole had looked out for him. Being half light fae was not easy for Varo in the dark fae realm.

There was one time, when Varo was fifteen, Cole came across a group of dark fae kids beating him up after school. Cole broke it apart, kicked more than a few of them in the ass, and scared the shit out of them. They all ran screaming for the hills.

As he dusted Varo off and wiped away the blood under his nose, he assured his brother it wouldn't happen again.

"Of course it will," Varo replied. "I'm a target in this realm. I always have been and always will be."

"What do you mean *have been*?" Cole asked.

When Varo didn't respond, Cole pressed. "This isn't the first time this has happened, is it?"

"No, and it won't be the last. The light fae are the opposites of the dark fae, and no one in this realm likes them."

"Father obviously liked at least one of them," Cole had pointed out. "And there are others here who like them too. *I* liked your mother."

"It wasn't enough to keep her here."

"No," Cole agreed. But then, he had no idea why the woman left, only that she was here one day and gone the next.

"And most of the dark fae don't like the light fae. They consider them weak."

Cole did too, but he didn't say that. "Why didn't you tell Father or *me* about this?"

Varo had shrugged as he dug the toe of his boot into the sandy ground. "This is my battle to fight."

"Five on one aren't battles you fight."

Varo shrugged again. Cole grasped his bony shoulder and led him away. After that, he followed Varo to and from his school, staying in the shadows and ensuring his little brother was never a target again.

That instance had created a soft spot in Cole's heart for his youngest brother. He never saw anyone try to beat Varo up again, but though he watched him during those times, there were many times when he wasn't there. And Varo never would have told him if someone went after him again.

He'd always been too kind, too gentle, and too fucking good for the rest of them, but he'd also been prideful. Out of all his brothers, Varo was the last one Cole expected to survive the war.

Yet here he was. Thinner and with shadows under his haunted eyes, but still standing and *alive*. Cole hadn't expected him to choose any side in the war, let alone go against their father, but he had.

He'd never understood it, but he didn't harbor the same resentment toward Varo as he did toward his other brothers who chose the other side. Whatever Varo's reasons, he knew none of them involved pride, glory, or anger.

Varo did what he did because he believed it was *right*. Not to prove something or to make his mark on the world.

"Varo," he whispered.

The familiarity and warmth of the grin on Varo's face tugged at his heart. Out of them all, Varo was the one who could brighten a room with his smile and presence. Cole hadn't realized how much he missed that smile until he saw it again.

When Varo stepped toward him, Cole broke away from Lexi and strode toward his brother. He opened his arms, and Varo walked into them.

Bones that weren't prominent the last time they embraced poked Cole's palms. In response, Cole hugged him tighter as Varo's fingers dug into his back.

Realizing his brother was crying, Cole bent his head and rested his cheek against Varo's. "I'm happy to see you too, brother," he whispered.

Varo's shoulders shook, and his words came out in a tremulous whisper. "I've missed you."

"And I you."

~

TEARS BURNED Lexi's throat as the brothers embraced. When one of them fell down her cheek, she glanced at her father. Earlier, she was so shocked by his revelation and angry about him and Sahira keeping everything from her that she hadn't taken the time to appreciate what she'd been given...

A miracle.

He must have seen something on her face as he rose and crossed the room to embrace her. Lexi melted into him when the arms that held her so often as a child enveloped her again.

The familiar scent of mint and the outdoors filled her nostrils. It was the scent of her youth, the aromas of comfort and love.

Lexi closed her eyes against the rest of her tears as she listened to the heartbeat she'd believed forever deadened. She opened her eyes as Cole and Varo pulled apart. They clasped each other's arms while they studied one another.

"I heard about father," Varo said. "That must have been horrible for you to witness."

Cole winced. "At least it was fast."

Varo's already prominent cheekbones stood out more as a desperate gleam filled his eyes. "We have to get the Lord off that throne."

"We will," Cole promised as he released Varo and turned to face the rest of them. "How did things go here?"

"The spell has been cast," Brokk said. "The clones are in the tunnel waiting for us to take them to the Lord."

"Where's Sahira?" Lexi asked.

"She was going to put the harrow stone somewhere safe before getting something to eat and drink. Last night took a lot out of her," her dad said.

A twinge of guilt and sorrow tugged at Lexi's heart. She wasn't entirely thrilled with everything she'd learned, but she didn't want Sahira drained or weakened.

"What happened with the dragon in the Gloaming?" Brokk asked. "How much damage did it cause?"

As Cole crossed to Lexi, her father released her but remained standing at her side. Cole rested his hand on her hip as he stood on the other side of her.

"None near the palace, but the fires and the craz had already done more than enough damage. There wasn't much for it to destroy or eat. It did eat some horses in Underhill," Cole answered.

"It made it to Underhill?" Orin asked.

"Yes," Cole said. "In case you forgot, dragons can fly."

Orin gave Cole the finger. His anger wasn't all that menacing, considering the end of his nose resembled Rudolph's. She still had no idea how Cole hit him or whatever he did, but he had.

Sahira appeared in the doorway. In one hand, she held a steaming mug of tea; in the other was a plate of cheese. She stopped when she saw Lexi and Cole. A large smile lit her face before her gaze settled on Lexi, and it faltered.

Lexi smiled and gave a tentative wave that caused her aunt to beam. Maybe she'd discovered her father and aunt weren't her blood relatives, but they were her family, and they always would be.

It would still take some time to get over being lied to and suppressed her entire life, but they'd done it out of love and to protect her. After what happened at the inn in Underhill, she understood why.

CHAPTER FIFTY-FIVE

"Is the dragon still in the Gloaming?" her dad asked.

"No, it stayed on a mountain for a little bit before disappearing through a portal it created. I left some men behind in case it, or one of its brethren, returns to Underhill now that they've discovered a food supply there," Cole said. "Niall is going to help them herd the wild horses somewhere safe before he takes Torigon and meets me back at the palace. If the dragons do return, there won't be a food supply readily available to them next time."

"What else happened while you were there?" Brokk focused on Lexi. "Why are you so covered up?"

With everything that happened after their return, Lexi had forgotten she was still wearing the thick cloak and hood over her hair. She went to pull it off before hesitating.

Her skin and everything else had gone back to normal once she was out of the sun, but she was still hesitant to remove the hood. What if she started glowing again?

Cole looked to Varo. "Have they filled you in on everything that's happened?"

"Brokk filled me in on all of it." Then his eyes flicked to Brokk, and his brow furrowed. "At least I think he has."

"He doesn't know everything," Brokk said. "You said he could know, but there was one thing I kept from him."

And Lexi knew what that one thing was... *her*. Or at least her true heritage.

"It's up to the two of you to reveal it or not," Brokk continued. "Though, I'm sure Orin will tell him eventually."

"No, I wouldn't," Orin said, and Varo looked a little hurt. "Sorry," Orin apologized. "But this is one secret that's not mine to tell."

"Fair enough," Varo murmured.

Cole looked questioningly down at her. "Can I tell him?"

"Do you trust him?" she asked.

"To keep this secret and protect you, absolutely."

Lexi bit her lip as she studied Varo. She trusted Cole completely, but she already felt too exposed and uncertain in this strange new world she was trying to navigate.

"You do *not* have to do anything you don't want to do," Cole reminded her.

"I know I'm a stranger to you, and all you know about me is that I stood against my father and Cole in the war, but I'm not a cruel man, and I do not break my vows. I promise that whatever you reveal here will go to my grave with me," Varo said.

Lexi studied Varo. Despite his haggard appearance, she saw the resemblance to his brothers. She also saw the depth of caring and honesty that shimmered in his striking eyes.

He went against his father and some of his brothers in the war, but his love for his siblings, especially Cole, was evident. So was his obvious desire to do right by his brothers.

"I believe you," she said.

When she went to pull back the hood, Cole clasped it and helped pull it back. Her body felt as if someone was jolting it with electricity and she resisted the impulse to run from the room.

Instead, she stood her ground as she undid the tie around her neck and took off the cloak. Her dad took it from her and draped it over his chair. She glanced down at her hands, but they remained normal.

Del rested one of his hands over hers and held it until she looked at him. "What happened?"

"Her arach powers are starting to show themselves," Cole said.

Varo sucked in a breath. "*Arach?*"

"Yes."

"But how?" Varo whispered.

"We'll fill you in on everything later."

"How are they showing themselves?" Sahira asked as she sank into one of the chairs. She set her untouched plate of cheese on the ground but sipped her tea.

"I haven't displayed any powers, just an ability to glow and... and... to look like a dragon," Lexi said.

When no one spoke, she listened to the grandfather clock in the other room as it ticked away the seconds.

"You looked like a dragon?" her dad finally asked.

"Yes. I mean, I didn't turn into one or anything like that. I just... changed."

"You look fine to me," Orin said.

"She was in the sunlight when it happened," Cole said.

"Did anyone else see this?" her dad asked with a sharp edge to his voice.

"No," Lexi said.

"*How* did you look like a dragon?" Orin asked.

Lexi glanced at Cole, who was studying the windows. "Do you want to show them?" he asked her.

"Might as well because I'm not sure how to explain it," she replied.

"Someone go and make sure no one is outside," Cole commanded.

Brokk walked over to the window and pulled the curtain back to peer outside before settling it back across the glass. "I'll be back," he said.

Before anyone could reply, he left the room. A couple of seconds later, the front door opened and closed. While he was gone, Cole filled Varo in on some of the details of her history. By the time Brokk returned, Varo knew most of it.

"There's no one out there," Brokk said.

Cole stayed by Lexi's side as she walked over to stand next to the window.

"Stay mostly out of the sun," Cole said. "They'll see enough to understand without you having to expose yourself too much. We can't take the chance of someone arriving and seeing something they shouldn't. We'll do this fast."

Lexi waited while he pulled back a small section of the curtain. When the sun's rays filtered into the room, they illuminated the dust particles dancing in the air.

For far too many heartbeats, she could only stand there and watch those particles as she worked up the courage to do this again. She wasn't frightened about seeing the glow again, but once she did, she would have to part from the sun once more.

She'd always relished being outside; it was where she was happiest. As a child, she spent hours playing under the willow tree in the yard, floating in a canoe on the lake, fishing, sitting on the shore reading a book, or riding horses.

As an adult, she didn't have as much time for all those lazy moments, but she still snuck away to enjoy them when she could.

But now, that light stirred a bone-deep excitement inside her; she almost lunged toward the rays spilling across the floor. Somehow, she managed to keep herself restrained, but she gulped before stretching her fingers toward the sun.

And then, they came into contact with the light.

CHAPTER FIFTY-SIX

LIKE A SPONGE ABSORBING WATER, she felt those rays penetrate her skin and creep into her muscles before slipping into her veins. As they coiled deeper into her, a rush of power filled her.

She had no idea what to do with that power or what she was capable of doing with it, but she *relished* it. The radiant glow started emanating from her fingers again as the silver scale-like marks broke out across the back of her hand.

That was all she exposed to the sun, but it was enough, as the others inhaled sharply. When she lifted her head to look at them, Sahira gasped, and her father's eyes widened.

"Holy shit," Orin breathed.

Lexi pulled her hand away from the rays, and Cole let the curtain fall back into place. The minute her connection with the sun broke, a sense of loss descended over her.

However, she still felt that light pulsing through her body. With every beat of her heart, it awakened something she'd never known was there. Something she didn't know how to control, but something that felt as right as it did unnerving.

"Your eyes," her dad said.

Cole stepped closer; his chest brushed her shoulder, and his hand settled on the small of her back. He surveyed the others with a look that clearly warned them to tread lightly.

She trusted everyone in this room with what she'd revealed. Orin was an asshole of the highest order, but he would keep her alive. And not just to bring down the Lord, but also because of Cole. The two of them were like oil and water, but if something happened to her, it would destroy Cole, and Orin wouldn't allow that.

She didn't know Varo, but if Cole believed in him, then so did she.

"Were my mother's eyes like this when you met her?" she asked her dad.

"No," he said. "She had beautiful brown eyes and hair the same shade as yours."

"Oh," Lexi whispered as sorrow for the woman she'd never met stabbed her heart. Her hand instinctively went to her hair.

"You look *so* much like her," her dad whispered.

Lexi blinked away the tears pricking her eyes. Now was not the time to let her emotions get the better of her. She still had so much to learn, and her father was the one who knew the most.

"Maybe she didn't look like this because you found her at night," Lexi suggested.

"I found her during the day. She was fully exposed to the sun when I carried her out from under the willow."

"So that means I should be able to control it eventually. I mean, if this is happening to me, it had to have happened to all the arach, right?"

She couldn't keep the hope or desperation from her voice. She couldn't imagine anything worse than being locked away from the sun for days, weeks, or *months* it took her to control herself better.

Okay, death was worse, but if she had to spend the next fifty years locked in the tunnels, she far preferred death.

"I would guess so," her dad said and looked to Sahira.

"I would assume so too, but I don't know for sure," Sahira

said. "If your mother wasn't glowing like this in the sun, and those other changes weren't visible, then there is no reason to believe you won't gain better control of it over time."

"What if only an arach could show me how to do that?" Lexi asked.

"We'll have to hope that's not true. We *can* figure this out, and we will, Lexi. You'll walk freely during the day again, I promise."

"We're not sure about moonlight either yet," Cole said.

Lexi's spirits deflated further. If she couldn't have the day, she needed the night, but what if she couldn't have it?

Then, she would have to get through it. She wouldn't let her morose thoughts bring her down. She *would* learn to control this. She *would* figure it out, because there was no other alternative.

"I still don't know what powers I have," Lexi said.

"You'll learn with time," Cole said.

"And that time is coming soon," Orin said.

"Too soon," Cole agreed. "It's time to take the clones to the Lord. The sooner he stops breathing down my neck about Orin and Varo, the sooner we can work on Lexi learning to control her abilities."

∼

LEXI WAS TRYING NOT to be creeped out by the bodies lying on the floor, but she was failing. She kept looking from Varo, to his duplicate and back again before shifting her attention to Orin and his clone.

She couldn't find any differences between any of them. If the idea of it didn't freak her out so much, she'd kneel beside them and pull up in their eyelids to see what color their eyes were.

Lexi half expected they would be the opaque color of a dead man's eyes, or worse, their freaking eyes might *move*. She'd run screaming from here and never look back if that happened.

She rubbed her hands up and down her arms as she tried to

ease the goose bumps breaking out on them. It did nothing to help her bone-deep chill as she waited for one of the bodies to sit up and come after them.

They're not zombies. She'd never had the misfortune of encountering a zombie before, but these were not those immortals who feasted on the brains of others. This was just a *really* good spell.

"They're so real, Sahira," she whispered. "It's amazing."

"I couldn't have done it without the stone," her aunt replied.

"And we couldn't have done it without you," Cole said. "But I can't take them into Dragonia and to the Lord with them looking this perfect."

"What do you mean?" Lexi asked, though she suspected she already knew what he meant. They weren't *actual* bodies, but they looked so real that the idea of doing anything to them made her stomach churn.

"He means he's going to do what he's always wanted to me," Orin replied.

"You know me so well, little brother," Cole replied sardonically.

He pulled his father's sword from its sheath still hanging on his back. Lexi cringed and edged away as he approached the bodies. This was a necessary evil, but it was so twisted.

The blade spun and reflected the beams of the flashlights as Cole twirled the hilt of the sword. He studied both bodies before gripping the handle in both hands and bringing the blade down across clone Orin's neck.

CHAPTER FIFTY-SEVEN

LEXI KEPT her mouth clamped against her rising nausea as the head made a strange thumping sound while it rolled across the floor toward Orin. Raising his foot, Orin stepped on the head to stop it and that awful noise.

"Did that make you feel better?" Orin asked.

"I won't feel better until the Lord believes you're both dead."

Orin's small smirk vanished at Cole's words. Cole turned to Varo's duplicate and plunged the sword into its chest, right where its heart should be. He pulled the weapon free and rested the tip on the ground as he examined both bodies.

"We're going to need some of your blood to mark the wounds and make them look real." Cole held the sword out to Orin. "I don't care where you cut yourself; just do it and do it quickly. We'll also probably require a fair amount of it, so make sure it's deep."

Orin took the sword from him and lifted it to examine the blade. "This is father's sword."

"Yes."

Orin rested the blade's tip on the ground as his eyes narrowed on Cole. "You carried this into the battle against the rebels, didn't you?"

"Yes."

Orin gaped at Cole. "*What* were you thinking? Why wouldn't you carry fae metal into a battle against them?"

"Because, even if it's my own people turning against me, I will not go against the unspoken rules of the dark fae. Those who remain loyal to me now know their loyalty is well-placed."

A muscle twitched in Orin's cheek. "One day, your foolish pride and a misplaced sense of always doing the right thing will get you killed."

"Well, if this goes wrong with the Lord, then today is that day."

Orin flinched at the reminder before setting his jaw. He lifted his arm and ran the blade from his forearm to his palm. Blood swelled forth and spilled on the ground. With every drop, Lexi knew it was Orin's way of showing his love for Cole.

"No, it won't," Orin said.

Lexi hoped he was right. If this failed....

No, she wouldn't think about that. She was shoving a lot into the darker recesses of her mind, but if she dwelled too much on all of it, she *would* go insane.

When he finished, Orin bent to lift the head. He smeared his blood across the neck and the ligaments hanging there before turning his attention to the body.

The worst part was the ligaments hanging from the head and the white piece of spine showing on the body. Fake or not, it was unnerving.

"How can they be so real?" she whispered.

"Magic," Sahira said. "The only thing they don't have is a pulse."

"Please tell me they don't have a brain," Lexi said.

For some reason, that would make it worse.

"It doesn't function," Sahira said. "But if they were cut open, they would have organs."

"Bloodless organs?" her dad asked.

"I'm not sure," Sahira replied. "They don't bleed, but that's probably because they don't have a pulse. Orin and Varo's blood helped weave them into existence, so I'm sure their blood is inside the doppelgangers too."

"Shit," Brokk muttered, and he looked almost as disgusted as Lexi felt.

Varo took the blade from Orin. He admired it for a second before closing his eyes. A wave of grief passed over his face before he composed himself, opened his eyes and slid it across his palm.

Varo bent to smear blood over the chest of his clone before brushing some across its cheeks. Orin splashed some blood across the face of the head on the ground.

"Let's get your clothes on them," Cole said. "So they'll have your smell too."

Lexi averted her gaze as Varo and Orin stripped. When their clothes were in place, Orin splattered and smeared more blood over the tunic now adorning his clone's body.

Cole lined up the blade of the sword with the hole he'd already pierced through Varo's chest and shoved it through again, so the hole in his clothes and chest lined up. Varo bent to add more blood to his clothes.

Next, the three of them used dirt to smear the hands and faces of the duplicates. In some places, the soil resembled a bruise. It wasn't so obvious as to be apparent that the dirt was trying to replicate a bruise if the Lord decided to examine them more closely.

When they finished, everyone stood back to examine their handiwork.

"I don't think it's getting any better than this," Brokk said.

"Neither do I," Orin agreed.

"It's my turn now," Cole said.

"What do you mean?" Lexi asked.

"I can't go before the Lord looking as if I haven't been

touched," Cole said. "Orin and Varo are survivors; they wouldn't go down without a fight."

"What do you expect us to do? Punch you in the face?" Orin asked.

"And a few other places," Cole said.

"Shit," Orin muttered.

Lexi wanted to protest against this, but she bit her lip and turned away. Cole was right; this was necessary, but that didn't mean she could watch it.

She walked over to stand near the closed door separating this tunnel from the next one. It was solid metal, but she was well aware of what lay beyond. In her mind, she pictured the tunnel twisting its way toward the stairs leading to the fireplace.

She winced and her shoulders hunched up when the thwack of a fist hitting flesh rebounded off the concrete walls. Her teeth ground together when the scent of Cole's blood wafted to her. It took all she had not to scream at them to stop.

She yearned to cover her ears, but she couldn't. She couldn't watch this, but she couldn't completely shut it out either.

Another thwack sounded, and Cole grunted. She was about to shout for them to stop when silence descended. Holding her breath, she counted the seconds to see if it was over or if they were taking a break.

When those seconds stretched into a minute, she braced herself before turning to face them. If she didn't get control of herself, the second she saw Cole, she might fly across the room and beat Orin.

Even prepared for what she was about to see, the blood oozing from Cole's nose and the black already surrounding his swelling eye unleashed a torrent of fury inside her. Most of the time, she only half despised Orin, but right then, she *loathed* him.

Another bruise shadowed Cole's jaw while a streak of blood ran across his cheek. She didn't see any cuts on him, and it took her a minute to realize the blood was from Orin's scraped knuckles.

She kept her attention averted from his nakedness as she stared at those knuckles before looking at the bodies. No one had considered that while they were working on making the corpses look real.

"You have to mark up their knuckles somehow, too," she said in a voice far steadier than she anticipated. "The clones don't look like they could have inflicted Cole's injuries."

"Good point," Brokk said.

"Use the walls," Cole said as he wiped away the blood trickling down from his bottom lip.

The bodies scraped against the floor as Varo and Orin dragged them over to one of the walls. Grasping the doppelganger's wrists, Varo and Orin scoured their knuckles against the surface. Then they smeared more of their blood on the doppelganger's hands.

Lexi tried to suppress the tremor making its way through her, but it wouldn't stop as it rattled its way through her bones. Soon Cole would walk into the Lord's palace with all those dragons and these magical bodies.

Soon, they would learn if this was good enough to trick the Lord. If it wasn't, Cole would never return. She hugged herself to try to calm herself, but it was useless.

"I'll take them now," Cole said.

"I'll carry Varo—"

"No," Cole abruptly cut off Brokk. "You're staying here."

"You can't go alone," Brokk protested, and Lexi nodded her agreement.

"I can, and I am," Cole said. "I saw what happened to father; if you think the Lord won't kill you too just to make sure I have no family left, then you're mistaken. You're not walking into that hall to become dinner for those dragons."

"Then I'll go with you," Lexi blurted.

CHAPTER FIFTY-EIGHT

"No," Cole said at the same time her father said, "Absolutely not."

Lexi restrained herself from rolling her eyes at their overprotective nature. "If the arach can control the dragons, then I'm the *best* one to send in there."

"Your powers are just awakening; we have no idea what you can do and no way of knowing if you *can* control the dragons. You can't walk down that hall, with its open ceiling, and through a field of dragons to stand before the Lord. He'll know what you are before you make it two feet into the room."

"So will the dragons," she retorted. "And maybe they'll turn against him."

"Or maybe they won't. It's not a chance we can take. If it backfires on us, it will get us both killed."

Lexi ground her teeth together as she tried to come up with another reason why she should go, but she had to admit he was right. That didn't mean she was willing to relent on this.

"You can't go alone," she insisted.

"I'll go with you," Del offered. "We can tell the Lord your brothers were keeping me prisoner and you freed me."

"No," Cole said. "Anyone else I bring in there will be nothing but a target. He also knows Lexi is my mate and will see you as a threat. He's aware you provided a lot of the military strategy that helped him win the war. If he thinks we have a tighter bond because of Lexi, he'll have no problem killing you."

"True," Del admitted.

"Besides, it's better if you remain dead," Cole continued. "That way, Lexi, Orin, and Varo aren't the only secrets we have against the Lord. Also, it's daylight there too, and unless that somehow changed in prison, you can't handle the sun."

Del's mouth quirked in a small smile. "True."

Cole lifted Orin's clone and hefted it over his shoulder. Lexi left the shadows of the tunnel behind as she stretched her hand toward him. "Cole—"

"I'll be fine," he assured her. "The Lord doesn't want me dead. Or at least he doesn't want me dead *yet*. He still has a use for me."

"Which is?" Orin asked.

"Because of Lexi, he thinks he has a way to control me. He might not get so lucky or have that kind of leverage over the next dark fae king or the dark fae council. Right now, he mistakenly believes he has control over the Gloaming because of me."

"He could turn his dragons loose on the Gloaming," Brokk said.

"He could, but then he'll be starting a war with *all* of the dark fae, and he's not ready for that. He lost a lot of fighters during the war, too, and the dark fae were a large part of his army. He can't afford to alienate them now.

"Besides, some, if not *all*, the other realms will realize he'll come for them once he finishes with the Gloaming and band together against him. He won this last war because the realms and fighters were divided, and many believed humans should know about the existence of immortals. The realms won't be divided if he starts attacking us."

"You're far more optimistic than me," Orin said. "I'm not so sure some of the realms, especially the warlocks; they've always had a darker side. Or the vamps, they'd love to get their realm back."

"Not all of them," Del said. "Many of us have made the human realm our home and wouldn't go back. Many have never lived anywhere else; I haven't."

"But some would," Orin pressed.

"Yes, some would."

"I think the Lord could start a massive civil war between all the realms," Orin said.

"Quite possibly," Cole agreed. "But it doesn't matter. I still have to deliver these bodies to him, or he's coming for Lexi and me soon. And I have to do it alone."

Before any of them could speak, he drove his sword through the neck of the decapitated head. He shifted the blade into his other hand before grabbing Varo's clone by its shirt collar.

"I have to go," he said.

"Where are you going to tell the Lord you found them?" Sahira asked.

"The human realm," Cole answered. "There are plenty of places for them to hide here, and the Lord can't punish humans for hiding immortals they would never even know were immortal. Besides, I will be coming out of the human realm portal when I exit near the palace. The Lord will know that."

"Where is the portal to Dragonia in this realm?" Varo asked.

"There's one near the city, or what remains of it. It's well hidden from the humans," Cole answered. "From here, I'll open a portal close to it. Once I'm there, if someone sees me with the bodies, it shouldn't be a problem as I'll be taking them straight to Dragonia."

"Won't opening a portal weaken you?" Lexi asked.

"I'll be fine."

Arguing with him was pointless, and she didn't want to spend what might be their last moments together fighting. Instead, she walked over and rested her head against his chest.

"You better come back to me," she whispered.

"Always." He rested his cheek against the top of her head. "I'll be back as soon as I can."

She tried not to think about the possibility that it could be days or weeks from now. None of them knew what the Lord would do. Lexi reluctantly released him and stepped away.

"When does the harrow stone have to go back?" Cole asked Sahira.

"Tomorrow morning," Sahira said.

"Wait for as long as you can before returning it. I want to go with you to thank the crones for letting us use it."

"I will."

Without another word, Cole opened a portal and walked away. Lexi watched until the darkness swallowed him completely. Something inside her deflated when he vanished.

CHAPTER FIFTY-NINE

COLE STEPPED out of the portal from the human realm and into Dragonia. No one could open a portal into and out of Dragonia without the Lord's knowledge. The entire kingdom was protected against such a thing happening.

Thanks to the arach before him, the Lord controlled the portals that remained permanently open to the realms. All of those portals led to an exit point near the palace, where the Lord's men watched over them.

When an immortal was leaving Dragonia, all they had to do was locate the portal to the realm they sought, picture where they wanted to go in that realm, and they would return there. The amount of magic behind the system the arach established was incredible.

He suspected the elaborate portals were a group effort, and one alone couldn't have completed them, but there was still a *lot* of magic behind them.

And that magic was manifesting inside Lexi right now. He had no idea how they would help her learn to control and use it, but they would.

Cole tilted his head back as he took in the Dragonian realm.

Rising above him, the golden peaks and turrets of the palace stretched high into the purple sky. Only a few pink clouds floated through the air.

When he walked a few feet away from the portal, some of the Lord's men turned toward him. By the looks of them, they were young, barely trained warlocks, but he couldn't be sure.

They lifted their spears and pointed them straight at his heart. One lunged a little too far forward; the pointed tip rested against Cole's chest. When the shadows stirred inside him, Cole suppressed them.

He lifted his eyebrows at the Lord's men. They'd been far too lax on their duty. If they'd been his men and he'd gotten this close before they noticed, they wouldn't be one of his guards anymore.

He'd have them removed from their duties immediately, but he welcomed this incompetence from the Lord's men.

Without blinking, he dropped one of the bodies, grabbed the spear resting against his chest and snapped it in half before shoving it away from him. The guard gawked at him and then the broken pieces of his spear. Cole doubted the guy had seen him move.

The rest of the guards kept their weapons aimed at him but backed away when he stepped toward the man who nearly speared him.

"I am the dark fae king," he snarled at the guard. "Don't *ever* point a weapon at me again unless you want it shoved up your ass."

The man hesitated before starting to swing the broken remains of the spear toward him again. Then he wisely thought better of it and lowered the broken shaft to the ground.

Cole hefted Orin's head into the air for them to see. "Tell the Lord I've brought him presents."

They gaped at the head before one of them blurted, "It's Orin."

"Aren't you observant," Cole drawled. "Now, run along and tell the Lord I'm here and I have the bodies of my brothers for him."

Their gazes shifted to Varo's fake body, but it was impossible to see its face.

This didn't matter as the tallest one nudged the shoulder of the one to the left of him as he spoke. "Go tell the Lord."

The other man hesitated before bowing his head and scurrying away like a rat with cheese. He kept his head down, and his shoulders hunched forward like he was bracing himself for a blow while he ran.

Cole doubted the Lord was ever easy to deal with and *never* kind to those who served him. He didn't care to think about the number of times the Lord abused the man. The man had chosen his path and would suffer the consequences of it... just as Cole would if this all blew up.

He refused to let that possibility enter his mind. He had to maintain his confidence while here. A lack of confidence would get him destroyed if he didn't.

Cole and the guy who'd nearly speared him eyed each other before Cole dismissively shifted his attention toward the palace. The portal opened near a large river that cut through the land.

A thousand feet above the river was a single bridge made of gray rocks. It stretched across the river for over two hundred feet before reaching the open palace gates.

The man who'd left disappeared behind the enormous stone walls surrounding the palace. After a couple of minutes, he came back into view as he ran up the hill toward the bridge.

One of the dragons circling lazily overhead roared before twisting to its side and making a sharp right. Sunlight glinted off its blue underbelly and the lethal talons tucked against it.

What would happen if Lexi got near one of these creatures?

The idea of it petrified him, but it would have to happen; it was as inevitable as the tide. If they were going to find out more about the connection between the arach and the dragons, she would have to get near one.

He didn't know how they were going to pull that off, but he would figure out the safest way to do it.

He wasn't sure how much time passed before the man who went up the hill sprinted out of the palace and onto the bridge. Cole kept his face impassive and heart rate calm as the man ran down the hill toward them.

At least the Lord didn't kill the messenger. But then, to that monster, this was a happy message to receive.

When he finally reached them again, the man skidded to a halt a few feet away. He rested his hand against his side as he bent over and wheezed out words.

"The Lord… would like to… see you… and the bodies… immediately."

Cole smiled at the one with the broken spear; the man scowled back. Without another word, he turned and strolled toward the open gates leading into the palace's courtyard.

He passed through them and into the bailey beyond. It was teeming with immortals looking to trade their wares and purchase things, but the crowd was abnormally subdued. None of the familiar shouts of merchants looking to hawk their wares filled the air.

Instead, immortals went quietly from one worn-down booth to the next. Some of them scurried around the bailey, and none of them made eye contact for long.

After the arach killed each other, Dragonia became home to an assortment of immortals. They all lived peaceably together, but none of them seemed happy. Despite that unhappiness, most stayed because they were outcasts from their realms.

He barely felt the weight of the bodies he carried, though they must have weighed the same as Orin and Varo. Everything else about them was so realistic, he doubted this detail was overlooked.

Feeding on Lexi again had bolstered his strength once more. And this last feeding had empowered him more than any of the others.

When he arrived at the top of the mountain path, he turned toward the rocky bridge and strode onto it. Cracks zigzagged across the rocky surface. With every step he took, pebbles broke away.

They clattered as they bounced against the rocky walls of the mountain before spiraling into the river. Once he was further out on the bridge, those pebbles stopped knocking against the sides of the walls, but he was certain they still broke away to spiral into the rushing water far below.

Cole ignored the quaking of the bridge beneath his feet. If it fell apart now, there was nothing he could do about it. Besides, this bridge had been here for more than a few millennia; it would last a little longer.

He was almost to the silver portcullis, with its lethal tips hanging above the front of the open gates, when he spotted a slender, stoop-shouldered man standing in the shadows.

"Hurry, hurry," the man encouraged as he waved a hand at Cole.

CHAPTER SIXTY

COLE STRODE past the golden gates shaped like dragons and into the palace. The man's feet thudded heavily against the stone floors as he rushed toward the hallway leading to the Lord's throne room.

At least, unlike the last two times he was here, he wouldn't have to wait to see the Lord.

Before they got to the hallway leading to the throne room, the man turned left and walked across the foyer to a set of glass doors. Cole had to shift his step away from the closed doors of the throne room.

Where was this guy taking him? He'd never seen the Lord outside the throne room.

He continued onward as if this didn't faze him, but he wasn't expecting to go anywhere other than the throne room. The man opened the glass doors and scurried into the large, beautiful room beyond.

The only light filtering into the room came from the windows all around it. There were more windows than golden walls here, and the combination cast only a few shadows across the well-lit floor.

Sunlight spilled across a white marble floor. The colors

swirling through the floor reminded him of the different hues of the dragons' scales. As he walked, this pattern shifted and changed in such a way that he had the disconcerting notion he was actually crossing dragons.

Trying to reorient himself, he tipped his head back and looked at the sky as a dragon soared overhead. When he felt more centered, he lowered his head to take in the room again.

It was empty now, but he doubted it had always been that way. After seeing the way Lexi reacted to light, he suspected this room was once a place where the arach would come to relax.

A place where they would bask in the sun and possibly moonlight as it shone through the windows and lit the floor. It was probably once opulently furnished and filled with things that made the arach happy.

This Lord, or one of the other lunatics before him, had changed all that. And now, it was nothing more than a barren, beautifully lit space.

As he walked, the shadows shifted around him. They didn't move to touch him, but he sensed the power they possessed, and something inside him stirred in response. There weren't many of them here, but if he needed them, they would come.

Across the way, another set of double glass doors were set into the wall. The man pulled one of them open, but this time he stepped back and gestured for Cole to go through alone.

CHAPTER SIXTY-ONE

COLE STEPPED through the doors and into a massive, open space. At first, he wasn't sure what he was looking at as the barren trees bowed beneath the weight of the sunlight beating down on them, but then he realized it was a garden.

More remains of dead plants spilled across the red, stone walkway that twisted through the acres of dead foliage surrounding him. The deadened tendrils of plants, shrubs, and trees stretched out as if they were seeking life from those who passed, but there was no life here.

Whatever beauty used to lay in what he was sure was once a magnificent, vast garden before the arach died, was gone. This was a garden for the dead; it was only fitting he brought the clones here.

Through the broken remnants of gnarled tree branches, Cole spotted the Lord. He stood a thousand feet away, near a fountain.

On either side of him were two guards; they each held a spear and had swords strapped to their backs. More guards moved amongst the dead plants and the endless acres of land.

Overhead, a dragon roared as it swooped across the sky, but none of them were on the ground in the garden. Cole ignored the circling beasts overhead as he strode toward the Lord. Rocks clattered beneath Varo's clone as Cole dragged it along the pathway.

Most of the guards watched as he approached the Lord, but some kept their attention focused away from the fountain to search the land. These men and women were better trained than the ones by the portal.

Cole didn't know if the Lord always had this many guards to protect him when he didn't have dragons near or if he'd called them to him when he heard of Cole's arrival. Either way, the Lord was making it clear *no* one was going to get at him.

Which meant the Lord had a very *big* false sense of security. He had no idea what was coming for him, but Cole did. Even if he'd never learned about Lexi's true heritage, he would have found a way to kill this man.

He looked forward to the day it happened.

However, the Lord was also making it clear Cole would not escape here. As if to reinforce this, the shadows of two dragons swept across him as they circled overhead.

"Cole!" the Lord greeted with false cheerfulness. "How good it is to see you, and I hear it's under the *best* of circumstances!"

Cole kept his ire over that statement hidden as he gave the Lord a tightlipped smile. This asshole didn't know the two bodies he carried weren't really his brothers, but if they were, then this would have been *far* from good circumstances.

But he was insane. That insanity shone from his red eyes, eyes that were once hazel and twinkled with merriment.

Before becoming the Lord, Andreas was a good man. That man died centuries ago.

"Your Highness," Cole greeted.

He didn't say how good it was to see the Lord again; it would have been a lie, and the Lord would have known it. Cole planned to spin a giant lie to him right now, but he wouldn't lie if he didn't have to. It would only get him caught if he did.

"Aren't these gardens magnificent?" the Lord asked as he waved a hand at all the rotten things surrounding them.

At one time, it was probably one of the most beautiful places in Dragonia; it was far from that now.

"They are something, my Lord," Cole replied.

The Lord chuckled and turned his attention to the fountain. In the center of it was a dragon carved out of gray stone. Its wings were open, its two feet remained on the ground, and its tail curled over its back. Its neck rose high as its chin rested against its chest. Red water spilled from its mouth and into the basin beneath.

"I suppose most wouldn't find them beautiful," the Lord said as he studied the fountain. "But that's only because they don't know what to look for."

"And what should one look for?" Cole inquired.

"What's not to love about the blood of your enemies?"

Cole's attention shifted back to the fountain and the red liquid spewing from the dragon's mouth. He'd only glanced at it before, but now he couldn't deny what the thick, red liquid was. When he scented the air, he caught the coppery tang of blood on it.

He composed his expression into one of indifference, but he knew something passed across it when the Lord smirked at him. Cole had no idea where the blood was coming from, and he had no intention of following the pipes to discover the answer.

Is it fresh blood or recirculated?

He'd prefer to believe it was at least partially recirculated, but he wasn't a fool. He wouldn't put it past the Lord to have someone slaughtered as often as it would take to keep fresh blood spilling from the dragon's mouth.

"And it seems you have brought me more enemies," the Lord said.

A tendril of unease crept up Cole's spine as he stared at the Lord. He wasn't sure how much blood was in these bodies. But then, no dead body that had been decapitated or stabbed through the heart would retain enough blood to fill this fountain.

He'd wager those whose blood fueled this fountain were alive when it was taken from them. Their screams and suffering would be part of what the Lord relished about this fountain.

"I have," Cole said.

"You know I'm aware of what Orin and Varo look like," the Lord said.

"Of course, Your Highness."

It was now or never. He'd come this far, and there was no turning back. If this didn't work, it would soon be his blood filling that fountain.

Cole shrugged Orin's body off his shoulder and let it hit the ground. It thudded off the stones before its hand slapped against the side of the stone fountain. He set the head down on the clone's chest before dropping Varo's duplicate beside it.

The Lord studied him with a tilt to his head and narrowed eyes that brimmed with maliciousness.

Finally, the Lord shifted his attention to the duplicates while Cole studied the fountain. Though they weren't his real brothers, he could barely stand to look at their bodies.

"You know I can sense magic too," the Lord said.

Cole looked the Lord straight in the eyes as he replied, "I know."

CHAPTER SIXTY-TWO

THE LORD STEPPED CLOSER and bent to touch Orin's head. He poked at it with his index finger before inspecting Varo. After ten minutes of poking and prodding, sighing, and smirking, he lifted his gaze to Cole once more.

"It looks like they put up a fight," the Lord said.

"There is a reason they lasted this long," Cole said.

"Until you."

"Until me."

"I wouldn't have thought the light fae could fight," the Lord murmured.

"Neither would I," Cole agreed. "But Varo was always full of surprises."

"Not anymore," the Lord chuckled.

Cole remained stone-faced. "Not anymore."

"And all they needed to do to die was come up against their brother. I made the right decision in killing your father; he *never* would have allowed this to happen."

Despite his attempts not to let it happen, Cole's face hardened. The Lord's eyes danced in amusement as he waved a finger at Cole.

294 BRENDA K DAVIES

"But you, you, Cole. You're a good lapdog. But then, there isn't anything a lycan won't do for their mate, even kill their brothers. So much for blood being thicker than water, am I right?"

The Lord clasped his hands behind him and rocked from his heels to his toes and back again while he waited for Cole's reaction.

Think of Lexi. He's trying to bait you into attacking him. If you fall for it, you won't make it out of here alive.

Cole pictured Lexi's striking green eyes, radiant smile, and the way she warmed the coldest recesses of his soul. He recalled the awe on her face as she held her glowing hands before her and the confusion on her face as she gazed at him.

She needed him too much for him to ruin it all now. But one day, he would rip this fucker's throat out and piss down his windpipe.

When Cole remained unresponsive, the Lord grew tired of his taunting and focused on the bodies once more.

"I'm curious how you had time to track them while fighting a rebellion in the Gloaming," the Lord remarked.

"Brokk tracked them."

"Is Brokk the one who killed them?"

"No, that was me," Cole said.

"So, I'm not able to count on your brother to do what has to be done?"

Cole buried the rage that rocketed through him. He was a fae, they lived to taunt and toy with others, and he was still tired of this man's games. And he would not allow this bastard to put a bull's-eye on Brokk's back.

"Of course you can," Cole replied with a calmness he didn't feel. "He is the one who found them after all, and he knew what fate awaited them. He could have let them slip away; he chose not to. I instructed Brokk to wait for me before doing anything because this was *my* kill to make. Their blood was mine to have on my hands. Brokk would have done it, but I ordered him not to."

SHADOWS OF BETRAYAL 295

"If I ordered him to do something different than you, whose order would he choose to obey?"

"You already know who he would obey, my Lord," Cole said. "He chose to fight for you during the war; you are where his loyalty lies."

"Hmm," the Lord murmured. "I guess we shall see."

With those words, Cole had no doubt this man would one day try to pit them against each other, but he was also certain as to where his brother's loyalty lay. And he would not allow it to happen.

He had no fear of Brokk turning on him, but he did fear what might happen to his brother if the Lord got anywhere near him.

Cole didn't respond. The Lord didn't want one from him anyway; he was making his point, playing his games, and in the future, he would make another move against someone Cole loved.

When that time came, Cole would be prepared for him. The Lord would *not* get another loved one of his.

For now, the Lord was enjoying playing with him, but that would end. Cole was his number one target on the list of immortals he wanted dead, but it would be his loved ones that the Lord tried to destroy first.

It would be a fun game for him—a way to destroy Cole before he actually went for the killing blow.

It was a game Cole would win.

The Lord seized Orin's hair and lifted the head from the ground. Its mouth hung slightly ajar to reveal the teeth within. The work they'd done on it still looked good. Bringing the head closer to his face, the Lord studied it before scenting the air.

"I sense no magic here," he muttered.

Outwardly, Cole remained unmoving. Inwardly, his shoulders sagged and he wiped the imaginary sweat from his brow. This wasn't over, but so far, so good.

"Where did Brokk find them?" the Lord inquired.

"The human realm," Cole replied.

"Interesting." He poked Orin's nose, and the head swayed in his grasp. "Was he anywhere near your little girlfriend?"

"No. They were near the city, hiding amid the remains of the buildings and the humans."

"Oh, they were living with the rats. How suiting. It's strange though; I have men searching the city."

"You've had men searching for them since the war ended, and none found them."

The Lord stopped poking Orin's nose and looked up at Cole over the swinging head. "Are you calling my men inadequate?"

"I'm not calling them anything; I'm simply stating a fact."

He may be pushing the Lord too far, but he wasn't going to stand here and take everything this madman dished out.

"How is it your brother found them so quickly when he couldn't find them before?" the Lord inquired.

"I don't know. I'm assuming they had only recently entered the human realm when Brokk was alerted to them. We've had spies searching for them for months," Cole replied. "Where they were hiding before they arrived in the human realm, I have no idea. But our allies in the human realm alerted us as soon as Orin and Varo were spotted. And now, they're dead."

"Yes, they are."

The Lord released Orin's head. A wet thud sounded when it hit the ground and rolled a few feet away.

"I hear you took a fae sword to the heart and lived," the Lord said.

Cole was not surprised that the Lord had this knowledge. He already knew someone in the Gloaming was feeding him information. With the number of people who witnessed what should have been his demise, Cole hadn't expected it not to make its way back to the Lord.

It didn't even have to be the traitor who was feeding him information. Any dark fae could have come here to trade, or anyone from Dragonia could have gone into another realm and heard the tale. For all he knew, the troubadours were already singing about it.

He despised the fact they sang about him, but he was good fodder for the musicians, and they loved it.

"I did, milord," he said.

The Lord eyed him from head to toe. "How very interesting, but then, fae metal does not kill a lycan."

"It doesn't."

"Perhaps the fae should weld a fae sword made of silver and fae metal. Maybe that would do the job."

Cole smiled at him. "Maybe."

The Lord smiled back at him. "How is your girlfriend, Colburn? I heard she went onto the battlefield after you."

"She did."

"How brave of her."

"Yes," Cole agreed.

"Did she enjoy her visit to Dragonia?"

"She thought it was a beautiful realm."

"I'm sure she enjoyed seeing Malakai again. He's quite taken with her and a very loyal subject to me."

Cole kept his mouth shut. The Lord was trying to bait him; he refused to rise to that bait. A dragon bellowed, and a shadow fell over them as it swooped low. Cole kept his gaze focused on the man across from him as hatred churned in his stomach.

The shadows inside him stirred as they crept through his veins. When a small shifting occurred in the garden, he became extremely aware of the shadows beneath the dead plants as the Lord stared at him.

And then the madman broke into a wide grin as he slapped Cole on the shoulder. "But you are also a very loyal subject!" he declared. "Malakai has reported many an enemy hidden amongst my allies, but *you* killed your brothers for me. We must celebrate!"

So *that* was what Malakai had done to earn a sun medallion

from the Lord. The amulet allowed him to walk in the daylight and was achieved by spilling the blood of countless others.

Cole wondered how many of the immortals Malakai reported were truly enemies and how many had just been standing in Malakai's way.

During the war, Cole hadn't been in his way; he was too far up the ranks to be a hindrance as Malakai clawed his way up the ladder. But had the bastard tried to turn him in for something when he realized Cole was competition for Lexi?

Cole was pretty certain he had.

"Come," the Lord said and kicked Orin's head out of the way as he turned Cole toward the palace. "Let's go celebrate the deaths of those who would have done us harm!"

Real or not, the last thing Cole wanted to do was celebrate the deaths of his brothers, but he couldn't say no to the Lord, and they both knew it.

CHAPTER SIXTY-THREE

FOR A WHILE, Lexi paced the library before retreating upstairs. Once there, she tried to occupy herself by taking a shower and putting on some of her comfortable, familiar clothes.

None of it took as long as she would have liked. Less than an hour later, she found herself pacing the library again. Orin and Varo retreated to the tunnels; Brokk muttered something about "annoying" before taking his newest Harry Potter book and retreating to the guest room he'd occupied before.

Sahira and her father checked in on her but left her alone when she refused to sit. After a while, exhaustion started seeping in. Still, she refused to sleep as she went from the bookshelves to the curtains and back again.

Sometimes, she would circle the room to change her pattern, and then she started walking in a grid-like sequence, but none of it kept her mind occupied. She tried reading, but sitting still made things worse.

When the grandfather clock in the other room chimed ten, she turned to look at the covered windows. She studied the thick drapes with a growing feeling of dread, but throwing her shoulders back, she stalked toward the curtains.

She was anxious about Cole, but *this* had also been weighing heavily on her mind. Stopping beside the curtain, she grasped a small piece of it and pulled it back. She couldn't see much outside, but the reflection of the half moon shimmered across the lake's glass-like surface.

Though it wasn't full, the moon was bright enough its glow illuminated the other side of the curtain. She peered outside the best she could but didn't see anyone there.

It didn't matter; she didn't have to expose herself much to learn the answer to this anyway. Her father and Cole wouldn't approve of her doing this, but if she didn't have an answer tonight, it would drive her *crazy*.

With a steady hand, she stuck the tips of her fingers into the moon's rays. It took a few seconds, and it wasn't anywhere near as bright as earlier, but a golden glow sparked to life at the tips of her fingers.

Lexi's breath came in small pants as she snatched her hand back and released the curtain. Only sheer will kept her from smashing the curtain, kicking the wall, and screaming as she struggled to get her rapid breathing under control.

She did none of those things as her mind spun and panic nearly overwhelmed her. If she didn't learn how to control this ability of hers, she was *screwed*. She couldn't spend the rest of her life trapped inside; she'd never survive it.

There had to be a reason she was like this, but she had no idea how to find out what that was or what it could be. *You'll get through this. Just relax. You'll figure this out and get through it.*

She kept trying to talk herself off the ledge, but she remained teetering there. One small shove would be more than enough to push her off.

"The same thing happened."

She jumped and bit back a squeak as she spun to face her dad. He stood in the doorway of the library, leaning against the frame as he studied her.

"I didn't mean to scare you," he said.

"I'm fine."

"You don't look it."

Lexi imagined she looked a mess. Her hair had straggled loose from the bun she'd thrown it into, she was breathing like she'd run a race, and her eyes felt wild, but she still shrugged.

His gaze shifted to the curtained window. "Did the same thing happen in the moonlight as the sunlight?"

"Yes, well, mostly. It wasn't as strong of a reaction."

Sadness crept across his features as he kept his focus on the window. "You shouldn't have done that."

"I *had* to have an answer. It would have eaten away at me until I got it."

"I understand." He finally looked at her again. "You can always take the potion again. It will suppress this, and you can go back outside."

It was so tempting that she almost leapt at the opportunity, but she couldn't. "How long would that last?"

"It probably wouldn't be long before your powers broke through, but it would give you time to adjust to what you are instead of plunging into it."

"And we need the answers to what I can do so we can use it against the Lord. I can't take the potion again."

He gave her a sad smile. "I knew you were going to say that. You're too stubborn for your own good sometimes."

"You raised me."

"And I'm going to keep you safe and make sure you have the happy life you deserve."

Her heart warmed as she smiled at him. "I know."

"Why don't you go upstairs and get some rest."

"I can't. I have to know Cole is safe."

"He might not return tonight."

"I know," she muttered. "But I'd rather stay here."

When she started pacing again, he remained standing in the doorway. After a few minutes, he spoke again.

"I'll be in the kitchen if you need me."

"Okay," she murmured as she reached the fireplace and turned to walk toward the chairs. "I'll be here."

"I love you, Lexi."

She paused before walking over to hug him. "I love you too, Dad."

CHAPTER SIXTY-FOUR

IT WAS WELL past midnight by the time Cole returned to the library. The Lord had been good and drunk when he left Dragonia, but Cole had mostly pretended to drink while sipping his goblet.

He'd "accidentally" knocked one goblet over on the table and another into the deadened plant next to his chair while sitting in the Lord's private solar. The Lord laughed and immediately ordered that Cole's goblet be refilled.

Like the rest of the palace, Cole imagined that the solar was once full of beauty; there was none now. Instead, dead potted plants and one barren tree sat in the corners of the vast room.

A portrait of the Lord hung above the fireplace that took up the entire far wall. In the painting, the Lord glared down at him from vivid red eyes, and it was still the nicest thing in the room.

The heads of far too many immortal creatures decorated the rest of the room. Unicorns, sasquatches, pegasusses, dark and light fae, and many others hung in the room. He even had the head of a giant, which took up most of the right wall.

Cole wasn't a fan of giants; not many who valued their lives were, but seeing one's head, along with so many others, mounted to the walls made his stomach churn. Cole didn't examine it too closely, but it looked like the giant's head had been scalped to get it to fit beneath the wooden beams crisscrossing the ceiling.

And nailed to those beams were the bodies of countless pixies. Their tiny bodies contributed to the stench of rot that permeated the room. From the looks of the nails holding them in place, they were silver.

Pixies couldn't tolerate silver. For however long the tiny immortals survived up there, it was a painful, agonizing existence until they finally died.

Most were dead, but a couple remained alive. Their tiny voices and incessant pleas for mercy filled the room. Pixie music was some of his favorite in all the realms, but this was far from the beautiful songs the creatures could weave. This was utter misery and grated like nails on a chalkboard against his skin.

"I do so love their song," the Lord said.

Cole didn't respond.

A rectangular table with ten chairs around it took up the center of the room. Though the chairs were comfortable, the room was not. Or at least, it wasn't anything that anyone else enjoyed.

The Lord had himself a grand old time as he drank goblet after goblet of wine. He slapped his hand on the table and laughed loudly while he celebrated the deaths of Orin and Varo.

Cole played the game too. He smiled and sipped his wine, but all the while, he plotted how he was going to destroy this man.

As he played the game, it took everything he had not to leap onto the table, race across it, and beat this piece of shit to death. His father was dead because of this man. And this douchebag was celebrating what he believed were the deaths of Cole's brothers.

Cole would never make it to the Lord before the twenty-five guards crammed into the room intercepted him. And then the Lord would kill him and throw Lexi to Malakai.

Since she couldn't keep her powers hidden anymore, it would only be a matter of time before Malakai turned her over to the Lord or figured out some other way to use her to his advantage.

He would *not* let that happen.

Shadows danced in the corners of the room and crept through his system. They beckoned to him with their power, but he had no idea what that power was or how to use it.

If he unleashed the shadows here on the Lord, as he had on Orin, then the Lord would know there was something more to him. And if he failed to bring the Lord down, then his surprise would be gone, and he would end up dead.

Still, he grated his teeth and twirled his goblet between his fingers as he labored to keep the power of the shadows suppressed while listening to the fucker go on about himself. He contented himself with the knowledge the Lord was so sure of himself that he'd never see his death coming.

By the time the Lord called it a night, his eyes were bloodshot and his words slurred, but he walked out of the room on his own. "Come with me," he slurred to his guards. "Get out of my home, Cole."

Glad to have finally been dismissed, Cole rose as the Lord's men fell into step behind him. They all filtered out the door.

When the door shut behind them and he found himself alone in the room, Cole's attention shifted to the pixies in the rafters. He couldn't leave them to such a horrible fate.

He climbed onto the table and located the two who'd cried all night. One was a male completely drained of color. By the time Cole got to him, the pixie was dead.

The other was a female so weakened that almost nothing of her orange color remained. When she lifted her head to look at him, he saw the truth in her nearly translucent eyes... it was too late to save her.

The silver used to crucify her had taken too much of a toll on her delicate body.

"Please," she whispered in the tiniest voice he'd ever heard.

Bile churned in his stomach, but they both knew what she was asking for; it was the only option left to her. "I'm sorry."

Gripping her head between his thumb and index finger, he twisted it until her neck snapped. A broken neck on most immortals wasn't a fatal injury, but she was so drained she wouldn't recover.

Her head dropped to her chest. Her breathing slowed before stopping. He'd never felt dirtier in his life, but he couldn't have saved the broken creature.

He contemplated removing her from the wood and taking her to be buried. Pixies were creatures of the outdoors and nature and deserved better than this. They should be buried in the earth they loved.

However, the Lord might notice she was missing. He'd taken a chance by ending her suffering; he couldn't put Lexi at risk by taking the pixie's body from here.

Climbing down from the table, he stalked toward the door and opened it to leave the room. There, he discovered the stoop-shouldered man who'd led him in earlier.

Cole followed him from the palace. He crossed the bridge on his own and didn't acknowledge the new guards outside the portals as he left Dragonia behind.

When he entered the mortal realm again, he stood on the outskirts of the broken city. He didn't bother to take in the wasteland before he opened another portal into Lexi's manor.

Glad to be free of that hideous room, the Lord, and Dragonia, all Cole craved was his mate, a shower to scrub himself clean, and a bed. Now back in the manor and staring at his mate, some of the dirtiness he felt faded.

CHAPTER SIXTY-FIVE

STEPPING AWAY FROM THE PORTAL, Cole closed it behind him as he studied Lexi. Her legs were tucked beneath her in the chair, and her head had fallen onto the armrest. She wore a baggy T-shirt and a pair of yoga pants. The book in her hand was still open to the first page.

He could picture her trying to read but unable to concentrate as she got up to pace before forcing herself back to the chair. She must have been worried sick about him before exhaustion finally took over.

He'd hoped to be back here long before now, but the Lord, as always, had other plans. He tiptoed closer, determined not to wake her.

Her mouth was parted, and her loose bun dangled against her shoulder. She looked so peaceful and at ease, something he rarely saw from her anymore.

His heart raced as love for her swelled inside it. Cole didn't care what he had to do or who he had to destroy; he would keep her safe. She deserved that.

Some of his self-disgust ebbed as he approached her. It was easy to hate himself when he was sitting in that room, pretending everything was fine. It wasn't so easy to hate himself when he was with her.

Though he'd done some terrible things in his life, things he would never forget—like killing that pixie—she still loved him and had faith in him. And she was the most amazing, loving immortal he'd ever known.

He was broken, battered, unrelenting, unforgiving, and often vicious, but her love made him a better man.

He was about to kneel at her side when a board creaked in the hallway. Resting his fingers on the armrest near Lexi's head, he scented Del before the man arrived in the doorway.

Del froze when he spotted Cole standing near his daughter; his gaze briefly fell to her before returning to Cole. A flicker of sadness went through his eyes before he gave Cole a tired smile.

"I was coming down to make her go to bed. She'd been waiting up for you," Del said, "but she must have fallen asleep."

"I'll carry her upstairs," Cole said.

"How did it go with the Lord?"

"As good as it can ever go with the Lord, but he believes Orin and Varo are dead, and I'm still alive to tell the tale, so...."

"As good as we hoped."

"Yes."

"Did he threaten her again?"

"In his little, subtle ways. He also threatened Brokk. I have no doubt he wants me dead and will one day try to see it happen."

"We'll figure out a way to destroy him before that day comes," Del said.

"We will."

Cole's gaze fell to Lexi, and his heart warmed as he gazed at her. She was beautiful, and she'd always been stronger than she realized, but now, she was becoming more so as her powers emerged.

He brushed his fingers across her cheek and the smattering of freckles there. Touching her didn't erase the horrible events of this night, but it helped ease some of the revulsion swirling inside him over that room and the fountain.

He would have far preferred to have showered before touching her, but he wasn't going to leave her here while he went to do so. She had to rest, and she would get more sleep in her bed than here.

"You really do love her, don't you?" Del asked. "It's more than your lycan seeking its mate; you love her."

Cole tore his attention away from Lexi to meet her father's gaze. "What's not to love?"

"Nothing," Del said. "And I'm glad you see that too. I'm happy she has you to protect her from what's coming. She's going to need it."

"I have a feeling that once she figures out how to use her powers, she won't need anyone to protect her."

A sad smile tugged at the corners of Del's mouth. "Oh, she will, but it will be from her own stubborn nature."

Cole chuckled, but before he could respond, Del walked away. He continued to smile at the place where Del just stood. It was good seeing his old friend again; he was glad he was back and more glad Del didn't intend to stand in his way when it came to Lexi.

The last thing he wanted was to end up fighting his friend and her father. She wouldn't handle that well.

Bending, Cole slid his arms under Lexi and picked her up. She murmured in her sleep and snuggled against him. Her head fell onto his shoulder, but she didn't wake.

Her sweet scent assailed him as he carried her from the library and up the stairs to her room. Del was nowhere in sight by the time he opened Lexi's door and carried her inside.

He adjusted his hold on her to pull back the blankets. When he finished, he slid her onto the bed and tucked the sheets and comforter under her chin.

He stepped away from the bed and went back to shut the door.

He poked his head into the hall, but it remained empty, and the house was quiet.

In the moonlight streaming through the windows, he stripped off his clothes and tossed them in a corner of the room. He would burn them tomorrow.

When he finished, he padded into the bathroom, closed the door, and turned on the light. He took a long shower where he scrubbed his skin until it turned red and the water ran cold. Even once the hot water ran out, he continued to rub at his skin.

He felt a little cleaner when he turned off the water, but he couldn't wash away the sound of the pixie's neck breaking and the feel of her small head between his fingers. The memories would haunt him forever, and she'd most likely become yet another figure in his nightmares.

He deserved that.

Cole toweled himself dry and turned off the light before opening the door. Lexi was still lying on the bed, but she'd rolled so he couldn't see her face. Certain she was still asleep, he padded toward the chair near the window where he would spend the night.

"You're supposed to be sleeping with me," she said.

Shit.

Cole was at the chair when he stopped walking and turned to face her. She was still burrowed beneath the comforter with her head turned away from him, but she didn't breathe as she waited for his reply.

CHAPTER SIXTY-SIX

"Lexi—"

"I wasn't kidding, Cole. No more sleeping apart."

She rolled to face him; he hated the dark shadows under her eyes, but he didn't miss the determined set of her chin. Anger glimmered in her beautiful, hunter eyes.

However, he'd never forget the magnificent, molten gold color they had become earlier. And he suspected it was only the first of many times he would see that color on her.

She was going to grow into a powerful force. And he would be there to help her every step of the way, but he could also become her downfall.

"And what if I hurt you again?" he asked.

"Then we'll go back to sleeping separately, but you won't."

"Neither of us can be so sure what I will or won't do while I'm sleeping," he said. "I could kill you."

"You won't."

"I'm glad you have so much faith in me, but I don't."

"I have the same faith in you that you have in me. You have to trust yourself."

That was the problem. "I don't trust myself around you while I'm sleeping. My nightmares are too intense."

And most of them were about the war, being attacked, and having to defend himself. He always woke primed for a fight.

"I know that, but let me trust you enough for both of us," she said.

She held her hand out, and though he wanted to argue further or leave so it wasn't an option anymore, he didn't move. Even after his shower, he still felt dirty from today, and she could help ease that.

He yearned to hold his mate, reassure himself she was safe and exactly where she belonged... in his arms. However, he was afraid he might somehow taint her.

"It was bad today, wasn't it?" she asked.

"I've seen worse."

But he hadn't seen much worse. What he'd seen before was done in the name of war and self-defense. What he saw today, the Lord did in the name of cruelty. What he'd done with the pixie was an act of mercy, but it still sickened him.

"That doesn't make it any better. Come on, Cole," she coaxed.

Unable to resist her, he changed direction and approached the bed. If anything, he would leave the bed when she fell asleep, like he always did. She'd be pissed if she discovered the truth in the morning, but he'd wake before her and return to the bed.

Pulling back the blankets, he crawled into the bed beside her, and she rolled into his arms. He discovered her T-shirt remained on, but she'd ditched the yoga pants. A small thrill went through him when she draped her bare leg over his.

Resting her hand over his heart, she snuggled closer. "I put my fingers into the moonlight."

"And?" he asked as he inhaled the crisp scent of her shampoo and stared at the moonlight spilling through the windows.

"It wasn't as strong of a reaction."

"But there was one?"

"Yes."

He hugged her closer. "We *will* figure it out."

"I know. What happened with the Lord?" she asked.

He didn't go into all the gory details, but he told her most of what happened. He also revealed how Malakai earned his amulet.

"That bastard," she murmured. "How many lives do you think he helped take?"

"Knowing the Lord, it took a lot for Malakai to earn the amulet."

"They're both pricks."

"That they are."

"But at least the harrow stone worked and you're here. I was so worried."

"I know." He ran his fingers through her hair, letting it fall back across her shoulders and his chest as he played with it. "But it will keep him off our backs for a little while."

"Good." She was silent for a minute before she whispered. "What else happened?"

He stiffened beneath her. "Lexi—"

"I can tell there's something else bothering you. Tell me."

"You don't need to know everything."

"Yes, I do. I'm going to help you defeat this monster; therefore, I have to know as much as possible."

"There's no need for all the horrible details."

"There is when those details are bothering you." She tilted her head back to look up at him. "You were in the shower for a long time; why?"

"There was no other woman, if that's what you're thinking," he said through his teeth.

He wouldn't put it past the Lord to try to make him sleep with other women. He was sure the monster had already considered it and was probably plotting a way to try to coerce Cole into it.

"I know that, but there was something," Lexi said.

Cole lifted his gaze to the ceiling, where the moon shining

through the trees created dancing shadows that called to him. Outside, the crickets chirruped.

He watched the shadows as he idly played with her hair and told her about the fountain and pixies. When he finished, she didn't speak as she caressed his chest.

Then her fingers tiptoed their way up to his chin. She clasped it and turned his head toward her. They stared at each other for a long while before she spoke.

"You did the right thing with the pixie."

"I still don't like it."

Anguish shone in her eyes before she leaned up to kiss him. She was exhausted, and the last thing she needed was him tiring her out more, but the second their lips touched, his body came alive.

It would be so easy to lose himself in her arms, to her tender touch and the warmth and love she emanated, but when her tongue stroked his lips, he pulled back a little.

"You should rest," he told her.

"I already rested."

"Lexi—"

"I'll take a nap tomorrow."

He didn't get the chance to respond before she hooked her leg over his and pulled herself on top of him. Resting her hands on his chest, she smiled as she pulled off her T-shirt.

She wore nothing beneath it. The moonlight caressed her skin, but out of its direct rays, she didn't react to it like she did the sun earlier.

When she tossed her shirt aside, his hands clenched on her hips while he drank her in. Bending, her mouth found his again, and their tongues entwined. The sweet taste of her washed away the bitterness of the memories haunting him.

As they kissed, she slid her arms around his neck and pressed her breasts against his chest. His cock throbbed in anticipation, but he didn't rush it. Instead, he savored her as he ran his palms along her back and down to her hips.

They spent a lot of time exploring each other, touching, and tasting and arousing. Eventually, they untangled enough for her to kiss her way down his body to his shaft.

When she took him into her mouth, his hips lifted off the bed, and he groaned as she tasted and teased him until he was on the verge of coming. When he couldn't take any more of her exquisite torture, he grasped her arms and drew her back up.

Clasping her hips, he flipped her over on the bed. She giggled before biting her lip to stifle it; she gave him a sexy smile and wiggled her hips enticingly.

She knew she was driving him nuts, but two could play that game.

With slow, deliberate movements, he kissed her belly as he moved lower, but when her legs spread wider and her hips arched up, he grasped her waist and turned her over. Lexi gasped as he leveled himself over top of her.

Clasping her hands, he nudged her thighs apart with his leg. And then, he slid his hand between her legs to caress her wetness.

She buried her face in the pillow as she moaned. Leaning over her, he kissed her shoulder and then her cheek as he guided his dick into her.

~

LEXI'S FINGERS curled into the sheets as Cole's body covered hers and his heavy weight pushed her into the mattress. The sensation wasn't uncomfortable; in fact, she enjoyed it because it reminded her that he was alive and *here*, and for tonight, nothing could tear them apart.

The future was so very uncertain, but here, in this room, everything was right. When his fingers entwined with hers, she grasped them and lifted her hips to meet his slow thrusts.

She forgot that she was changing into something none of them were familiar with, that the Lord wanted them dead, and the countless other horrors in this brutal world as he possessed her.

While they moved together, her love for him grew until it radiated outward almost as much as the light she emitted earlier. When he started feeding on her, the gentle tug of the sexual energy he absorbed aroused her further.

He released one of her hands and slid his palm down her belly to the junction between her legs. She reacted as if she'd grabbed a live wire when his finger stroked her clit before he moved it in a circular motion that almost made her scream.

Before she did cry out, she recalled the others in the manor and bit her lip as she turned into the pillow again. When she came, it muffled her loud cry.

Cole's fangs pierced her shoulder, marking her as his mate again. His bite muted his loud groan of pleasure, and the sound of it sent a thrill through her as his seed filled her.

CHAPTER SIXTY-SEVEN

WHEN COLE MET the others in the library the next morning, the scent of coffee brewing and bacon cooking on the stove filled the downstairs. Orin and Varo sipped coffee while Del flipped through the pages of an old book.

Sahira and Brokk shifted nervously from foot to foot as they stood near the fireplace. They'd had too much coffee already, or they were eager to be free of the stone. He suspected it was the latter.

The drapes remained closed over the windows, but it was still early enough the sun hadn't risen yet. They had a few hours before the stone had to go back, but Brokk knocked on their door early that morning, waking Lexi and him.

Cole wasn't happy to discover himself still sleeping in her bed, but she smiled and nuzzled closer. "*This* is where you belong," she'd muttered happily.

Cole wasn't anywhere near as happy. He hated that he'd put her at risk, but he'd made it through the night with her in his arms.

More than that, for the first time since the war ended, he hadn't experienced any nightmares. It was as if she chased them away.

If anyone could, it was Lexi, but he was still afraid they would come back, or she wouldn't keep them away. And if they returned, he could attack her again.

But she wasn't going to let him return to sleeping in chairs or on the floor; truth be told, after *finally* getting a really good night of rest, he didn't want to do that either. Waking to find her in his arms had been as exhilarating as it was terrifying.

Cole loathed the idea of putting her at risk, but unless something drastic happened again, he wouldn't sleep apart from her anymore. He had to make sure he didn't hurt her. He wasn't sure how to do that, but he would figure it out.

"Where's Lexi?" Sahira asked.

"Upstairs getting dressed, but she's not coming with us," Cole said.

Though the crones were mostly retired from the immortals, *no* one else could see Lexi in the light until they were ready to fight the Lord. Instead, she would remain here with Del, Orin, and Varo while he went with Brokk and Sahira.

He didn't like leaving her again so soon after returning from the Lord, but they would need the witches and crones on their side in the future. Besides, he should thank the generosity the crones showed by allowing them to use the harrow stone.

"I'll get the harrow stone," Sahira said, "and open the portal when I return."

"Are you strong enough to open it?" Brokk inquired. "Or would you prefer if I did it?"

"They'll sense if it's not a witch opening it and might attack if it's a vamp. That spell drained me, but I have enough energy to open a portal."

She left the room and returned less than a minute later. With her shoulders back, she glided over to the fireplace and set the stone on the mantel. Her mahogany hair was in its customary bun, and her amber eyes glinted with determination as she turned back to the room.

With a wave of her hands and a few muttered words, she opened a portal and lifted the stone from the mantle.

"We should go soon," Sahira said as Lexi stepped into the doorway.

"Good morning, everyone," Lexi greeted with a smile that warmed Cole's heart.

"We were getting ready... OW!" Sahira cried.

Cole turned toward her as smoke coiled from Sahira's hand, and she released the stone. It glowed like it was on fire as it plummeted toward the ground. Just before it would have crashed into the floor, it stopped. For a few seconds, it hovered above the ground.

"What the...?"

Whatever Brokk was about to say died away as the stone shot like a bullet across the room toward Lexi. Her hand flew to her chest, and she staggered away as the stone stopped to hover a couple of inches away from her face.

Her eyes widened as the stone's radiance grew. Cole was too stunned to move at first, but then panic slammed his heart against his ribs, and he lurched forward. He had no idea what was happening with the stone, but he didn't want it near Lexi.

Then the stone began to shine brighter. It bathed the room in a brilliant red glow that illuminated her sun-kissed skin and reflected in her now golden eyes.

Awe parted her mouth and caused her eyebrows to rise. Cole was sure his astonishment mirrored hers, but he didn't know what was happening. He was only a few feet away when the stone swung forward and hit the hand Lexi had lifted to tuck a loose strand of hair behind her ear.

"No!" Sahira shouted.

Cole was reaching for Lexi when a loud pop reverberated through the air, and she flew backward out of the library.

CHAPTER SIXTY-EIGHT

"No!" Cole bellowed as he sprinted out the door.

Lexi had hit the wall opposite the library so hard she dented it. After the impact, her body hung in the air for a second before sliding to the ground.

Her head fell forward, and her chin rested against her chest. Her hands fell open at her sides, and the stone landed in one of her open palms. And then, she didn't move at all.

She was so still.

Too still!

He was almost to her side when something slammed into him, knocking him off course. Arms encircled his waist as he toppled to the ground. Turning into the embrace, Cole prepared to kill whoever was keeping him from Lexi.

Fury rocked him when he spotted Brokk. His brother rolled with him, but before Cole could tear his head off, Brokk leapt to his feet and danced away.

"Don't touch her!" Brokk shouted at him. "She's holding the stone! If you touch her, it will kill you."

He didn't say kill you *too*, probably because he knew Cole

would lose his mind if she died. And how could she be anything other than dead? The stone was cursed; they *all* knew that.

No one other than the immortal granted access to it was allowed to touch it. It killed anyone else who dared to try. How could she possibly be alive?

Terror buried his rage as his gaze swung to Lexi. She hadn't purposely touched it; the thing had sought *her* out. And then it had fallen into *her* hand.

How could she be made to bear the brunt of this curse when it hadn't been her choice to touch the stone?

He couldn't lose her; he'd tear every one of the realms apart if he did. He would shred everyone and everything in his way. As the murderous impulses churned in his mind, the shadows lurking in the hallway crept closer.

Through his strengthening bond with them, he sensed their excitement. They would help him to destroy everyone in his way. They would welcome the blood, just as they had in his nightmare.

Cole almost pulled them closer to him, but he realized that though Lexi should be dead, he didn't feel the loss of his mate through his mark on her.

If he did, he wouldn't be able to keep control of what was building inside him. And the first place he would unleash it was on the crone realm. If she died, he would make the crones pay for her death.

Cole shoved himself to his feet as something vile and volatile clawed at his insides. He'd never experienced anything like it before, but it felt as if someone had turned a hundred rats loose inside him, and every one of them was trying to dig their way out.

The shadows of the hall shifted and slid toward him while the shadows residing inside him woke. They screamed for vengeance and roared to be set free, but he kept them restrained.

The only enemy here was the stone, and the shadows couldn't destroy it. And that *thing* might be the only chance he had of saving her. He didn't care what it took; the crones would break the curse.

Already at Lexi's side, Sahira knocked Lexi's hand to the side, and the stone tumbled out. "Lexi?" Sahira whispered as she brushed the hair back from Lexi's face.

Clasping Lexi's cheeks, she lifted her head to peer at her pale face and nearly bloodless lips. He'd seen dead bodies that weren't as pale as her.

Orin and Varo hovered in the library's doorway while Del knelt at Lexi's other side. Brokk remained standing between him and Lexi. The look on his brother's face, as he glanced nervously between them, said he'd prefer to crawl into a pit of vipers.

"She's alive," Cole stated as he stalked toward them.

For how long, he didn't know, but he would save her.

Brokk held up his hands and backed away from him. Orin and Varo remained where they were. Varo watched with frightened eyes while Orin's gaze went from Cole to Lexi and back again. His brother was calculating exactly how close Cole was to losing it.

"Yes," Sahira said. When Del leaned closer to her, Sahira waved him back. "Don't touch her. I'm not sure how the curse works now that it's activated. If you touch her, it could spread to you."

Sahira turned her attention to the stone. The brilliant glow was gone, but when she tried to lift it, she yelped and jerked her fingers away. She stared at it in disbelief.

"It certainly no longer welcomes my touch," Sahira muttered.

She turned her hand over to reveal the nasty burn in the middle of her palm and two on the tips of her fingers.

"What is going on?" Del demanded.

"I don't know," Sahira said. "She should be dead, and because she touched it…." Her voice trailed off as she looked at Brokk.

"We're next," he said.

"We're next," she confirmed.

"Who put the curse on the stone?" Cole growled.

Sahira turned toward him, and when her gaze met his, her mouth opened, but she didn't speak. He didn't know what she saw on his face, but she leaned away from him.

"Cole...." Orin started, but he closed his mouth and glanced at Brokk, who shook his head in warning.

"Who controls the curse?" Cole enunciated.

"Kaylia gave us the stone."

"Take me to her."

"I... uh... I don't think it's such a good idea for you to enter the crone realm right now. I'll go—"

"No," Cole said. "Take me to her. Now."

Sahira glanced nervously at the others.

"Cole, the crones won't take kindly to you... ah... entering their realm like this," she said. "You have to calm down."

"I don't give a *fuck* what they take kindly to. They are going to save her."

"I'll go with you," Brokk offered.

"Um... yeah... ah... okay," she whispered.

"I'll come too," Varo said.

"No," Cole said harshly. "We did all of this to ensure everyone believed you were dead. Even if they know the stone was supposed to be used on you, you're not going to waltz into the crone realm and confirm it."

Varo glanced at Orin, whose mouth remained clamped shut.

"Let's go," Cole snarled.

Brokk strode toward the library doors, but Sahira hesitated as she brushed Lexi's hair back from her face. With tender care, she adjusted Lexi to lie on the ground with the stone near her side. Then she lifted Lexi's hands and examined them before setting them on the floor.

"Don't let anyone touch her," she said to Del, who nodded.

"Is she going to be okay?" he asked anxiously.

Cole didn't miss the doubt in Sahira's eyes when she met her brother's gaze. He also noted that she didn't reply.

The rage building inside him was becoming a bomb waiting to blow, and if this Kaylia didn't agree to save Lexi, she would get the brunt of it.

As Cole strode into the library, more shadows slid toward him, caressed his skin, and slipped inside him. He didn't care who he had to kill or destroy; he would save Lexi.

CHAPTER SIXTY-NINE

WHEN THEY FIRST ENTERED THE crone realm, the sweet, lyrical notes of the pixies filled the air, but their song was fading away as more and more became aware of their presence. And it was obvious it was a hostile presence as Cole stalked relentlessly forward.

Brokk didn't know what to say or do as he trailed Cole and Sahira toward Kaylia's lodge. He remained behind in case someone decided to go after Cole; he would have his brother's back. If someone tried to attack Cole, it would be the worst mistake they ever made.

He had no idea exactly what would happen then, but it would be *bad*. If Cole wasn't his brother, he'd be terrified of the man and the blackness oozing from his pores to form a small cloud around him.

But it *was* his brother. So then why was he growing increasingly scared of the man in front of him?

Cole had always been one of the most admirable and steadfast men Brokk knew. He wouldn't do anything crazy; he wouldn't harm an innocent to get what he wanted, but...

But staring at him, Brokk wasn't so sure this was the Cole he'd always known. The trials had changed him, his bond to Lexi had made him stronger, and he was a lycan whose mate was in danger.

All those things made for a *very* dangerous combination—one that might unleash on this realm if Kaylia wasn't able to help them.

The crones stopped what they were doing to watch as they passed. They held their brooms closer, stopped stirring their cauldrons, edged closer to the phoenixes, and watched them with wary eyes. And then they started to follow.

Brokk kept an eye on the crones as they weaved their way through the lodges to the biggest one in the center. So far, none of the crones had been foolish enough to try to stop them or attack them, but that would change if Cole released whatever was going on inside him.

He did not want to be attacked by a bunch of crones. They'd probably turn him into a toad or crisp fry his ass.

He had no idea what was about to unfold, but these witches already despised him and Sahira because of their vampire blood. They'd come up with an extra cruel punishment for him, if they didn't kill him outright.

With every step they took, more darkness seeped out of Cole. The witches might try to curse them or blow them up, but he had no idea what Cole on edge would produce. He'd never seen anything like what was unraveling before him, and it *was* an unraveling.

It had started the second the stone blasted Lexi into the wall. The black emerged then as madness filled his brother's eyes. And that unraveling had sent tendrils of black across the whites of his eyes.

It had pushed aside the *lycan* whose *mate* was threatened. He found that the most unsettling aspect of all this.

Everyone knew a lycan with a threatened mate was the deadliest creature in all the realms, but whatever was inside Cole was stronger. Brokk saw the second when the lycan gave way to the black taking over.

Brokk gulped and almost tugged at the collar of his shirt, but he wouldn't let anyone else know how much *this* Cole unsettled him. Instead, he wiped his sweaty palms on his pants as he studied the crones creeping closer to them as more emerged from their lodges.

The now silent pixies zipped away while the unicorns stopped munching grass to watch them. A couple of pegasus took flight and soared low over the land. Brokk didn't see any sasquatches by the lake, but they weren't always there.

The phoenixes by Kaylia's lodge roused from their slumber and lifted their heads. The tufts of gold on their heads stood up in all different directions. They blinked their amber eyes and looked as if they were trying to process what was happening. One released a small squawk, but none took flight.

One of the older ones opened its wings and swept the babies close against it. When its wings settled around the chicks, they vanished. Brokk hoped they could keep the young protected as Sahira stopped before Kaylia's lodge.

Sahira raised her arm to knock on the flap, but before she could hit it, the flap pulled back, and Kaylia emerged. Her undeniable beauty struck Brokk like a fist to the gut.

He hadn't thought he could react to anything other than the growing tension settling over the land; he was wrong. He didn't like the woman, but he hoped she didn't do anything stupid enough to get herself killed.

As Kaylia surveyed the three of them, the only reaction she showed to Cole was a slight widening of her pewter-gray eyes before she focused on Sahira.

However, she couldn't completely conceal the fact Cole alarmed her. Her face remained impassive, but her shoulders tensed while she spoke.

"You're back," Kaylia stated. "Did the spell work?"

"Yes," Sahira replied.

Kaylia held her palm out to Sahira. "Good. I'll take the stone."

"We had to leave it behind," Sahara said. Her eyes also darted to Cole before settling on Kaylia again. "There was an incident with it."

"What do you mean there was an *incident*? Where is the stone?"

"Someone touched it," Sahira said.

"So why would that make it so you couldn't return the stone to me? They're already dead, you'll die soon, and it will be your fault for allowing such a thing to happen."

Brokk winced when the darkness spread around Cole until it obscured parts of Kaylia's lodge. The crone had to realize she was playing with fire, and if she didn't, she was an idiot.

And while she was an abrasive, unlikeable ass, he didn't take her for an idiot.

"We did not *allow* such a thing to happen," Cole snarled. "She didn't touch the *fucking* thing willingly."

Kaylia's face remained blank as she studied Cole. Brokk shifted uneasily. *Choose your words wisely.*

"Did you force it into her hand?" Kaylia asked Sahira.

"I would never do such a thing!" Sahira retorted. "And she's not dead."

It took Kaylia a few seconds to cover her shock. "Not dead?"

"No."

"Then she will be soon. I don't see what the problem is here."

So much for choosing your words wisely, Brokk thought with a sigh.

The woman knew something wasn't right with Cole, but she was too stubborn to walk on eggshells in her realm. If he wasn't afraid Lexi might die and his brother would lose his shit, he might respect and admire Kaylia for her courage.

Instead, he considered shaking some sense into the infuriating creature.

"The problem is," Cole grated, "she is *not* going to die. And *you* are going to save her."

Brokk barely recognized Cole's voice anymore as what came out of his brother was a strange mixture of something guttural and inhuman. And he swore it was also a mixture of *different* voices, but that wasn't possible.

"When they took the stone, I told them what would happen if another touched it. They will also reap the consequences of this," Kaylia said. "I will not interfere in the curse."

Cole stepped closer to Kaylia, and Brokk felt a fracturing inside his brother as something cracked across the air. He started to reach for Cole, but his hand froze as more blackness seeped out of him.

CHAPTER SEVENTY

"DID you set up the stone to kill innocents?" Cole hissed in that strange, inhuman voice.

"Of course not," Kaylia retorted. "A witch would never do that. If they did, they would suffer the consequences of it, and we *never* hurt innocents. If she sought to use the stone's power when it wasn't given to her—"

"She didn't seek anything of the sort."

Brokk had known Cole his whole life; they'd fought together, played together, killed for each other, and been the best of companions, but his brother's voice wasn't just *almost* unrecognizable anymore... he didn't recognize it *at all.*

For the first time, Brokk wasn't just unnerved by the power emanating from his brother; he was also scared he was losing his best friend.

"Cole," he said.

He sucked in a breath when his brother's gaze swung toward him, but Kaylia drew his attention away again when she spoke.

"If you've come here to threaten us, then all you'll succeed in doing is unleashing hell upon yourself. You may be the king of the dark fae, but there are many of us here, and we will fight you."

When Cole stepped toward Kaylia, her chin rose and her head tipped back. Brokk moved forward to intervene if Cole tried to kill her, but he wasn't so sure his brother wouldn't kill *him*. That was a thought he never believed he'd have with Cole.

If Cole believed Brokk was standing in the way of saving Lexi's life, he would smack him down.

"She did *not* seek out the stone; it sought *her* out," Cole replied.

This time, it sounded as if dozens of different voices issued from Cole. Confusion swam in Kaylia's eyes. Finally giving way to common sense over pride, she edged away from Cole. Brokk suspected she'd realized she was dealing with something more than the king of the dark fae.

"I don't understand," she said.

"The stone. Sought *her*. Out," Cole said through his teeth.

With every clearly enunciated word, shadows slid across the earth toward them. The ones beneath the phoenixes slipped away to leave the ground bare and exposed.

Moving like snakes escaping a fire, they twisted their way toward Cole. Brokk sidestepped some of them as they slid beneath his feet. He knew they were just shadows and couldn't harm him, but something about all of this felt completely wrong.

When he exchanged a glance with Sahira, he was certain the horror on her face more than mirrored his. He wanted to reach out to his brother, connect with him, and bring him out of whatever held him.

He didn't move.

Though they'd fought countless battles together, nearly been killed more times than he could recall, and killed more than he ever wanted to remember, he didn't know the man before him.

It wasn't just that Cole was losing it; something far more sinister was unfolding here, and he had no idea what it was or how it could be possible. He wasn't as connected to the earth as the witches, but even he felt a shift in the world around them.

Then one of the shadows surrounding Cole twisted around and rose over the top of his brother as Cole hissed out. "If you take one more step, I'll take that pouch you're holding and choke you with it."

The hair on Brokk's nape rose. Slowly, he turned his head to see that one of the crones had approached and had her hand in a pouch.

Brokk's mouth went dry as he tried to understand what was happening. He hadn't seen the woman coming, and there was *no way* Cole could have seen her.

Brokk turned his attention back to his brother. Cole's back remained to the woman, but the shadow remained raised over him like a scorpion's tail about to deliver its killing blow.

Cole never could have seen the woman or the pouch, but the shadow could. But how did a shadow report anything to anyone? How could a shadow *see* anything?

The more he tried to make sense of what was happening, the more lost he felt. His head spun as he looked from the crone to Cole and finally to Kaylia, whose mouth had parted.

Then his hand dropped to the blade at his side. No matter what was happening here, it was still his duty to protect his brother.

He was about to pull his sword free, but the crone removed her hand from the pouch and backed away. The shadow behind Cole didn't turn away; instead, it remained twisted to survey the crowd.

Sahira's hand went to her mouth as the crones started whispering as more shadows slid toward Cole....

No, that wasn't right. The fucking things were slithering *into* him.

He'd never seen anything like what was happening, and he hoped never to see it again, but he couldn't tear his eyes away. The shadows filling Cole oozed back out of him in a way that made him look as if he were ten feet tall.

They also seemed to be protecting him as more of them rose to survey the crowd. Some of the formations even looked like *wings*.

And maybe they *were* protecting him, but what else are they doing?

Destroying him.

And once Brokk had that thought, he couldn't rid himself of it. Whatever was happening here, whatever Cole had undergone during the trials, it was destroying him.

Brokk didn't know if it was because Cole was only half fae and therefore unable to handle the power granted him after the trials or not. And it didn't matter.

What caused this was not the issue. All that mattered was making sure his brother didn't completely lose himself in trying to save Lexi.

Then the whispers of the crones pierced through his confused and jumbled ruminations.

"My gods and goddesses," some of them whispered.

"Hecate save us," others murmured.

But amid all the whispers, a stronger one was growing and spreading. More and more crones were uttering four words over and over again...

"It's the Shadow Reaver."

CHAPTER SEVENTY-ONE

"YOU WILL COME WITH US," Cole told the crone, Kaylia, he recalled her name was. "And you will save her, or I will level this realm. I swear it."

The woman searched his face as she stared at him with a look of dawning horror. Throughout their entire exchange, she'd kept her uneasiness of him well hidden; he'd sensed it, but she refused to let it show.

It was there now as her heartbeat increased, and she took a small step away from him. He'd never wanted others to fear him before, to respect him, yes, but not to tremble at his approach like they did the Lord.

He no longer cared about that. He hoped her fear got her to cave to his will, because if it didn't, he'd meant what he said. And if these witches refused to help him reverse the curse they created, he wouldn't feel one ounce of remorse over doing it. He'd make them suffer for what they did to her.

This entire realm would be nothing but ashes by the time he finished with it, and then he would move on to the Lord. Because if Lexi wasn't alive, then there was nothing holding him back from unleashing his wrath upon that bastard too, even if it killed him.

He was on the verge of losing it, but whereas for most of his life, he prided himself on his levelheadedness, he didn't now. Lexi had rattled that rational side of him when his lycan half recognized her as its mate and sought to claim her.

Cole lost some of his control then, but this was different and worse than anything he'd endured after meeting her.

As the whispers around them grew louder, Cole caught some of what they said. He didn't pay much attention to them, and his main focus remained on the woman across from him.

"Did you put the curse on the stone?" he demanded.

"I... I..." Her voice quivered before her eyes narrowed. "I did."

"Can you remove it?"

She looked toward the shadows creeping toward him. He was aware of them stealing into his body and gathering around him; he welcomed their power.

He had no idea how they would help him do it, but he *knew* he could somehow unleash these shadows on this realm, just as he'd unleashed them on Orin. Then he'd been trying to hold back because, although his brother had pissed him off, he was still Cole's brother.

These crones were nothing to him.

No, that wasn't right. They were the women who held his mate's life in their hands, and they would fix it.

Kaylia's gaze flicked to one of the women to his left, and from the corner of his eye, Cole couldn't see her, but the shadows could. He didn't understand it and didn't question it, but he did welcome this growing connection to them and the new sets of eyes the shadows offered.

The shadows saw the woman give a brief nod while the others hovered nervously around her. He kept his attention focused on Kaylia, but the shadows watched his back.

"I can remove the curse," Kaylia said. "*If* she's still alive."

Brokk's head dropped into his hand. Sahira closed her eyes as if Kaylia's words hurt her. Something inside Cole recoiled and broke at the possibility Lexi may have already succumbed to the curse.

A hiss filled the air. It took Cole a couple of seconds to realize it was coming from the shadows. It wasn't quite a serpentine hiss, but something more, something darker and harsher. Something that promised death and the kind of agony he would endure if Lexi were dead.

"I will come with you to see what I can do," Kaylia offered.

"Thank you, Kaylia," Sahira breathed.

"We'll use the portal you came through."

"I closed it when we arrived," Sahira said.

Cole wouldn't let Sahira leave it open and take the chance someone might go through it and discover Lexi.

"I'll open one to return," Brokk offered.

"Fine," Kaylia replied.

"You're not able to open one into the manor," Sahira said. "I've only granted Cole permission, and I'm not strong enough to open another portal right now."

Brokk didn't look offended by this. "Understandable."

"I will do it," Cole growled.

He reined in the shadows seeking to strike out and drew them closer to him. They encased his arms, wrapped around his chest, and gripped his legs, but they didn't make moving difficult as he opened another portal a few feet away.

The shadows' steady, constant presence lent him power as they slid beneath his skin and out across the ground. When they spread, the crones closest to them backed away. They gazed at him from wide eyes and pale faces that would have bothered him before, but it sparked no emotion in him now.

He'd intended to come here today to offer them thanks for the stone, but *that* wasn't going to happen. Their fear had gotten Kaylia to agree to leave with them; that was all he cared about now.

Cole didn't take his gaze off Kaylia's back as she walked with her head held high toward the portal. He didn't trust her not to change her mind and try to make a run for it, but she remained calm and docile as she entered it.

Cole glanced back to make sure no one followed them. No one so much as breathed as he stepped into the portal.

When they returned to the library, he turned and closed the portal immediately after leaving it. The fireplace came back into view. Cole studied it for a minute as he took a deep breath and tried to prepare himself for the possibility Lexi was dead.

There was no way to prepare for it. He simply had to face what was to come.

On the journey through the portal, he'd relinquished most of the shadows, sending them back to where they belonged. He could draw more in if it became necessary to scare Kaylia into helping them.

And if Lexi were dead, he wouldn't need the shadows to help him destroy the crone. The witches and crones would declare war on him if he killed her, but he didn't care.

And if Lexi was still alive, then he had to get this woman to her now.

"This way," he commanded.

He strode across the room and into the hall. The few shadows he'd kept with him stayed by his side while he walked.

Lexi remained where Sahira had left her on the floor. Varo and Del sat beside her; their hands were close to hers but not touching. Orin stood near the front door, leaning against the wall with his arms folded over his chest. He stood away from the wall when Cole strode into the hallway.

"Co-Cole?" Del asked incredulously.

"We brought help," Cole said. "Is she still alive?"

Even he heard the raw anguish in his voice, but at least it was *his* voice again and not whatever came out of him in the crones' realm. If they managed to get through this, he would have to figure out what was going on with him and the shadows. But that could, and *would*, wait.

"Yes," Varo answered.

"Move away from her," Cole commanded.

Cole turned toward Kaylia as she glided out of the library and across the hall toward them. Her head tilted to the side while she studied Lexi before kneeling beside her. She went to lift the harrow stone, but the second her fingers touched it, she squeaked and ripped her hand away.

Smoke coiled up from the burns at the ends of her fingers. The incredulous expression on her face soon turned to anger.

CHAPTER SEVENTY-TWO

"WHAT DID YOU DO TO IT?" Kaylia demanded as she cradled her hand and glowered at Sahira.

"Nothing," Sahira said. "It worked great for the spell, and it was perfectly normal when we were getting ready to bring it back to you. But that abruptly changed. I was holding it when it suddenly burnt my hand. When I released it, it nearly hit the floor before it stopped and flew across the room to Lexi."

Kaylia blinked at her. "That's impossible."

"It's what happened!" Cole snapped. "It must be part of your curse."

"That's impossible. Nothing like that has *ever* happened before. The few times the stone has gone out, it has always returned to us the same, and it has *never* flown across the room at someone."

Then her attention shifted back to Lexi, and the look on her face was one of disbelief. She gawked for a few seconds before shaking her head as if she were trying to clear it.

"What happened when it flew across the room to her. Did it hit her? Did it hit the ground and bounce into her? Did she try to smack it away out of instinct? Tell me everything," Kaylia said.

Sahira looked at Cole as if she were unsure if she should say anything more, and no one else spoke. Cole wasn't sure how much to reveal to this woman. They needed her to save Lexi, but they also had to keep Lexi's heritage a secret.

"I can't help you, or *her*, if you don't tell me *everything* that happened," Kaylia said.

Cole debated this for a few seconds before he nodded to Sahira. If this woman learned too much, he could always kill her. She wasn't entirely innocent in all of this, and if it came between her life and Lexi's, there was no choice.

"The stone flew across the room and stopped before her," Sahira said. "As it hovered in the air before her, it started to glow. She lifted her hand to brush back some hair, and the stone flew at her hand. The second they connected, the stone launched her off her feet and into the wall."

Kaylia's head tipped back, and she took in the dent in the wall. "*That* was the curse, but it should have killed her. The fact she's still alive…."

Her voice trailed off as her eyes fell on Lexi again. Unlike in the crone realm, where she kept her emotions mostly hidden, her disbelief, awe, and uncertainty were evident.

"The stone shouldn't have reacted like that. She *shouldn't* be…" she hesitated before whispering, "alive."

There was something about the words that made Cole wonder if she meant *now* or at all. He was beginning to suspect she knew more than she was letting on and had really meant to say Lexi shouldn't exist.

"Don't," Cole warned when she stretched a hand toward Lexi.

Her fingers froze in the air, and she twisted toward Cole. "If I'm going to help her, you have to let me touch her."

"How do I know you're not going to make it worse?" Cole demanded.

"Because I don't want to die, and you're going to kill me if *she* dies, aren't you?"

"Yes," he confirmed.

The only one who didn't suck in a loud breath was Orin.

"I thought so," Kaylia said.

She turned her attention back to Lexi. Her fingers moved toward the harrow stone but stopped when they were a few centimeters away. And then she grasped Lexi's hands and turned them over to examine them.

"Did the stone burn *her?*" Kaylia asked.

"No," Sahira said. "I checked before we went to the crone realm. She had no burn marks on her."

Kaylia set Lexi's hands down. As she did, Lexi's pinky brushed the harrow stone, and a spark of light flashed inside it. Kaylia's hand trembled as she lifted Lexi's and turned it over once more, but no burn marred her flesh.

"Oh, Hecate," she breathed. "Oh, it can't be."

Cole no longer had any doubt this woman knew what Lexi was and therefore posed a threat to her.

"Is she...?" Kaylia gulped, and her shoulders hunched up as if she could feel the weight of Cole's stare on her back. She finished in a tremulous whisper. "Is she arach?"

When no one spoke, some of the color came back into Kaylia's face, her shoulders went back, and she met Cole's eyes. "If I'm going to help her, I have to know the truth. *Is she arach?*"

He ground his teeth together. He didn't want to kill her if she saved Lexi, but he didn't trust this woman. There was no way she could walk amongst the realms with her knowledge of Lexi's heritage.

But if she didn't have the truth, she might not be able to save Lexi.

"Yes," he confirmed.

Her hands trembled as she rested them against Lexi's face. "How is that possible?"

"How is anything possible?" Sahira asked. "Can you save her?"

"Yes," Kaylia replied. "The stone protected her from the full brunt of the curse; that's why she's still alive. I can remove the curse from her and the stone."

Then she turned to Sahira and Brokk. She examined them like they were alien life-forms she'd never seen before. They both frowned at her in return.

"Neither of you has asked about yourselves in this," Kaylia said.

"We're not the ones lying on the ground right now," Brokk pointed out.

"No, but the curse also affects you, and you *are* vampires."

"What does being a vampire have to do with anything?"

"*No* vampire has ever cared for anything beyond themselves."

"Lady, you've got a lot to learn about vampires," Del said.

"I know all I need to know about the monsters. Sometimes, there is a small exception to the rule, but not when it comes to vamps. Perhaps they didn't ask because they knew it would piss him off," she said and thrust her finger at Cole.

"*This* is pissing me off," Cole said. "Can you lift the curse from all of them?"

Kaylia hesitated before replying. "I can."

"Good, then do it."

Kaylia turned her attention back to the stone. She leaned so close that she was almost kissing it when she whispered a few words Cole didn't hear. When she finished, nothing happened to the stone, but she gave a satisfied nod.

"The curse has been lifted from the stone, which means the two of you will not be affected by it." She glanced pointedly at Brokk and Sahira before turning her attention to Lexi.

Kaylia rested her fingers against Lexi's cheeks. As she leaned closer, Cole watched the small rise and fall of Lexi's chest. If she stopped breathing, he'd tear Kaylia's head off before she realized he'd moved.

Kaylia released Lexi's face and lifted her fingers over Lexi's chest. Her hands rose and fell in a rhythmic, mesmerizing motion.

He couldn't understand the words she spoke, but he thought it might be the language of the ancients. A language he'd believed lost many centuries ago.

If it was the language of the ancients, then there was a lot of power in the words she uttered and the woman herself. The air beneath Kaylia's fingers crackled and popped as she drew on its power. Cole tensed, and the shadows around and inside him stirred.

When he stepped closer to Kaylia, Sahira held out her hand to stop him and gave a subtle shake of her head. He scowled at her, but she didn't back down. Kaylia said something more before bending closer to Lexi.

Her mouth hovered above Lexi's. It was so close they nearly kissed when Kaylia inhaled deeply. From between Lexi's barely parted lips, a tendril of black, wispy smoke rose to hover in the air between them.

Once all the smoke stopped, Kaylia leaned back a little. With a small wave of her hand, Kaylia brushed it aside, and it dissipated in the air before she kissed Lexi's forehead.

"Awaken," she murmured before leaning back and resting her hands on her knees.

Lexi's eyes flew open, and her back arched off the floor as she inhaled a large, gulping breath. Cole's heart leapt in excitement, and he pushed past Kaylia to drop beside Lexi. She coughed and wheezed as he gathered her into his arms and cradled her against his chest.

"It's okay; you're okay," he assured her as he ran his hands over her silken hair.

Her fingers dug into his back as she clung to him, and her entire body shook. The sounds she emitted were ones of terror as her tears wet his neck. She tried to speak, but all that came out were more gasps for air.

"Shh, love," he whispered as he clasped her nape. "Don't try to talk. You're safe now, and I'm not going to let you go. Relax and breathe slowly. In and out. In and out."

He coaxed her through some relaxation techniques until her breathing finally became more natural and her death grip on him eased. Movement from the corner of his eye caught his attention as Kaylia edged away from them.

"Don't you dare try to leave," he told her.

She didn't reply, but Orin and Del stepped closer to keep her penned in.

"You're okay," Cole said again to Lexi when she shuddered. "I've got you. I'm here for you. I love you."

Her only response was to hold him closer. Cole forgot about everyone else in the hall as he buried his face in her hair and inhaled her sweet, strawberry scent.

CHAPTER SEVENTY-THREE

BROKK COULDN'T TEAR his attention away from Cole and Lexi as they held each other. Their evident love for each other warmed his heart and gave him hope for a better future, but it also scared him.

He'd never expected to see Cole like this. He'd known his brother loved Lexi, there was no denying that, but he never thought Cole would go from threatening to destroy a realm—and probably attempting to do so if Kaylia hadn't agreed to leave—to hugging someone so close while whispering words of love.

And as much as this tender moment touched a heart he'd considered mostly deadened since the war, he was aware something was really wrong here. He kept hearing the whispered words of the crones when Cole started to lose control.

What the fuck is a Shadow Reaver?

He glanced at Kaylia and edged closer to her as the rest of them all fell back toward the library to give Lexi and Cole privacy. He maneuvered his way through the others until he stood beside her.

He'd bet she was thrilled by his presence near her, given his monstrous half-vamp status. Del and Orin moved away from her once he took over the responsibility of watching her. They stood near the fireplace but didn't approach as their attention remained on Lexi and Cole.

"I'll get us something to drink," Sahira said.

"Make it something strong," Orin said.

"I'll help you," Varo offered, and the two of them left the room.

"What is the Shadow Reaver?" Brokk whispered to Kaylia when he was sure no one else was close enough to hear him.

Kaylia's striking eyes were troubled when they met his. At first, he didn't think she would answer him—probably because he was part vamp—but then, she spoke.

"It's a witches' legend about a dark, lethal entity who would one day rise to power. They whispered the scary tale around cauldron fires. It was told to misbehaving children to get them to fall in line. It was a ghost story meant to scare and always believed to be nothing more."

"What is the legend exactly?"

"That one day the Shadow Reaver will rise and use the shadows he controls to bring darkness to the world before destroying it. I grew up listening to the story and always believed it was a cautionary tale, a little bit of harmless, scary fun. It was never anything we ever gave much attention, until...."

"Until now," Brokk finished when her voice trailed off. He pondered her words before replying. "Just because the shadows responded to Cole doesn't mean he's this Shadow Reaver thing. All dark fae have some control over the shadows. It's how we cloak ourselves with them."

She gave a small snort of derision. "*No* dark fae has *that* much control over shadows, and we both know it. Those shadows didn't just respond and cloak him; they *obeyed* his command. They were his *eyes*. They let him know things he *never* could have known. Have the shadows ever done that for you?"

Brokk wanted to say yes, but he couldn't. They'd never done

that for him. They'd never done that for anyone he knew… not even his father.

"No," he admitted.

She glanced around to make sure no one else was listening. When she shifted her attention back to him, he saw the dislike in her gaze. But even though she considered him about as likable as dog shit on her shoe, she stepped closer.

"There's more," she whispered.

"I'm all ears."

Her gaze remained riveted on Lexi and Cole while she spoke. "There's a prophecy about the Shadow Reaver too."

"Prophecies are garbage. None of them ever come true."

"Normally, I would agree, but some have come true. Very few, but some."

"Usually the smaller, inconsequential ones. Like the one about a pixie who would have no voice. The pixie who couldn't sing would become king," he quoted.

"And it happened."

"Because he was born a pixie prince who couldn't speak. *That's* how he became king of the pixies."

A small smile twitched at the corners of her mouth. "Yes, that one was rather silly, but someone saw it coming." She nodded her chin at Lexi and Cole. "And someone saw them coming too. Except, this time, I don't think it's going to be as inconsequential."

"Saw *them* coming?"

"Yes, and I can tell you half of this prophecy has already come true."

Brokk watched as Cole settled Lexi in his lap and sat on the floor with her. His head fell into her hair as he nuzzled her cheek.

A look of such pure love and joy lit his face that it awed and frightened Brokk. When he looked at Kaylia, he saw the same emotions playing across her face.

"How is it possible she's an arach?" she whispered.

"That's a long story. Tell me what the prophecy says."

She shot him an irritated look, and when her jaw locked and her nostrils flared, Brokk was certain she wasn't going to speak again, but she did. "I'll tell you, but I want her story too."

"Are you sure? It involves a vampire doing something good."

When fury darkened her face, he realized he probably shouldn't have taken that jab at her, but he couldn't help it. He resented that she'd stuck him into this tiny box without getting to know him, simply because of his bloodline.

"I'm sure," she grated through her teeth.

"Okay then, I'll tell you when we have time, but tell me the prophecy first."

He wasn't sure Cole was going to let her live anyway, so he didn't see the harm in telling her. Hell, he might not get the chance to do so.

"The prophecy states that when the last light shines, the Shadow Reaver shall rise. But when the last light falls, the Shadow Reaver will destroy us all," Kaylia said.

A chill ran down Brokk's spine. If the prophecy was true, then Lexi was definitely the last light. He'd seen the way she reacted to light, and she was the last of her kind. He'd also seen the way the shadows responded to Cole.

"Okay," he said. "So, if by some one-in-a-million chance this prophecy is real, then all we have to do is stop the light from falling."

Which meant they couldn't let Lexi die, and since he had no intention of ever letting that happen, he would make sure it didn't.

"That's far easier said than done, especially given what she is," Kaylia said. "The second the Lord learns of her existence, he'll come after her with everything he has and tear the realms apart to find her."

"Then we will keep him from learning what she is until we're ready. He knows she exists and that she's Cole's mate, but he doesn't know *what* she is."

"How is that possible?"

"She didn't have any powers before and only recently started coming into them."

Kaylia shook her head. "That's impossible. The arach were too strong not to have powers before becoming adults."

"That's part of our other conversation, but we'll keep her safe from the Lord until we're ready to face him."

"Not to state the obvious here, but you just failed at keeping her safe. If the harrow stone wasn't originally an arach possession, the curse would have killed her."

"So *that's* why it reacted to her like it did," he muttered. "It recognized her as its rightful owner."

"Yes, and it also has a *lot* of power. All of which belongs to her now."

"We never could have seen *that* coming. How were we supposed to know about the stone? But we will keep her alive, and we *will* bring down the Lord."

"There are going to be a lot of obstacles you're never going to see coming."

"I know," Brokk said. He was beginning to suspect this woman might be one of them.

"She's also his mate," Kaylia whispered.

"She is."

"No wonder he was so furious, and it will only get worse. Both of their powers are going to keep growing."

And Brokk was afraid neither of them would know how to control them.

He and Kaylia didn't speak as they studied the couple. Lexi pulled back to rest her hand against Cole's cheek before they kissed.

"But if she does fall, or if he can't control whatever has turned him into the Shadow Reaver... because this is a new development for him, is it not?" Kaylia asked.

"It is," Brokk confirmed.

"I thought so. What he can do would have gotten out long ago, and we all would have known about him, if it was something he could always do. But if he can't control what he is becoming and if she *does* die, who will save the rest of us from *him*?"

Brokk didn't reply, mainly because he'd been contemplating the same question before she voiced it. Never in his life had he ever thought Cole could become the enemy, but after what he'd seen today, he was beginning to fear that a bigger danger than the Lord was emerging.

And this one may be the brother he'd always considered his best friend and strongest ally.

∼

Turn the page for a sneak peek of book 4, *Shadows of Fury*, or download now and continue reading: brendakdavies.com/SFuwb

∼

Stay in touch on updates, sales, and new releases by joining to the mailing list: brendakdavies.com/ESBKDNews

Visit the Erica Stevens/Brenda K. Davies Book Club on Facebook for exclusive giveaways and all things book related. Come join the fun: brendakdavies.com/ESBKDBookClub

SNEAK PEEK

SHADOWS OF FURY, THE SHADOW REALMS
BOOK 4

COLE HELD Lexi in his arms as he studied the crone and his brother while they spoke. He couldn't hear what they were saying, but judging by the way their eyes continuously flicked to Lexi and him, *they* were the topic of conversation.

Of course, he couldn't expect anything less after what just transpired with Lexi and the harrow stone, Brokk's face had drained of color and Kaylia looked extremely uneasy, which meant that whatever they were discussing wasn't good.

He imagined they were discussing that Shadow Reaver bullshit the crones were muttering about while he was in their realm, but he didn't care. He'd done what was necessary to save Lexi's life, and even if it meant drawing *every* shadow in *all* the realms to him, he would do it again.

When Lexi shuddered, he squeezed her tighter as he tried not to recall what it was like to stare at her unmoving body while she lay on the floor. That stone had nearly killed her.

He glanced uneasily at the red stone, still lying on the ground only a few feet away. If he could have reached it without disrupting Lexi too much, he would have kicked the thing clear across the room.

Instead, he glowered at it before shifting his attention back to Brokk and the crone. His gaze locked with Kaylia's, and for the first time, true fear shone in her pewter gray eyes. She had a right to be afraid; she had to know he wouldn't let her put Lexi's life in danger.

Which meant she most likely wouldn't leave here alive.

"What should I do with you?" he asked.

Kaylia's shoulders went back as her elegant, blonde eyebrows rose. "What do you mean, *do* with me?"

Lexi stirred in his arms and lifted her head. She was still far too pale but alive and moving, and that was what mattered.

"Yes," Cole said. "*Do* with you."

"You won't be *doing* anything with me. I'm free to do as I please."

When Lexi woke, he'd released the shadows that came to him, but the ones inside him stirred at Kaylia's tone. Recalling how hostile they'd been, he tamped the shadows down again. He *would* keep them away from Lexi.

"No, you won't," he replied. "Not with what you know about her. I can't let you walk free with that knowledge."

"Cole," Lexi whispered.

He kissed her forehead before adjusting his hold on her. He made sure she was comfortable against the wall before releasing her and rising. Kaylia braced her feet apart as she faced off against him.

"It doesn't matter *what* you are," Kaylia said, "or what you can do. If you kill me, the crones will come for you. They'll hunt you down—"

"And what?" Cole demanded. "*What* will they do? I'll burn them *all* down to keep her safe, and anyone else who gets in my *fucking* way."

Kaylia gulped, but she stubbornly raised her chin. "Cole—"

Kaylia cut off whatever Lexi was about to say.

"You're not indestructible, and neither is she!"

Despite his resolve to keep the shadows suppressed, they shifted and stirred inside him. Their power swelled into his fingertips as they sought release. They ached to break free and destroy, but he fisted his hands against the impulse.

No matter what, he didn't want to make enemies of the crones. They would be far better allies than enemies. But he would unleash hell on them if it became necessary.

"Are you threatening her?" Cole's voice started taking on the hint of distortion it held while he was in the crone realm.

∽

"Whoa! Slow down here," Brokk said as he stepped between them and held up his hands.

"Yes," Del said as he moved away from the fireplace and closer to Brokk.

Orin remained standing with his arm resting on the mantle. Though an amused smile curved his lips, his posture said he wasn't as relaxed as he was pretending to be.

Behind him, Lexi placed her hand against the wall and rose. "What is going on? What exactly happened with the stone, with *me*, and the curse? How am I still alive?"

When Kaylia looked at her, Cole growled as he stepped between them. It didn't dissuade Kaylia from speaking to her.

"The stone reacted to you in such a way because it is an *arach* possession, and it recognized *you* as its rightful owner. Unfortunately, the curse still had some effect on you, but the stone protected you from the full brunt of it, so you didn't die. Then *I* removed the curse from the stone so Sahira, this vamp—" Her lip curled in disgust as she jerked her head toward Brokk. "—and you wouldn't die."

Kaylia's gaze shifted back to Cole. "You're welcome."

"Thank you," Lexi breathed.

"Finally, someone with some manners. You're welcome," Kaylia replied with a tight-lipped smile that was far from warm.

"I'm Brokk, *not* vamp," Brokk said to her. "And maybe you should show some manners considering I'm standing between you and my brother who wants *you* dead."

Kaylia glared at him but didn't respond before turning her attention haughtily away. Cole was beginning to like her less and less. *No* one treated his little brother like that.

"You're not going to leave here knowing what you do about her," Cole told her.

"*I* saved her life."

"And you could destroy it by revealing what you've discovered."

"I aligned myself and the rest of the crones with you and your cause when I gave Sahira the harrow stone. There is no turning back for them or me."

"That was before you knew about Lexi," he reminded her.

Sahira and Varo appeared in the hallway. Sahira held a tray of cheese and apple slices while Varo carried one filled with glasses and two decanters. One decanter had a reddish liquid, while the other contained an amber one.

They couldn't see into the library where Kaylia and the others stood, but Cole's stance and Lexi's uneasy glance told them things weren't good. Sahira set her tray on one of the stairs, and Varo did the same before coming closer. They stayed to the side of Cole but positioned themselves so they could see into the library.

Lexi rested her hand on his arm and stepped out from behind him. "Thank you for everything you've done, including letting us use the stone," she said.

"Don't thank her; she's a danger to you," Cole said.

"No, I'm not," Kaylia replied as she focused on Lexi. "Not only did I save your life, but when I gave you and your friends the harrow stone, I put my own life, and the lives of those I love, at risk. I'm not going to turn you over to the Lord; he'll kill me once he learns of my role in this."

"She's clearly not the enemy," Lexi said.

Orin groaned and dropped his head into his hand. "Save me from the ones with hearts and scruples."

"Oh, shut up!" Lexi snapped. "She's helped us multiple times."

"Yes, please shut up," Del said. "You're not helping the problem."

"She cannot leave here with the knowledge of what you are," Cole said. "None of the other crones know of your heritage, and it has to stay that way."

"I wouldn't tell them," Kaylia replied. "Not until you're prepared for the war her existence will bring, or until you give me permission to do so. With her abilities—"

"What *are* my abilities?" Lexi interrupted.

"How do you not know?" Kaylia blurted.

"Lexi," Cole warned. "We can't trust her."

"But I do."

"For fuck's sake," Orin muttered.

"I trust her too," Varo murmured in his soothing way that took a small edge off Cole's distrust.

"Oh, goodie," Orin said. "Now we have *two* of you with scruples. We're never going to win this war."

"Yes, we will," Kaylia retorted.

Cole's eyebrows rose over the vehemence in her tone. She'd just gotten involved in this, but for the first time, he believed she might be on their side and wouldn't have to die.

"I trust her as much as I do you," Del said and shot a pointed look at Orin.

Cole suspected it would be a long time before his friend forgave Orin for imprisoning him. But they would work together, for Lexi's sake. That didn't mean either of them was going to like it… which was evident as they scowled at each other.

"Why don't you know about your abilities?" Kaylia asked again. "*How* have you managed to stay hidden for so long?"

"How did you end up with the harrow stone if it's an arach possession?" Brokk asked.

"What about my questions?" Kaylia asked.

"Later," Cole replied brusquely.

Kaylia sighed, and one of her eyes twitched as she spoke. "I knew some arach; that's how I ended up with the harrow stone. When the war between them was really starting to ramp up, my friend Fenmenor showed me how to use the harrow stone and gave it to me for safekeeping.

"I placed the curse on the stone because I wasn't as capable as an arach to guard it. I figured that when he returned for it, I would remove the curse, but I never saw him again."

Cole wasn't sure if it was an act or what, but he saw true emotion in the crone's eyes for the first time. That sheen in them might have been tears, but she blinked them away too fast for him to be certain.

"So, the arach trusted you," Lexi said.

"Fenmenor did, and I knew others too," Kaylia replied. "I can help you with your abilities."

"Do you know what her abilities *are*?" Cole demanded.

∾

"WELL," Kaylia hedged. "No, not really. The arach were very private about that and kept a lot of what they could do hidden. But I can show you how to use the stone, we know they could withstand fire, and we also know they could throw fire. You must be able to do those things."

"Not yet," Lexi admitted.

"And why not? No one has answered that for me yet."

"Because we kept her powers suppressed from the time she

was a baby," Sahira replied. "We believed it was the best way to keep her safe."

"Who did?"

"Me and my brother," Sahira said and nodded toward Del.

"They're my aunt and my dad," Lexi said. "They kept me alive and safe."

"She didn't know what she truly was until recently," Del said.

Kaylia studied Del like he was some kind of alien frog monster. "*You* took care of her."

"I told you, you have a lot to learn about vampires," Del replied.

"He's a great dad," Lexi said defensively. "I never would have guessed he wasn't my real father or that Sahira wasn't my aunt until they told me the truth. I've always been loved, and if you don't like them, then we *are* going to have a problem."

Cole smiled at the crone while her mouth opened and closed as she tried to form words and failed.

"We're not going to have a problem," Kaylia finally said. "I'm just surprised to learn such a thing about vampires."

"We're not monsters," Brokk retorted.

"Most of you are."

"That's enough," Lexi interjected. "I understand you may be able to help, but these are my friends and family. I won't let you treat them like shit. I'd prefer you didn't help with this if it means you're going to treat them badly."

Which meant Cole would have to kill her or lock her away somewhere.

Kaylia's shoulders went back again. "You need my help, and I can give it. Few are more in tune with nature and magical abilities than me. I am the oldest living witch, and I can sense and intuit things no others can."

"This is true," Sahira said. "Kaylia is an extremely powerful witch who has helped many master their abilities."

"Many *witches*," Cole said. "She knows what witches are capable of doing; she doesn't know what the arach can do."

"That is true, but I can help her figure it out," Kaylia insisted.

"And why would you do that?"

"She is"—Kaylia's eyes locked on Lexi's—"*you* are needed to defeat the Lord, and that is something I want. He has to die."

~

Continue reading *Shadows of Fury*: brendakdavies.com/SFuwb

~

Stay in touch on updates, sales, and new releases by joining to the mailing list: brendakdavies.com/ESBKDNews

Visit the Erica Stevens/Brenda K. Davies Book Club on Facebook for exclusive giveaways and all things book related. Come join the fun: brendakdavies.com/ESBKDBookClub

FIND THE AUTHOR

Brenda K. Davies Mailing List:
brendakdavies.com/News

Facebook: brendakdavies.com/BKDfb

Brenda K. Davies Book Club:
brendakdavies.com/BKDBooks

Instagram: brendakdavies.com/BKDInsta
Twitter: brendakdavies.com/BKDTweet
Website: www.brendakdavies.com

ALSO FROM THE AUTHOR

Books written under the pen name
Brenda K. Davies

Bound by Fate (Book 8)

Bound by Blood (Book 9)

Bound by Love (Book 10)

The Road to Hell Series

Good Intentions (Book 1)

Carved (Book 2)

The Road (Book 3)

Into Hell (Book 4)

Hell on Earth (Book 5)

Into the Abyss (Book 6)

Kiss of Death (Book 7)

Edge of the Darkness (Book 8)

The Shadow Realms

Shadows of Fire (Book 1)

Shadows of Discovery (Book 2)

Shadows of Betrayal (Book 3)

Shadows of Fury (Book 4)

Shadows of Destiny (Book 5)

Shadows of Light (Book 6)

Wicked Curses (Book 7)

Sinful Curses (Book 8)

Gilded Curses (Book 9)

Whispers of Ruin (Book 10)

Secrets of Ruin (Book 11)

Tempest of Shadows

A Tempest of Shadows (Book 1)

A Tempest of Thieves (Book 2)

A Tempest of Revelations (Book 3)

A Tempest of Intrigue (Book 4)

A Tempest of Chaos (Book 5)

Historical Romance

A Stolen Heart

Books written under the pen name

Erica Stevens

The Coven Series

Nightmares (Book 1)

The Maze (Book 2)

Dream Walker (Book 3)

The Captive Series

Captured (Book 1)

Renegade (Book 2)

Refugee (Book 3)

Salvation (Book 4)

Redemption (Book 5)

Vengeance (Book 6)

Unbound (Book 7)

Broken (Book 8 - Prequel)

The Kindred Series

Kindred (Book 1)

Ashes (Book 2)

Kindled (Book 3)

Inferno (Book 4)

Phoenix Rising (Book 5)

The Fire & Ice Series

Frost Burn (Book 1)

Arctic Fire (Book 2)

Scorched Ice (Book 3)

The Ravening Series

The Ravening (Book 1)

Taken Over (Book 2)

Reclamation (Book 3)

The Survivor Chronicles

The Upheaval (Book 1)

The Divide (Book 2)

The Forsaken (Book 3)

The Risen (Book 4)

ABOUT THE AUTHOR

Brenda K. Davies is the USA Today Bestselling author of the Vampire Awakening Series, Alliance Series, Road to Hell Series, Hell on Earth Series, The Shadow Realms Series, A Tempest of Shadows Series, and historical romantic fiction. She also writes under the pen name, Erica Stevens. When not out with friends and family, she can be found at home with her husband, son, and pets.

Printed in Dunstable, United Kingdom

65801195R00211